RICHMOND ROAD

RICHMOND ROAD

A Novel

by

Miles Hughes

For Jemima McKenzie-Higgott

Acknowledgments

I wish to thank my wife, Bronwen, for being the long suffering partner of a writer locked away in his own world while writing this book and those before it. My thanks are also extended to the members of my writers' group: Thomas Lodge aka Thomas Ryan, Trisha Hanafin, MeeMee Phipps, Karen Van Eden, Anne Kayes, whose critiques of the evolving work proved invaluable. Also thanks to my external assessor, Stephanie Johnson and to my copy editor Stephanie Dagg. For assistance with preparation of the cover art I would like to thank George Buxton of Monkey Creative. Finally, for this soft cover edition I would also like to thank my layout editor Bev Robitai.

Kindle ISBN: 978-0-473-26595-3
PDF ISBN: 978-0-473-26596-0
Epub ISBN: 978-0-473-26594-6
Softcover ISBN: 978-0-473-26593-9

Chapter 1

It is still dark. The only light in the room sneaks its way through the viewing panels set into the doors. I reckon it's about four in the morning. There's a lingering odour of disinfectant. In my mind's eye I see gauze bandages, ointments, clean wash basins and scrubbed walls. This masks the smell of blood, so redolent when we arrived. Age is a killer and I've been fair buggered by the high drama of it all. I'm still sitting in the straight back chair I fell asleep in **the night before**. How I haven't fallen off escapes me.

The rows of beds lining both sides of the room look ghostly. They vanish into the gloom that is the other end of the ward. My eyes feel bloodshot and my back aches. I rub my hand over my cheek and feel the bristles. My clothes stick to me. I feel where his blood soaked into them, but it is too dark to see. The cloth feels stiff, like an old canvas sail. I should return home for a change of clothes and a shower and shave, but I can't bring myself to leave his bedside.

Tiny pips of sound emanate from the monitor behind Steven's bed. Little dots of light move up and down on its face, like three drunken sailors reeling their way home in the wee small hours. Steven is an amorphous lump barely moving under his blankets. In fact, I become alarmed and lean forward to ascertain that he's still breathing. A slight rise and fall of the blanket reassures me. His arm hangs limp down the side of his bed. Intravenous fluids feed into it through the cannula in his wrist. I stare, through eyes still partly glued together by sleep, at the bottles of life-saving liquids that dangle next to his bed. Why hadn't I read the signs? I wonder once again if he planned that I should find him. That is possible. It appears he waited **until his parents were away. I got to him just in time. God knows what led me to him, some innate instinct perhaps.**

When he was born, I was dismayed to see Steven was a living reincarnation of my brother. The resemblance bordered on the uncanny. Even his mannerisms are the same. I feel certain he has been sent back to haunt me and because of that, I feel in some way tied to him. I sometimes wonder if he feels any special tie to me. The family always put out that Daniel died soon after the Great War from wounds received. In part that was true, but it wasn't the whole story. Perhaps Steven is now of an age that he can be told the truth about Daniel.

I mull this around in my mind as I look at the still form in the bed. One of the other patients rolls over in his bed and emits a long snort, then begins to snore. It can't be far from dawn now. I sense the lightening of the sky outside. Within the ward the gloom is retreating, taking its ghosts and phantoms with it.

The doors at the end of the corridor open and two nurses with a chromium plated trolley enter the ward. They begin their odyssey from bed to bed taking heart rates, measuring blood pressures, taking temperatures and writing these down on the charts at the end of each bed. Some of the patients wake at this intrusion; others sleep on, blissfully unaware until they are rudely awoken by the jab of a needle in their arm or some other part of their anatomy. A general restlessness invades the ward. Somewhere outside the ward a floor polisher starts up. It is the start of a new day in the hospital. Now there will be no peace for the patients.

The nurses reach Steven's bed and I stand up to get out of their way. I walk across the room and stand between two beds, looking out the window. One of those new container ships is rounding North Head, about to enter Rangitoto Channel. It will meet a slight swell there, but in a ship that size those on board will hardly notice a thing. In my day we would be gybing, heaving on ropes, watching the set of the sail, while the skipper would be bawling out orders from the tiller to do this or do that.

That's a bygone era now. The world has moved on and the city has grown. Flashing lights from straddle carriers move back and forth at the new container terminal. Banks of floodlights banish the darkness of night letting them work twenty-four hours a day. Where the container terminal is now was all sea bed in my day. Some of the old city landmarks still survive. The Britomart Pub is still there though it's called something else now. No more do the watersiders have the 'Ups' there, in between their 'Downs' in the holds of the ships. Gleeson's has long gone, but the Rob Roy Hotel still survives, but with a new moniker. A wry smile creases my face as I envisage what all the old salts would think of it now being called The Birdcage.

The orange ball of the sun rises over Rangitoto, shedding a golden glow over the city.

The internal darkness of the ward gives way to a monochrome world of beige and white. Heads appear above blankets and bleary eyes cast glances about the room before the heads subside back onto their pillows to a series of grunts and grumbles. A waft of stale air washes over me from one of the beds nearby. No one claims responsibility.

The doors open at the end of the ward as a man with a floor polisher backs his way through. A smell of floor wax follows him in. The shrill whirr of the machine breaks the last vestiges of peace in the ward. Patients roll over and sit up, many cursing the man with their eyes for doing his job. A new shift of nurses comes bustling into the room to prop up the patients, fluff pillows and prepare them for their breakfasts. Some of the patients get up to go to the toilet. Steven remains motionless in his coma.

The Ward Sister marches in to survey her domain. Seeing me she comes across. She is a stern looking woman, built like a pit bull, but with a pleasant face. The white veil framing her face makes her look younger than she probably is.

"Still here Mister Bender?" she asks.

"That's right," I reply.

"How many nights is that, then?" she asks.

"Three now," I say.

"No sign of him waking then?"

"No," I reply.

"Any news from his parents?"

"I sent a telegram to their hotel in Australia, but haven't heard back yet."

"You should go home and get some sleep. You look terrible."

I give a wry grin. "No one has said that to me for years".

She looks at me quizzically before brushing past to pick up Steven's limp arm and check his pulse. She looks back at me while marshalling her thoughts. "We can ring you if he wakes, you know."

"Nah, I'll stay, so long as I'm not in the way."

"He means a lot to you, doesn't he?"

"The world," I say, realising the truth of the statement. I hadn't articulated the feeling into words before now. She is holding up an eyelid and shining a torch into his eye. I need to see that he is still breathing. I stand up and she senses my presence close to her. She turns to me and gives me a flicker of a smile. "Would you like some breakfast?" she asks.

"I could do with a cuppa and some toast."

"I'll see to it," she says. She hovers there, as if about to say more. I feel a need to reach out and take her hand. There's warmth there. Instead, I mutter "Thanks."

"If you like, I can arrange for you to use the staff bathroom."

I look at her as if she is an angel. Indeed, the morning light coming through a window on the far side of the room casts a kind of radiance about her head. I shuffle my chair further out of the way and the effect is gone. Sisters and matrons aren't usually noted for their looks, but this one has something special, an inner calm and a sweet disposition. That beats good looks any day of the week, if you ask me. Still I'm too long in the tooth to have any illusions in that department. After swallowing the lump in my throat and chastising myself for being an old fool I say, "That would be mighty welcome. I guess I'll just have to turn my underclothes inside out for now."

She gives me a hint of a smile. Even that transforms her otherwise impassive features. Still she doesn't move. I'm sure that she has plenty of duties other than chatting with me.

"You could try talking to him," she says. "They say that people in comas can hear you." I read concern, or is it pity, in her eyes. Whatever it is, she comes across as a genuine person. She continues. "A familiar voice might bring him out of the coma sooner. Why not try reading to him."

"I haven't a book and anyway I've never been much of a reader."

"Well, no matter, perhaps you could tell him your life story then."

"Hah, that would take a long time."

"I'd say he's got plenty of time, wouldn't you?"

Looking at Steven under his blankets, I reply, "Yeah, I suppose so. What about the other patients? They won't want to listen to me rabbitting on all day."

"We can put him in a private room."

"You'd do that for us?"

"I'll see what can be done after breakfast," she says before walking off. I stare at her fulsome form with its starched uniform, practical shoes with low heels, white stockings enclosing her sturdy legs until she vanishes through the **doors at the end of the ward**. She reminds me of the Vindex with her clipper bow and broad beam under full sail. Something a man could trust his life with. When no one is looking I take a quick peek at Steven's chart. The only thing that means anything is the hour, 8:00am and the date, 15-9-72, scrawled at the end of the last line.

When I return from a shower and shave, I feel a new man, a bit like an old car that's had a wax and polish, still with a few dents and a little crusty underneath maybe. The razor was blunt and there are a few cuts and grazes here and there, but hey, who cares. I see that Steven hasn't been moved to a private room, but has been relocated to the end of the ward where he is now separated from the others by an empty bed. The Sister leads me to his bedside and pulls the curtain around us to give us some privacy.

I have no idea how I'm going to begin. I mull over in my mind what I want to say. I sit close to Steven's head and begin talking softly, lest the others overhear. At first I tell him how much I love him and implore him to return from the grey world he is in.

It isn't as hard as I first thought. My voice steadies, a bit louder than before. "My life as a young man wasn't always easy. In fact, it was hardly ever easy. Not by the standards of today anyway," I say. I pause and lift my head to see, or perhaps sense, if anyone else out there is listening to me. Realising the stupidity of this I carry on. "If circumstances had been different I wouldn't have had to make my way in the world at such an early age. But that's history now. The world was full of possibilities back then. A young man could have put together a small fortune if he'd had the right breaks. Sadly, those breaks didn't come my way. Then again, money isn't everything and I can say I've had an adventurous life, if nothing else."

Now I've got through the preamble, as it were, I pause to consider where to begin my **story**. I decide to begin with my earliest memories.

7

Chapter 2

When I was little we lived in a kauri cottage in Lincoln Street, Ponsonby. It had a veranda along the front facing the street and out the back there was a separate dunny and washhouse. The house was located on the lower side of the road in the dip before it climbs up to the cart track, later to be given the grand name of Richmond Road. The backyard had a big plum tree and several peach trees and dropped down into a valley full of scrub and tall grasses where, as children, we played our make-believe games with the neighbouring kids.

You won't remember much about my Ma and Da; they died before you were born. Ma was from Ireland. She had the endurance of a mule and could be as stubborn as one as well. My Da was from Liverpool. I daresay he had plenty of Irish back in his ancestry too, though he was not so much of the faith as Ma. He was quiet and thoughtful, always considerate of how others might feel. That said, he could still be firm when the need arose. I never saw him smoke a cigarette or drink anything more alcoholic than a beer and that was never at home. Ma wouldn't have alcohol in the house. She said she had seen too many men ruined by it back in the old country.

I guess Da was a man of moderation in all things, but you couldn't say that about Ma. There were no grey areas for her. Everything was black and white. In her mind everyone was the sum total of their family background, race, occupation, and religious belief. Too bad about the individual inside, but then her take on people was right more often than not. She was very intuitive when it came to people, as if she had the sight, though she downplayed this. Possibly some priest had told her this gift was evil. Who knows for sure?

We still had the night cart in those days. All the waste from our area was dumped down at Victoria Park. As kids we used to laugh at the things that might happen to the night cart men. I hope you're listening to all this because don't think I'm going to repeat it when you wake up.

I went to school at the Catholic Boys' School in Summer Street. I had the misfortune to be instructed by Father O'Riorden pretty much the whole way through my schooling. Ma thought Father O'Riorden was wonderful, being a priest and all, and coming from County Sligo. For her he was a link back to Ireland and they would jaw away for hours. To me he was a man to avoid at all costs. He had long ago decided that I was not gifted and therefore not worthy of his time. As a consequence I never did well at school and was put off Church for a good part of my life.

One of my earliest memories is of us all in the parlour of an evening. My brother, Daniel, was just a baby in arms back then. I must have been about five at the time. It must have been during the winter because one of Da's jobs after coming in from work was to light the fire. He would kneel before the fireplace and place some crumpled-up newspaper in the grate before piling up pieces of kindling in a little heap that resembled the poles used to hold up an Indian tepee. I liked this as it was how we built our huts down by the creek. He always took his time placing these, like they were works of art. He then placed a single sheet of newspaper over the pile. My job, as his assistant, was to then pass him the ti-tree logs from the basket. They had thick fur-like bark which always caught fire on the tips. He piled these up once again like the spokes of a tepee over the newspaper.

"The ti-tree's wet!" he would mutter sometimes, more to himself than me. "It will take a bit of starting,"

"The rain drove in under the veranda last night," Ma would say.

"I know!" Da would say. "George, go and get me some more sheets of newspaper."

I would jump up off my knees and run through to the washhouse to get some more newspaper from the pile behind the door and return to give this to my father.

"Thanks son," he would say, taking the papers and placing them on the floor beside him. He then selected two large sheets and opened these out before lighting the newspaper in the grate. We would all watch until the kindling took, then he held the sheets of newspaper over the fireplace to let it draw. Da's bent form stayed motionless for ages, as if in supplication to the god of fire. I remember him vividly like that; the set expression on his face, his matted hair, often wet from the rain, the worn leather soles of his slippers and his old brown cardigan that he wore about the house. A small orb of light would appear behind the newspaper. An orange glow would now light his face and I half expected the sheet of newspaper to burst into flames in his hands, but he was experienced at his craft and always withdrew the paper before this happened. The ti-tree would then catch alight with bright orange embers dancing across the bark. The excess moisture was driven out of the logs as steam. Wisps of undulating smoke would spiral up the flue like entwined serpents. At the back of the fireplace bright orange embers marched across the face of the brick, like a colony of army ants. Da and I would stare at their staccato motion back and forth across the soot-laden bricks.

"Right!" he would say, standing up on his creaking knees. "That's that done. Have you washed your hands? Dinner will be ready soon."

Another memory I have of my childhood was when I was twelve. I had just celebrated my birthday when news came that the American Great White Fleet was putting into Auckland. That would have been in August 1908, a long time ago now. Bunting and ceremonial gateways and arches were put up to welcome them.

It was a Friday when the fleet arrived and the whole city took the opportunity to make a long weekend of it. Da got us up early. We dressed and were given a hurried breakfast before we joined the throngs making their way to a vantage point. When we got to Point Erin we were disappointed to see the harbour wreathed in mist. We waited expectantly in the chill air, hoping the sun would break through and disperse the mist before the ships arrived. Then the boom of heavy guns sounded, one after the other like rolling thunder.

An old sailor near to us told us it was from the leading ship as it rounded North Head. I suppose he knew about the protocols of such things. Immediately another series of rolling booms sounded, rolling on and on. The old sailor nodded his head and said, "They be the shore batteries replying."

From where we were, none of this could be seen, due to a thin layer of fog blanketing the harbour. People about us bobbed up and down declaring they could see a mast here or a mast there, but I felt it was mostly in their heads that they saw these things. The rolling thunder of salutes carried on and on to such an extent that our initial enthusiasm soon died away. After they finished there was a deathly silence.

I quickly became bored and began looking for trees to climb with Daniel when there was a hush, followed by some "oohs" and "aahs" from those around us. I turned back to see the mist lifting to expose the fleet. The first thing that struck me was that the battleships were white. Every depiction of an ironclad ship I had seen up till then had been of grey vessels. As the mist dispersed I saw two lines of battleships stretching from a line out from the Western Wall in Freeman's Bay all the way to North Head. Black smoke hung in the air above each of the ships. Dozens and dozens of small craft had sailed or steamed out to meet the fleet. I could make out sailing scows, open sailing boats, steam launches, gaff-rigged yachts of all kinds, steam ferries and steamers sailing up and down the line of ships. It seemed as if everyone with a boat had gone out. I wouldn't have been surprised to a see a man in a bathtub. Little did I know then that the sea would one day have a hold over me.

On the Saturday, Da took us all out on a steam ferry to see the fleet. It was the first time I had been out on the water. Daniel and I were thrilled by the steam ferry as much as anything else. We looked down at all the machinery going up and down and at the stokers shovelling coal into the boiler. The red glow coming from the door of the firebox held me transfixed. Everything smelled of oil, coal and sweat; all brought to a fine head by the heat. Da had to pull us away from the engine room to look at the lines of battleships at anchor. All of the ironclad battleships had between two and four funnels, great cantilevered bridge structures and guns housed in deck turrets or in blisters along the sides of their hulls. There were guns everywhere. Most of the ships still had steam exhausting from their funnels. Da, being an assistant engineer, told us that they had to keep the boilers going even when anchored so that everything aboard could still operate. The wooden vessels moving about on the harbour looked frail compared to the battleships. I was exhilarated at the raw power of these ships, but also daunted by the destructive power they were capable of meting out. It gave me comfort to know that our batteries on North Head and Fort Takapuna were there to protect us.

After we arrived back at the ferry terminus, we were met by the stench coming from the fish market at the bottom of town. We walked up Queen Street past all the hoardings outside the railway station advertising soap, tea and businesses, to take in all the decorated arches, bunting and pavilions erected to greet the Americans. Someone had gone mad decorating the arches with fern and palm fronds. Each archway looked like a living forest. The big one past the tram terminus even had a whole cabbage tree on top of it. American sailors were everywhere in their navy blue jackets and flat topped hats. Many people thought the Americans were the same as us and had saved us from the Russians or Japanese just by sailing into our harbour. I wasn't so sure of that, after listening to their strange accents and watching their shenanigans. They seemed to me to act in a manner quite foreign to the way we did. Anyway, it was a good day out.

Da insisted that Daniel and I remained at school when we reached twelve. Most of the boys in the neighbourhood left school then. Da said that leaving school at twelve condemned you to a life as a labourer or being a navvy, as my Ma would say. Da wanted better for Daniel and me. He saw our staying on until we reached fifteen as the means for us to get a trade's ticket or even to become part of the new merchant class. He had seen how most of the wealthy merchant class in town had come from meagre backgrounds and become self-made men through investments in the timber or mining industries. Some of my schoolmates at the time had gone on to apprenticeships in the various trades around the port: shipbuilding, boilermaking, gas fitting, carpentry, bricklaying or solid plastering. Some even took up apprenticeships in the new field of electricity. After they went, I felt a bit like a fish out of water staying on at school. It wouldn't have been so bad if it wasn't for the fact that I still had Father O'Riorden. Not only was he our form teacher, but he took us for history, arithmetic and religious studies, at least three hours every day. Nothing you did was good enough for him. I was constantly berated in front of the class and cuffed about the head. To make matters worse, my old schoolmates ridiculed me in the street when we met and called me names. Since leaving school they had become more "worldly," while I remained a naive schoolboy. I received a good grounding in arithmetic, English and history, but I could not for the life of me see how this was going to be of any benefit. As I approached my fifteenth year I was more than ready to leave school and to get Father O'Riorden out of my life.

Chapter 3

On the day my Da took me down to the mill for a job interview Freeman's Bay was covered in thick fog. Our breath hung in the air like steam in front of us. Da explained to me that the fog formed in the creeks and mudflats of the upper harbour. It then stole down the harbour in the early hours, like a thief in the night, to enfold the city and port in its embrace. Foghorns wailed and bells clanged out their warnings to ships. These sentinels, sad and abandoned in a blind world, always left me with a sense of loss.

At the mill, Da took off his cloth cap before mounting the wooden steps up to the office, that sacrosanct domain of the bosses. I paused before mounting the first step to look up the long flight. Moisture lined the handrail and covered the treads. Cobwebs lined with droplets of dew hung from the eaves overhead, like Christmas decorations. By then, Da had reached the top landing outside the door to the office. He turned and motioned me to hurry up. Something about the servile manner he had put on, like an old coat, made me uncomfortable. His hands fumbled with his cloth cap, constantly rolling and unrolling it. This action transmitted something to me I could not define. I had heard him talking to Ma and to other men about the General Waterfront Strike a couple of years before. Not everyone had supported the waterfront workers, who kept a pretty closed shop, but when the government came in with mounted police and clubs, most of the workers around town came out on support of the watersiders and there was still a deep resentment against the bosses. Da shared this view, but there he was, cap in hand, waiting on the landing. He straightened my collar and ran his big hand across my hair, patting down any unruly tufts, before turning to open the door.

Inside, we edged past a clerk sweeping the worst of the mud mixed with sawdust and shavings, brought in from the yard. The room smelt of floor wax, old leather and cigarette smoke. It consisted of one large room with three offices leading off it. The lower walls were wainscoted in dark wood, varnished so that they gleamed in the yellow light cast by the electric lights. These had large bulbs and green witches' hats, and hung down from the ceiling on long chords, like those in billiard halls.

Da walked up to the receptionist. The counter in front of her was so highly polished I could see her reflection in it. Further along there were two order clerks in their shirtsleeves and waistcoats dealing with the merchants and trades people. In front of each of them were arrayed their order books, inkwells, blotting pads, pens, pencils and spikes on which the various invoices, receipts and orders were stacked.

While Da was speaking to the receptionist I studied the rest of the room. Behind the counter were eight desks with typists in white puffed-sleeve blouses pounding away on typewriters. I had heard about these machines, but had never seen one. The women's hands danced across the keyboards at a speed bewildering to watch. Suddenly, a bell dinged and the operator would pull the top part of the contraption back. I wanted to go over and get a closer look, but the main counter acted as a barrier and Da had just placed his hand on my shoulder, as if divining what I was thinking. He motioned me to sit with him on a couch by the wall.

Once I sat down I was left with only the main counter and the receptionist to look at. She was in her late twenties or early thirties. She also wore a high-necked blouse, though hers was a deep burgundy colour which brought out the colour in her face which was made up, like a tart's, as Ma would say. Her hair was piled up and pinned, making her seem taller than she probably was. She was the most beautiful woman I had ever seen.

A door to one of the offices opened and a tall, well-dressed man came out to meet us. He wore a conservative blue serge three-piece suit; open at the front to give us a glimpse of his waistcoat and his gold fob watch chain. His slightly auburn hair was parted down the middle and threatened to turn into unruly curls unless kept tightly trimmed. His long aquiline nose and clearly formed eyebrows delineated his penetrating blue eyes. These were slightly veiled by drooping upper eyelids, like those of a lizard. Below his nose was a neatly trimmed moustache. I wondered if the starched collar he wore was uncomfortable. He wore a silk tie knotted in a manner I had not seen before. He obviously knew Da as his face broke out into a polite yet guarded smile when he put his hand out in greeting. I noted the long fingers and the nails pared back and carefully trimmed. Da leapt off the couch, his left hand grasping his cap while his right

18

hand shot out to take hold of the hand offered to him.

"Mister Bender, how are you this damp old morning?"

"Fine to be sure. I trust you are well also?"

"Never better. How may I be of help?"

"I've brought along my son, George. He turns fifteen soon and will be looking for employment. I was hoping that you might be able to find a position for him in the mill. I've kept him at school until now in the hope that he will find a job in one of the trades."

"Is that so? Well then George, what would you like to do?"

By now I had risen to my feet, feeling like a prize calf on show at the fair. It was only after prodding from Da that I found my tongue.

"Ah, I, I don't know." This sounded lame even to me, so I tried again. "I suppose I'm ready to have a crack at anything."

"That's the spirit. A young man should be prepared to look at many things. Only then will he find his true calling. Do you think that you would like to be an assistant engineer like your father here?"

"I'm not sure. There would be a lot to learn."

"That's true, but the firm could help you get your ticket, if that was what you wanted."

"Perhaps when I'm a bit older."

"Fair enough," he replied. "We'll start you working in the timber yard."

I was about to thank him when he turned to my Da, effectively dismissing me. I was still feeling a tinge of resentment at this when he addressed Da saying, "On your way out introduce George to John Dowd, the yard manager, and tell him when young George here will be starting. Mrs Gallagher at reception will take care of the paperwork to sign him on."

With that he turned back to me and put out his hand. I put out my hand to have it gripped by one that was firm yet not callused like so many I had shaken. He held my hand in a steely grip and I was forced to look up into his eyes. They held my gaze in a steady and unblinking glare, as though a spotlight had been shone on my soul. His strong grasp had to be the result of some sort of physical work, even if it was on a yacht, or with a cricket bat instead of labouring.

"Welcome aboard, George," he said, showing enough animation in his face for me to believe he might mean it. "We try to run a happy ship here, but you have to be alert at all times. A timber yard can be a dangerous place for the unwary."

"I'll be careful, sir."

"Make sure you do."

As he released both my hand and his focus on my face, a slight smile curled the ends of his lip. He watched us take our leave, making sure that Mrs Gallagher filled in the name of George Bender in the employees' register, before turning on his heels and marching back to his office where he shut the door. By now my thoughts had transferred to the receptionist who was taking down all my details. Right then it was hard for me to get my head around the fact she was a Mrs Gallagher. The name made her sound so much older than she looked. When she had finished writing everything down in her neat copperplate writing she looked up and gave me a beaming smile. It seemed like the sun had come out again after the chill of meeting the boss, whose name I still did not know. This knowledge came over me like a wave. Why hadn't Da told me his boss's name? Did he not think I was worthy of knowing? As we reached the bottom of the stairs I turned to Da and asked, "What was that man's name?"

He looked down at me with a crooked grin on his face before saying, "Why, that was Mr O'Connor.

Everywhere you looked, great stacks of sawn timber rose up into the air. Each stack looked like it might collapse at the first puff of wind. They reminded me more of how a bird built a nest than anything men might have put together. Pile after pile of these mountains of timber covered every spare bit of ground around the perimeter of the yard. Running and jumping across the tops of these were the yardmen who picked up boards and planks to order and passed these down to the men on the ground that loaded the wagons and drays the customers brought into the yard. The stockpiles went right around the sides of the mill building and the engine room with its brick chimney spouting out grey smoke. I could see that it was a dangerous place to work. I was half expecting one of the towering stacks of timber to fall down around me at any moment. Even then, I jumped each time that a piece of wood crashed to the ground behind me.

We walked around all this timber to reach the harbour side where booms of logs lay corralled between a jetty and the shore, some semi-submerged in the mud, waiting to be winched ashore up the ramps that projected out into the harbour. These logs had been floated down the harbour from Riverhead. I had been expecting to see some kind of gantry for lifting the great logs, but they relied entirely on hand winches to drag them up the ramps and along the rollers. If one of these logs was to roll off a saw bench I don't know how they would have got it back up.

Coming back around the side of the building we ran into the yard foreman, John Dowd. He looked a doughty sort of chap, not tall, but well-built with a barrel chest and looking like he could give a good account of himself in a fight, should the occasion arise. He was wearing a bowler hat and must have left his coat hanging on a peg back in his office when we met him, for he was dressed in his shirtsleeves which had been rolled up past his elbows to show arms well-tanned by the sun. His legs were slightly bowed and when he walked he had a gait that swayed from side to side, as though he had spent many years before the mast. He shook hands with Da, looking him in the eye and giving him a hearty "G'day, Cyril." This was the greeting I was used to between working men who had known each other for some time. I had already decided I liked the man before he turned to me and offered his hand. A welcoming smile broke out on his ruddy face, which was framed by greying hair sticking out in tufts from below his bowler hat and by his long sideburns that stopped short of forming a beard.

"Gidday, young fellah," he said. "Starting off in the yard is always a good way to learn this business. If you prove your worth we can promote you to boiler assistant or sawyer. Maybe one day you could go all the way up to working in the office even."

I looked at him in surprise and then looked at Da to see if I had heard right. Da merely looked at Mr Dowd and put a hand on his shoulder before saying, "No need to get the lad's hopes flying too high now, John. We'll start him off in the yard and see how he likes it first. He's starting in a fortnight's time when he's finished school."

"Right you are then, Cyril. Just give me a few days warning so that I can have something ready for him."

"I'll do that John," said Da who put an arm over my shoulder and steered me towards the brick building next to the saw shed, leaving Mr Dowd to go about his business.

This was the engine room where my Da worked. A smell of burning oil and metal filled the room. Da was an assistant engineer, one of two who worked under the chief engineer. I could tell by the way he looked at the boiler and by the way he explained everything to me that he was proud of this machine and the way it drove all of the machinery in the saw building.

The boiler sat in the middle of the little room in all its steel-plated glory. You couldn't imagine the pressure inside it, but you could certainly feel the heat coming out of it. Next to it was a horizontal steam engine. This was a stationary engine with a huge piston that ran back and forth. It was bolted to a steel frame and had a belt drive running at knee height which I took great care to keep clear of. Pipes covered in huge spigot valves ran this way and that way and a huge exhaust pipe ran up through the roof. This engine was connected by a shaft, which we could walk under, to a giant flywheel that was as tall as me. Connected to this was a leather belt that ran through a hole in the wall to the saw shed. To one side there were a series of steam pumps and a dynamo which provided electricity to run the lights in all the buildings.

The room was full of 'putta-putta' sounds from the steam engine and 'clackety-clack' noises from the joins in the belts that travelled endlessly round and round the flywheels. Da showed me one of the pressure gauges and explained what would happen if the needle went into the red zone. I was allowed to pull a cord which sounded a high pitched whistle. When I wanted to do it a second time Da said, "No!" By then, the heat emanating from the boiler and the cramped conditions in the shed were making me feel sick so Da took me outside to recover before taking me over to the saw shed.

If I had been fearful in the engine room, I was scared, out of my wits in the saw shed. Whirling blades bit into the great kauri logs. Each time a saw bit into timber the log seemed to scream out in agony. Whines, buzzes, bangs, zings, zizzes and roars filled the air. The men had built up a series of hand signals to compensate for the noise. After the bark had been trimmed off the logs, the logs then glided along on rollers to more saws that cut them into planks and boards. Huge fly wheels and belts spun around at dizzying speeds driving all the blades. These were all connected to shafts driven by the steam engine which in turn was driven by the boiler. It was easy to see that the boiler drove everything and that it was the most important piece of machinery there.

The only thing I liked about the saw shed was the smell of freshly cut wood. It was as if the huge tree trunks gave up a bit of their living essence each time they were cut. The shed was filled with this living spirit. Even so, I reeled out of the saw shed back into the yard with my ears ringing. It took me several minutes for my hearing to come back. My Da was grinning at me and ruffled my hair with his great paw, proud of my having passed some sort of rite of passage.

"Well done, lad. Now go on home. I'll see you tonight."

Chapter 4

On my first day of work, I walked with Da down Franklin Road. A blustery nor-easter was coming in from the harbour making us both hunch forward into the wind. Clouds scudded overhead at great speed, yet it was surprisingly mild. Summer was definitely not far away.

At the bottom of the road we crossed Victoria Park well away from where the council dumped the contents of the night carts. On the far side we crossed the recently formed road on which The Kauri Timber Company had their premises. We walked along the side of this to where their rivals, the Leyland-O'Connor Timber Company Limited had their yard, and where both Da and I now worked. The roads all around the timber companies were full of horses and wagons, all waiting for the various yards to open. The horses waited with heads hung low. Da seemed to know a lot of the drivers, touching the peak of his cap and giving the time of day to them as we passed.

The timber yard was surrounded by an eight-foot-high fence made of timber posts and rails and corrugated iron sheeting. The staff entered through the yard foreman's office which had a door to the street. There a clerk by the name of Sam O'Grady signed in each person as they arrived. Coming out of his little office into the yard, we met the foreman, John Dowd. He stood there each morning to greet each worker and to give them instructions on what their task might be that morning. I didn't realise it at the time, but this was his way of seeing that the men were all fit for work and were not drunk. This morning he greeted Pa with a jovial "Morning Cyril."

"Morning John," said Da. "I've bought the boy along."

"Right you are. George isn't it?" he said, looking me in the eye.

"Yes sir," I replied.

"I'm teaming you up with young Charlie Hanson. He joined us about this time last year so he can show you the ropes."

"Sounds good!" said Da. "Well son, keep your wits about you. I'll leave you in John's capable hands for now. I'd best be getting over to the engine room. I'll try and get out and see how you are getting on at lunch time."

"Thanks Da, I'll see you later then."

I watched Da walk off towards the engine room, open the brightly painted door and disappear inside. It was a glossy red, which contrasted against the dull buff colour of the bricks surrounding it.

A steady stream of workers came through the little booth, each one being greeted by Mr Dowd. The longer I waited the more self-conscious I felt. The men and boys all went off to their tasks while I was left not knowing where to put myself. Then Mr Dowd turned around and called me over. He was standing with a youth maybe a year older than me, but one who, I am sure, looked far more streetwise.

"George, this is Charlie Hanson. He'll be showing you what to do for the next few days."

I stepped forward to shake Charlie's hand. He was taller than me by a couple of inches. He too was lean and wiry like me. He gripped my hand and gave me a grin.

"Do you play rugby?" he asked.

"No, why?" I asked.

"You look like you would make a good back, that's all."

I had taken no notice of rugby or football of any sort at that stage and barely knew what the duties of a back might be.

"Never mind the chit-chat. You can sort all that at during your lunch break," said Mr Dowd. "Right now, George, I want you to do whatever Charlie here says. He's in charge of you for now. Remember to keep your wits about you and be careful where you put your feet."

"Right you are Mr Dowd," I said, relieved to be finally about to do something.

That first morning Charlie had me on the ground loading carts while he climbed up and down the various stacks to select whatever was on the order form. I soon learned to differentiate between 3 x 2s, 4 x 2s, 6 x 1s, 6 x 2s, barge boards, fascia boards, rusticated and bevelled weatherboards, house piles and the rest. On one side of the yard there was a lean-to built against the outside fence where they kept the inside profile timbers such as the tongue and grooved boarding, wainscoting and profiled cornices, scotias, architraves, skirtings, dados, lacework for verandas, ceiling battens, ceiling roses and other intricately cut-out pieces for use in ceilings and other places.

By the end of the morning I was feeling pretty much at home and knew more or less where everything was. I also got to know a lot of the cart drivers. When the midday whistle went off some of these cart drivers came over to join the boys from the yard for lunch.

The lunch shed turned out to be the woodshed built on to the end of the engine room. The boys had left a space in the middle clear and had even made up seats with the logs on which they had placed planks and sacks to sit on. Da brought out a great pot of tea from the engine room and placed this on the end plank, evidently its rightful place, before he turned to me.

"Since you are the youngest it will be your job to get the tea from the engine room each lunch time. I'll show you where to get the water from. Have you met everyone here?"

"Only Charlie," I said.

"Right you are then. I'll introduce you to the yardsmen first. This here is Joe. He's probably been here the longest, is that right Joe?"

Joe was a small man, probably only about five feet four in height, though he had long arms, almost like an ape. It crossed my mind that he was perfectly suited to clambering about the stacks like a monkey. He looked at me intently for a moment when we shook hands. In that instant I feared he might have been able to read what I had been thinking and felt embarrassed at having thought such a mean-spirited thing.

"How long have you been here?" I asked, hoping to deflect any ill-feeling.

He looked around at each of us in turn before answering, as though his answer were a gem worth waiting for. Then, in a quiet voice he spoke as he looked straight at me. "I joined when I was a young whippersnapper, younger than you. That was back in 1877."

My mind raced through the numbers. He must have been about fifty-four. This came as a shock. The idea of me still working there at that age was beyond my comprehension.

The other yard man was called Zeb. He was in his thirties and looked to be a good bloke to stick around. He reminded me of Ma's brother, Declan. Da then introduced me to the two cart drivers who had joined us. One of them worked for the company and the other was a private contractor. Both were spooning sugar into their mugs as though it were going off the market tomorrow. Each of them gave me a weary grin.

Just then I remembered the comment Charlie had made when we first met earlier in the morning. Turning to him, I asked, "Why did you ask if I play rugby when we first met this morning?"

Charlie grinned before replying. It was a grin I grew to know. It became his hallmark and every time I think of him I can see that grin.

"Quite a few of the lads here play, that's all. We play for Ponsonby. You looked like you might make a good player."

"I don't know anything about the game. We kicked a ball around at school, but that was a round ball."

"Well, you should came along and see a game sometime. It's great fun."

"We'll see."

Meanwhile Zeb had brought out a pack of cards and was holding it up in the air waiting for us to finish our discussion.

"Right, who's in?" he asked.

"What're you playing?" I asked, feeling once more out of my depth in this company.

"It depends. If there are four or more we play poker or five hundred. If there is only one or two of us we play euchre."

"What's it today then?"

"I reckon we'll be playing poker."

"I'm in," I said.

When the whistle went to signal the afternoon shift Da took me with him into the engine room to show me the tap to use to fill the kettle each day. I then went back out into the yard to join Charlie. By the end of that first day my hands were full of splinters and bleeding. I was so pooped I could barely walk back up the hill home.

I discovered that there was quite a gang of the lads who worked around Freeman's Bay playing up at Blake Street for the Ponsonby District Rugby Club. I had been working for about six months when I first went to watch Charlie play. I recognised lots of faces among the crowd and among those playing. Not only were they from Leyland-O'Connor, but also from the Kauri Timber Company, the Auckland Timber Company, Sam White's, Parker Lamb's and from the various boatbuilding firms around Freeman's Bay. When I told Da about this he said I should join. He said it would do me good though I didn't get the drift of what he meant at the time. So that's how I began playing rugby.

By then the season had already started and I was one of those players who sat on a bench waiting to be called up. It was frustrating for the first few weeks, but then the injuries began taking their toll and I found myself playing regularly at centre or on the wing for one of the lower grades. Whenever they could, Da and Daniel came along to cheer me on from the side lines. Da was never that keen on rugby, being a supporter of Liverpool Football Club from his youth before coming to New Zealand. Anyway, I appreciated it when they came along to watch. Ma wouldn't allow Daniel to play the game, him being too young at the time. She thought the game too rough and this is from a woman who used to tell us about the local lads playing hurley back in Ireland.

Each week found me playing for a different team, depending on who couldn't turn up. It was in this way that I came to the attention of a lot of different coaches who soon appreciated that I could run fast and was developing quite a good side-step to boot. Eventually, Charlie must have put in a word with his coach, Bert O'Hearn, because I was called in to play in his team at centre outside Charlie. Just as at work, Charlie and I hit it off immediately, seeming to know instinctively what the other was going to do.

O'Hearn was a joiner by trade and worked at Sam White's, making sash windows. He was a big man with a big heart and a soft-spoke voice that made you want to listen to it all day. It was said that he came from County Waterford in Ireland. I didn't know whether someone actually knew this or was using his accent to pinpoint his origins. When I was talking to Ma about him, she too said the Irish from the southern counties had soft voices and a great way of telling a story; the blarney, she said. Anyway, I liked being around him. He hardly ever raised his voice, always getting his way through logic and persuasion. Even when he cursed, it was a gentle kind of swearing, almost humorous, usually a gentle reprimand against his Maker. After the match was over he always had a shaggy dog story or joke at the ready in case we lost the game.

The clubrooms and grounds were pretty crude in those days. The changing room was attached to the toilets and smelt just as bad, a melange of sweat, stale clothes and sewage common to all the grounds I played on. You took your life in your hands to go to the toilet there. Someone outside was sure to bang on the corrugated iron by your head, scaring the bejeezus out of you in a quiet moment, or pushing a clump of grass and mud through the louvres onto your head. Everyone skylarked and played practical jokes on one another. We had a lot of fun on and off the field and my circle of friends grew.

We had a full-sized field with an open grandstand holding about twelve tiers on one side of the field. The changing rooms were to the rear of the stand. Over the years, thousands of sprigs had driven any topsoil that had been spread back over the field deep into the clay. In the summer the field dried out to have a craze of cracks all over it. In the winter the rotting grass mixed with clay gave the field that distinctive rugby pitch smell that all players know. After heavy rain the field would often be under water. There were those games where a back running with the ball could avoid being tackled just by aquaplaning over the goal line.

The third-grade matches usually started around eleven in the morning. They were followed by the second-grade game at half past twelve followed by the senior grade match at two. We always stayed on to watch a senior home game before retiring to the nearest pub for the rest of the afternoon.

The pub was always wreathed in cigarette smoke such that you could barely see the other side of the room. Everyone smoked and it was not long before I experimented with it too. After all, you couldn't be the odd one out, especially with so many girls hanging around. A bloke had to have a packet on hand to offer a ciggie to any female who came up to you. It was part of the ritual. Bert O'Hearn came into his own when he had a jug in his hand. Da was a good man, but his conversations were a bit on the limited side. You could say he was economical in his speech. You couldn't say that about Bert. He could hold forth on any subject, dissecting it and putting it back in better condition than when he started. It didn't matter if it was politics, sports or religion. He taught me to think rationally about things. How to think things through before you leapt blindly ahead. The one thing that he never did was to say a bad word against anyone. He even had a good word to say about Jock McAlister, his rival at the club.

I matured a lot in that time. It was just what a young fellow needed. There were always plenty of potential mentors in all aspects of having a good time and attracting the opposite sex. My schoolboy awkwardness had given way to a new me. I was now more confident and putting on weight in the right places. Girls were now coming into focus, no longer being those unattainable creatures schoolboys dreamt about. Like a sapling in spring, I could feel the juices coursing through me. Da's words about it doing me good began to take on meaning though I guess I was still a bit thick back then.

Chapter 5

On the day that Da died, we had both walked, as usual, down through Freeman's Bay to the yard. It was 1913 and I was seventeen at the time. Spring blossom was out everywhere filling the air with heady perfumes and a hint of optimism. Once we signed in, Da went off to the engine room while I joined Charlie Hanson loading up the drays and wagons with their orders. Things were a bit slack that morning because both the yard foreman, John Dowd, and the chief engineer, Alex Sinclair, had gone off somewhere together. The lads got up to a bit of shenanigans around the yard, playing pranks on some of the regular customers. If John Dowd had been there none of it would have happened, but that was the way it was. By the time the midday hooter sounded there was still no sign of the foreman. When we sat down to have our lunch, one of the lads brought out the cards and we settled down for a few hands of euchre, as was our custom.

Da also came out to join us. After we had been playing for some time, Charlie Hanson made the comment that the whistle should have gone. I think we all thought that a bit strange, but I insisted on finishing the round. When it ended, I remember looking up at the smoke stack and observing there was no steam coming out. When I commented on this, a look of concern crossed Da's face. He got up and began running towards the engine room. We packed the cards away and went back to work, a good quarter of an hour or more later than usual. Charlie Hanson and I had begun to pull some timber off a stack when the hairs on my arms begin to prickle. A billow of hot air passed over me and the hairs on my arms began to burn on their tips, like it does on the bark of a ti-tree log.

Then the pressure wave hit me, knocking me face first into the stack, which itself seemed to move bodily to one side under the onslaught. A deafening roar followed, filling my whole being with noise. Something warm and sticky began trickling from my nose and ears. Bricks and debris rained down out of the sky. All I could do was huddle on the ground with my burning arms over my head to protect me from the falling debris.

When it was all over, echoes of the blast filled my head, like heavy surf lashing the shore. I rolled about on the ground and beat myself all over with my hands to put out what I thought were little fires on me. Charlie and I looked across at each other in the same instant. The backs of both of our shirts had been burnt off and we had scald burns all over.

Blisters erupted all over my skin. It was not till later that I understood that everyone in the yard had been hit by scalding water from the boiler. The pressure inside my head had then given way to a ringing sensation. I looked around. I couldn't take it all in. The engine room had vanished, as had half of the timber stacks nearby. There was no brick chimney poking up into the sky. Part of the saw shed had been demolished and what remained was bent and buckled. The boundary fence to the yard had blown clean across the road and most of the windows to the offices had blown in. I was still taking all this in when it registered on my brain that Da had been running towards the engine room only a minute or so before the explosion. I called out to Charlie "My Da!" I couldn't hear anything that I said despite yelling at the top of my voice. Charlie stared at my mouth, then put his hands on his ears and shrugged. He couldn't hear either. He then pointed at me and then himself, before pointing all around, then putting his hand over his eyes in the classic pose of seeking something among the wreckage.

We began clambering over the rubble and debris towards where the engine room used to be. Dust and smoke swirled about us. Voices began calling out and women began screaming from up in the offices. The concrete floor and plinths to the engine room were still there, as were the steel cradle and the bottom half of the boiler shell. The steam engine was still there minus most of the smaller pipes and valves. Everything else had gone, blown into a million pieces. I was amazed that I hadn't been struck by one of the pieces of flying steel.

Someone was shouting to our right. It was coming from the saw shed. A group of men had gathered around something lying on the ground. I tried to push through, but one of the hands turned around and held me back.

"You don't want to see, believe me," he said. He looked at the ground as he said this.

"Is it my Da?"

He nodded eyes downcast. A lump came to my throat and I had difficulty breathing. I knew then Da must have been badly injured. When I next pushed him, he relented and let me through. I saw immediately that Da had to be dead. There was no way he could be alive. He must have been flung a good twenty or thirty feet. He wouldn't have known what hit him. The first thing I noticed was the odd angle of the head. It took me a moment to realise that half his head was missing and that I was staring at the grey mass of his brain inside his shattered skull. More grey matter was splattered on the ground. I grew faint at that stage and fell to my knees. I could not take my eyes away even if I had wanted to.

Da's body had been ripped apart by the blast. His intestines protruded from the opening, looking like a line of steaming sausages at the butcher's shop. His flesh looked like it had been boiled in a pot. What skin remained was a mass of red suppurating bubbles. Here and there pieces of clothing still stuck to it. The worst thing was that I couldn't bring myself to touch him. Something snapped inside of me and I collapsed. I don't know how long I was lying on the ground curled up like a baby. I don't suppose anyone knew what to do with me. I was broken out of my daze by a hand clasping me on my raw right shoulder. I winced with pain and looked up to see John Dowd looking down at me. God knows how he had got there.

"Are you all right, George?" he asked.

When I nodded my head he looked relieved. "Don't worry," he said, "we'll look after your father from here. You need some attention yourself. The ambulance is on its way. You and Charlie stay here while I start a head count to see if we've suffered any more fatalities."

Small fires had sprung up around the yard and men were running about with buckets. I heard the clanging bells of a fire engine wending its way to the scene. Dowd organised any of the men still on their feet to tend to the fires while he went off to make a head count before the police got there.

There were about a dozen of us taken to hospital that day with scalds, burns, concussion and fractures. Amazingly, no one else had died. My clothes were peeled and cut off me before salves were applied to the burns. I was then wrapped up like an Egyptian mummy and taken to a ward smelling of antiseptic and boiled cabbage. Even this was better than the smell of burnt flesh that still filled my nostrils. To this day I can't bring myself to eat bacon. I found Charlie already there looking like my twin and a few of the other boys with plaster casts and hand bandages. One of them asked if anyone had brought along any playing cards. I don't know who said it and I suppose he was just trying to make conversation, but playing cards seemed the last thing I wanted to do.

The next day Ma and Daniel came in at visiting hours with a bag of grapes. Ma sat down on the only chair available while Daniel hovered behind, not quite knowing where to put himself or what to do. Ma took hold of my bandaged hand for an instant as if to make sure I was still there in the here and now. A spark shone in her eye, and then when she blinked it had gone, to be replaced by a tear. She withdrew her hand to pull out the well-worn rosary beads she used when troubled. She was dressed in her Sunday best, but even that didn't look quite right. Wisps of greying hair stuck out from beneath her hat, almost as though she had forgotten to brush it. Her Sunday dress, usually pressed, looked crumpled, as if she had slept in it.

Evidently, it had been a great shock to her. It was as if her inner sight had let her down. Even so, I detected that stoic defiance she always had when faced with adversity. I wished I could do more to help her, but I was in no position to. Daniel could help, but he still needed to go to school in the day. That left Ma alone for much of the day. It came as a bit of a shock therefore when she asked if I was all right.

"Yeah, Ma, I'll be fine. What about you?"

"We'll manage," she said. I noticed her use of the third-person to get around her feelings. "Mr O'Connor at the mill has been very sympathetic. They're going to pay us the week's wages and the holiday pay due to Cyril, as well as pay for the funeral costs."

I hadn't occurred to me that you had to pay for a funeral. Even so, I couldn't believe that that was all they were offering. Da had worked for the firm his whole working life. It all became clear to me. Ma was now going to have to meet the mortgage payments on the house, as well as feed and clothe us. Daniel was going to have to leave school and get a job. I didn't voice these thoughts, as I pondered my own future. What I did know was that if that was all the company was going to do for us then there was no way I was staying there. I guess we were all having thoughts along the same line as the room became quiet. I broke that melancholy mood by asking Ma if they had set a date for the funeral.

"On Friday," she said, her voice crackling like dry paper burning in the grate. She looked at me, her pale blue eyes rimmed in red to ask, "Will you be able to get there?"

"Nothing would prevent me being there, Ma, you know that."

"Thanks son. I'm going to be relying on you a lot from now on."

That's when it hit me that I was now the man of the house, the main breadwinner. It seemed insensitive, but it was as if I had been given a life sentence. I hadn't really thought much about what I wanted to do in life, but I was hoping I would be free to do whatever I fancied. Now I was going to be saddled with maintaining my mother in a house and bringing up my brother until he could fend for himself. A shadow had passed over me. I covered up my swirling emotions by asking, "Who's organising the funeral?"

"Father O'Riorden," said Ma.

"That's good," I replied. How I hated that man, but I couldn't state this in front of Ma. To her a priest was something saintly, who could do no wrong. To me Father O'Riorden was the hard-faced bastard who had taught me at school and dragged me shouting through my communion. After leaving school, I had done everything in my power to avoid him, but here we were once more about to come face to face. You could be sure he would make the most of his opportunity to remind me of my obligations to the Church and to my family. Was I looking forward to that?

"The funeral will be at the Church of the Blessed Sacrament then," I said.

"That's right. The interment will be at Waikumete," said Ma.

"How're we going to get out there," I asked. "It's miles away?"

"The timber company has arranged traps and wagons to take us to the railway station and we'll catch a train there."

"Right, good for them," I said, thinking all the time it was the least the bastards could do in the circumstances.

Chapter 6

It was a good turnout for Da as we milled about on the footpath outside the church. Most of the men from the mill were there, so too were a goodly number of relatives, regulars from the church congregation, and men from his workingman's club.

I had never been to a funeral before. Two of my grandparents had died while I was still at school, but Daniel and I weren't taken to their funerals. Red blossom from the pohutukawa trees covered the ground. Recent showers had washed the blossom off the trees. Some of it had now run into the gutter to mix with the rice that lay congealed there.

The slow clip-clop of hooves alerted us to the approach of the hearse. Four black horses, each glistening with sweat, came ambling down the road pulling the bleak conveyance of the dead, its ornate woodwork painted black, and glass-panelled sides seemingly designed to let onlookers get a glimpse of the beyond. Even the horses' harness ware was black, and so too were the plumes attached to the horses' heads. The driver and his assistant were lugubrious looking fellows, dressed in top hats and morning suits. They pulled the horses up in front of the church. A hush descended on those assembled there as the driver and his assistant climbed down. I walked across to the lead horse and put a hand on its neck. A shiver ran through it, so I stroked it some more. I could feel the warmth of the horse flowing through my hand and up my arm. This lessened the desolate anguish that consumed me.

Ma had had Da in the house for two days and two nights now, but I'd only been released from hospital last night. It gave me the heebie-jeebies having Da in the parlour with candles all around him. Because of his injuries it was a closed coffin, but I could still imagine what he looked like in there. It was a relief this morning when the men from the funeral home had come along to collect him. I suppose having seen him straight after the explosion it had left no doubt in my mind that Da had gone from this world.

My disabilities had somehow precluded me from being considered as a pall bearer. John O'Dowd and old man O'Connor stubbed out their cigarettes before walking over and grabbing the head of the casket with some of Da's workmates. Daniel and Ma's brother Declan brought up the rear as they pulled the casket out of the hearse, turned it around and led the rest of the congregation into the church. People stepped back to open up a pathway through to the vestibule.

The pall bearers continued past the baptistery and down the main aisle to lay the casket on the cradle prepared for it in front of the altar. The extended family then followed, dipping their fingers in the font to trace the points of the cross in the air, before walking down the aisle to genuflect at the crucifix above the altar. Light flooded into the church through the stained glass windows of the apse, though the musty smell of candle wax still lingered in the air. After mumbling an Our Father I sat back in the wooden pew to stare at the great effigy of Jesus on the cross. Whoever had made this had done a fine job of detailing the nails beaten through His flesh and the anguish on His face. He and I were as one in our suffering.

After mass the pall bearers once again came forth to pick up the casket and take it back out to the hearse. This was the time everyone came forward to offer the condolences to the family. I had not given a thought to how I looked when I arrived at the funeral, but obviously all the bandages made my wounds look far worse than they were. I felt a fraud as people came forward to see if I was all right and offer their sympathies. Even Father O'Riorden was somewhat taken aback by my appearance and this restrained him, I'm sure, from his launching into a diatribe about my new responsibilities. After the casket was reloaded into the hearse we all climbed aboard the various wagons, traps and buggies provided for the ride to the station.

The cortege wound its way down College Hill, past the mill and along Custom Street West to the railway station. Even the sky was overcast and a cold southwest breeze had sprung up. At the railway station the line of conveyances stopped at the kerbside beside the huge hoardings on Queen Street. The men got down from the various vehicles to help the woman and children off before filing through to the platform. The train was already waiting, as were a number of people from the neighbourhood who were not Catholic, but wished to pay their respects.

Among them were the Thompsons, father and daughter. They lived up the road from us at No. 76. Her family were Prods from County Down, so my Ma had told me. To her they were worse than the English and that was saying something. Despite Ma's attitude, Suzanne and I saw each other, off and on, nothing serious mind, just meeting in the street or in the park and spending some time together nattering, that sort of thing. I guess there was that forbidden element to it which made it more exciting. Ma and Mrs Thompson had fallen out long ago, but Mr Thompson and Da had always been on cordial enough terms. It was my guess that Suzanne had put her Da up to coming along, for which I was grateful.

"What are they doing here?" asked Ma when she saw them.

"Paying their respects, I would guess," I said.

"Well, they're not welcome," she said.

I looked at her drawn face and thin lips and decided there was no point in arguing about it.

By then we had reached the carriage and I helped Ma aboard before turning to give the Thompsons a wave and mouth a silent "thank you" to Suzanne. Even dressed in black she looked a picture with her blond curly hair hanging down to her shoulders.

The council must have been mad when they established the new cemetery for the city way out at Waikumete. It took the best part of an hour to get there by train. How big did they think this city was going to get? And what a god-forsaken place it was when we got there. Scrub and trees had regained a

46

foothold on land once cleared for farms. It was spitting large drops of rain when we pulled into the open platform and stepped down from the train.

There was no shelter anywhere except for the odd tree to stand under. We clustered together, like a school of fish seeking protection in numbers from a predator, while the casket was unloaded and put on a wagon. We followed this through the wet clay and leaves along rutted tracks. By then, the rain had intensified to a steady drizzle. I was wearing a cloth cap over the bandages still swathing my head and had on a heavy coat. Ma had wrapped some black cloth around her old straw hat for the occasion. Her winter coat and leather boots kept her warm and dry, but poor Daniel had no coat or leather boots and he got soaked. Fortunately, we didn't have far to trudge.

At the graveside Father O'Riorden put his surplice over his soutane and intoned the Rite of Commital while we bowed our heads and the rain ran off the peaks and fronts of our hats. At the end he gave a nod to the sexton and his assistants to lower the casket into the hole. We then silently tossed in a flower, token leaf or clod of earth, as was our wont, before filing back through the mud to the station to wait for the train.

No one said a word as we waited in the cold wind. My thoughts revolved around Da, and I looked back at the good times we had had together. Each time I pictured him I found I could see everything about him except his face. It was as though my image of him was vanishing, bit by bit. I was worrying about this when the sun broke through the cloud to cast a golden glow over us. That seemed to break the melancholy mood of the crowd and we all looked up to smile at each other, as though acknowledging that we were the survivors.

Da had been buried three days and during that time the three of us had barely said a word to one another. However, things needed to be said and we needed to make some hard choices. We were seated in the parlour having just consumed a meagre meal. It was a humid night and we had left the front and back doors open to let a breeze blow through the house. It was not yet summer, but a pending storm had driven up the humidity to such a point that we knew it would be a restless night for us all until the rain came. The tension in the room seemed to match the weather outside. Something had to break.

I knew Ma had been worrying herself sick about our plight. The company had given Ma the week's wages and holiday pay it was legally bound to. It was a paltry amount. Apart from a couple of quid in small change Ma kept in a tin that was all the money we had. It was no surprise therefore when Ma looked up and declared, "I don't know what I'm going to do now. Without your Da's pay packet each week we won't have enough to pay the mortgage, let alone all the other expenses."

It was finally out in the open. I had been waiting for Ma to admit it and get her worries out so we could discuss it as a family.

"I've been thinking of that," I said. "We've still got my wages coming in. I'm going to start looking for another job where the pay is better. If things get bad we can always pull Daniel out of school so he can get a job."

Ma looked up quickly at this, and gave me a baleful stare like I had suddenly become the enemy.

She then looked back down at the table before saying, "Your father would have been against Daniel leaving school so early."

I could see that she wasn't going down that path. In exasperation I asked, "What option do we have?"

"You and Daniel could share a room and I could take in a lodger."

"Christ, there wouldn't be room to swing a cat with two of us in together."

"Don't blaspheme. I've told you before I won't have it in this house and anyway, you said it yourself, what choice do we have?"

"Perhaps Daniel can get a job after school then."

Ma looked at me in that way she used whenever Daniel or I had done something wrong. It was as if she were cataloguing in her mind all the things that I had done wrong in my life and was planning on a suitable punishment. It grieved me when she did this. She remained silent for a time before saying, "Don't forget, George that you had the benefit of staying at school. I'm sure your father would have wanted Daniel to have the same opportunity if it was humanly possible. That said, I have heard the butcher on the corner of John and Vermont Street is looking for a delivery boy."

"Well, that's sorted then," I said, hoping that the idea of a lodger had been put on hold.

"It still might not be enough," she uttered as a parting shot.

"I'm sure we'll muddle through somehow," I answered with little conviction in my voice.

Chapter 7

Both Charlie and I were called as witnesses at the coroner's inquest into Da's death. It was held a month after the explosion and I had had time to come to grips with what had happened and how it had affected the family. The inquest was held at the Suffolk Arms Hotel, halfway up College Hill. The bar was closed for the morning while the inquest was being conducted. Probably about a hundred people attended, including the press and a large contingent of police. The inquest had been arranged so that the people who had witnessed the explosion, or were affected by it, were called up first. After that it was the owners' turn.

Mr O'Connor was the first of those to give evidence. He walked up to the witness box, took the oath and then imperiously looked around the room, his auburn hair slicked down with pomade and gleaming under the lights. Apparently the witness box was a permanent feature of the hotel and had once served as the pulpit in a church in Bristol. At the instigation of the coroner Mr O'Connor placed both hands on the top rail of the witness box and proceeded to outline the history of the company, the running of the mill and the number of employees.

When he had finished, the coroner said, "I understand that the chief engineer was not on site at the time of the explosion."

"That's correct. Mr Sinclair and the yard foreman, Mr O'Dowd, had both gone down to the docks that morning to clear some new machinery through customs."

"Who was in charge of the boiler?" asked the coroner.

"It is my understanding that the deceased and the other assistant engineer, Mr Edward Hay, were left in charge."

"And would you say that these men were reliable?"

"Until the events that day I would have, your honour."

"Does that mean you have your doubts now?"

"This was a tragic event, your honour. It was either caused by a mechanical failure or by human negligence, I do not know which. I will leave that for this inquest to decide."

"Thank you, Mr O'Connor. You may step down. Call Mr Samuel O'Grady to the stand."

Sam O'Grady made his way forward from the back of the room. Everything about him looked defeated. His hair hung down the side of his head in wisps. His old suit jacket hung down open at the front and his shoulders sagged so much it looked as if the jacket might fall off altogether. There was a man who must have been questioning what he could have done to prevent the tragedy. I felt for him as I had always thought he was a good sort.

His evidence was about who was and who wasn't on site at the time of the explosion. I suppose the coroner needed this evidence to confirm that the chief engineer, Alex Sinclair, was off-site at the time of the explosion and that Da had been on site and was the only person not accounted for after the explosion. This confirmed that the person killed could only have been Da. When this had been confirmed I saw how the coroner was piecing each morsel of the evidence together to make an inescapable conclusion which everyone in the room could see. However, I was taken aback at his next line of questioning when he asked, "You have given evidence that you clocked the deceased into work at 7:29 that morning. At what time did you clock in the other boiler assistant, Edward Hay, that morning?"

"I didn't your honour. It was my understanding that it was his turn to fire up the boiler that morning and he would have let himself into the premises just after midnight."

"I see. You may step down. Call Mr Edward Hay to the stand."

It was known about the yard that Hay was a teetotaller and a member of the Temperance Union. Not many of the men liked him because of his constant haranguing about the evils of drink. He had on his Sunday-best tweed suit. After taking the oath he looked across at the coroner ready to answer any questions put to him. After he had stated his name, address and occupation, the coroner said, "Thank you, Mr Hay. Can you confirm that you fired up the boiler around midnight on the night before the boiler explosion?"

"Yes, your honour."

Everyone waited for him to say something else, but it was evident that he was a man of few words.

"Please state the arrangement you had with the deceased about firing up the boiler."

"Mr Bender and I took it in turns to fire up the boiler. That day it was my turn."

"Does that mean that the deceased had worked a twelve-hour shift the day before the incident?"

"It does your honour."

"Would you say that he was tired on the day of the incident?"

"I can't answer for him, your honour, only to say that you get used to the long hours after the first week or so."

"Had the deceased been in any way ill before the incident?"

"Not that I knew of."

"Thank you, you may step down. Call Mr Alexander Sinclair to the stand."

Alex Sinclair had been sitting in the front row and stood up the moment his name was called and took the witness box. My Da had often complained that he was always up in the office sucking up to the bosses instead of being in the engine room doing his job. As a result, the assistants had had to look after the running of the mill on their own more often than not. Sinclair's short dark hair and his smoothly shaven face shone under the lights. The leanness of his figure could not be disguised by the charcoal grey three-piece suit he wore and which was buttoned up the front. I barely recognised him without his overalls on as he stood in the box with his arm raised to take the oath.

"Please state your name, home address and occupation."

"My name is Alexander William Sinclair. My address is 58 Chapel Street, City and I am the chief engineer for the Leyland-O'Connor Timber Company."

"Please state what qualifications you have and where you obtained them"

His answer was some technical school in Scotland, the name of which escapes me now. It occurred to me that Sinclair might also be a member of the Temperance Union since many of the Scots living in Auckland at the time were a pretty pious lot, always bible bashing and seldom seen in a bar unless making themselves unpopular with the patrons and the owner by handing out leaflets. It made sense when I realised that Hay was a Scottish name also. My reverie was broken when the coroner asked Sinclair what his duties were at Leyland-O'Connor."

"I'm in charge of all machinery and plant in the mill. It's my responsibility to see that it is all in working order each day and to minimise downtime due to machinery failures. This requires that the saw blades are kept sharp, bearings are replaced, belts are checked for wear, light bulbs are changed, flywheels are inspected, machinery is lubricated, and of course, that the boiler is working properly."

"With regard to the boiler, have you any opinion as to what might have caused it to explode?"

"I inspected the boiler that morning before going down to the Customs Building with Mr O'Dowd. The boiler was functioning perfectly at the time and I saw no mechanical reason for it to explode later in the day."

"You realise that by saying that that you are implying that it may have been human error that caused the boiler to explode."

"That can't be ruled out, your honour."

"What make of boiler was it?"

"It was made by George Fraser and Sons in Mechanic's Bay."

"Could you state when it was made?"

"The manufacturer's name and the date of manufacture were on a brass plate affixed to the boiler. That has not been found as far as I know. To the best of my recollection it was 1895."

"Would the boiler meet modern standards of manufacture?"

"Despite its age it held a current certification, as is required by law."

I, along with every other person in that room, I suspect, realised Sinclair had evaded the answer. I was fully expecting the coroner to say something along those lines when he instead asked, "I understand that the boiler in question was lap-jointed and not butt-welded, as is the modern practice."

"That is so, your honour."

"That being so, do you have any misgivings about the possibility of cracking, or grooving, as it is sometimes called, occurring at these lap joints and whether this might have been the cause of the failure of the boiler shell?"

"I inspected the vessel every day and saw no sign of that occurring."

"But you have no way of inspecting the inside of the vessel without decommissioning the vessel, is that correct?"

"Yes, your honour."

"So, in the circumstances you would not know if it had occurred?"

"No, your honour."

"Another possible cause of failure could have been corrosion, is that not so?"

"That is always a possibility, but once again I saw no sign of this occurring in any of my inspections."

"Again, if this had been taking place on the inside, you would not have known, is that correct?"

"Yes, that is correct, your honour."

"The explosion took place at 12:45pm. That is just after the men's regular lunch break. According to witnesses, the steam whistle signalling the end of the lunch break did not sound that day. Can you state why that might be the case?"

"No, your honour. I was not on the premises at the time. I can only surmise that there was some sort of blockage that prevented it working."

"That was my opinion also. Who would normally have been in charge of the boiler during the lunch break?"

"Either Mr Bender or Mr Hay. One or other would have been monitoring the boiler while the other had his lunch. I can't say for sure who was monitoring the boiler that day because I was not there."

"That poses a question, does it not? We have evidence that the deceased was outside of the engine room, possibly returning to it, when the explosion occurred. Mr Hay however was giving out Temperance Union leaflets to the men in the saw shop at the time. That would indicate that one or other was in dereliction of his duty."

"On the face of it, I would have to agree with that statement."

"Have either of these men been negligent in the past?"

"No. Both men have been assiduous in their duties, your honour."

"To what would you ascribe this dereliction of duty that day?"

"That is hard to say. It was known that Mr Hay was an avid member of the Temperance Union and perhaps his zeal got the better of him. Mr Bender has always been reliable, but I have heard that since both Mr O'Dowd and I were away that morning that things had become a bit slack. Heaven knows what the result of that was."

"Thank you, you may step down."

The next witnesses were so-called experts called in by the government to determine the cause of the explosion. They gave evidence about their investigations, none of which was conclusive, but gave the impression that they did not think that a mechanical failure had caused the explosion. The inquest then concluded with the coroner stating that he would release his report in the forthcoming days.

I left the room in a daze. It had been a long day and nothing seemed to have been settled. Even so, I had this gut feeling that the bosses would do all in their powers to free themselves from any blame. That only left one conclusion. I just hoped I was wrong. I also blamed myself for the whole debacle. If I hadn't kept him playing cards he may have gone back to monitoring the boiler and averted the whole thing. Then again, he may not. Who knew?

Chapter 8

The timber company was closed for six weeks
while they replaced the boiler and patched up
buildings to a state where they were once more
usable. A steel flue replaced the old brick chimney
and a tin shed served as the engine room. I noted
that it was the very latest model and wondered
whether Da would still be alive if they had
upgraded it earlier. A new office building was built
in that time. It was basically a shell when the staff
moved back in, the idea being to finish the interior
outside of business hours. That wouldn't happen
until well into 1914.

While all that was going on the yard men
salvaged what they could from the shambles, made
an inventory of what could be saved and stacked it
once more. This took the first three days and then
the yard was reopened for business. Without the
steady supply from the sawmill it was soon
apparent that the stocks would not last and
management then limited what supplies we had for
its most regular customers. There's no doubt that
they lost a lot of custom to their competitors
during this time.

We were having a break several weeks later
when Mr O'Dowd came across from his office
with a copy of the Observer.

"You'd better read this, George," he said.

I read the Coroner's verdict in the Observer. By then the event was old news and it made only a small mention on page 6. It stated that Da 'had been killed accidentally at the premises of Leyland-O'Connor Timber Co Ltd, Custom Street West, Auckland, by the explosion of a steam boiler'. What really incensed me was the rider that stated that 'great carelessness was manifested by the deceased'.

Too bad about the whereabouts of Hay, or the fact that it was an old boiler that didn't meet current safety standards, and what about Sinclair as chief engineer being directly responsible for its running.

I turned on O'Dowd. "This isn't right. They're blaming Da for the explosion."

"I know. You have every right to feel the way you do, but look at it from their point of view. Without any proof that there was mechanical failure the only conclusion the coroner could have come to was that it was human error."

"What about Hay, why not blame him?"

"It's always easier for them to blame a dead man. He can't defend himself and that way the whole incident can be forgotten."

"That's easy to say when it's not your father that bears the brunt of it."

"I'm sorry, that's just the way it is. There's nothing I can do about it."

"I'm sorry too. You've been a good mate through it all, but I can't leave it like this. I'm going to see the boss."

"Don't do anything rash. Take a deep breath and think about it before you go charging up there. You might say something that you will later regret."

"I don't care," I said, storming off towards the offices. I bounded up the steps three at a time to arrive at the top landing and flung open the door.

Mrs Gallagher and the order clerks looked up in surprise as I marched past them and through the typing pool to pound on O'Connor's door. I expected someone to say "Come in," but instead the door was wrenched open and I stood face to face with Mr O'Connor. He took one look at my face and pulled me inside before closing the door.

"Ah, George, sit down and be quiet for one second," he said, while steering me towards the chair opposite his desk. I was forcibly pushed into it by strong hands before I realised what was happening. Mr O'Connor then sat down in his chair and looked me in the eye with that unwavering stare that he had.

"I take it you've seen the coroner's verdict," he said.

"Yes."

"I understand that you might be upset. I don't want to believe that your father was negligent either, but then again it is highly likely that someone was."

"What about the boiler? There could well have been a fault in it."

"It's possible, but all the evidence is to the contrary."

"What's it all mean then?"

"It means that it's over. Your father is dead. The firm sustained considerable financial loss as a result of the explosion, but will survive. You are alive and well, and life must go on."

"Christ! Nothing's that cut and dried."

"Unless you are going to go around the rest of your life with grudges against all and sundry, I suggest that it is."

"What about my mother? Is she getting any compensation?"

"Ah, that's a bit awkward. Now that your father has been deemed culpable for causing the accident, our insurers have advised us that they will not be paying out any widow's benefit."

"What's Ma supposed to live on then?"

"She'll have to get a job like lots of others and hopefully you'll support her too."

"Is that it then?"

"It is," he said, his fine hands forming a little steeple in front of his face.

I wanted to punch his lights out, but knew that he would have me arrested for assault. "Well, I resign. I'm not going to work for a company that treats its workers like that."

"That's your prerogative, but I suggest that you go home and sleep on it. If you turn up for work tomorrow I'll think no more of this incident. If you don't turn up then I'll accept your resignation."

"I've made up my mind. I'm leaving," I shouted.

Right then, I hated this man and all that he stood for. If it wasn't for him and his cronies, Da would still be alive. His eyes held mine, watching to see what I would do next. It gave me some satisfaction to see fear flit across his face at the realisation I might do something stupid. I wasn't about to leap over his desk and punch him in the face even if the thought had crossed my mind. I turned to open the door to his office. A sea of blank faces stared at me from the typing pool. I put my shoulders down and charged past their desks and down the stairs like a front row forward. That afternoon I went to the Rob Roy Tavern to drown my anger.

It took a couple of weeks for the rage in me to die down enough to think straight. I realised the best thing I could do was get a better paid job than I had had at the timber company. The only reason I had gone there in the first place was that Da had taken me there. I suppose he had visions of me being an engineer like him, but I now knew I could do better for myself. After trolling through the classified sections of the papers and applying for several jobs I was interviewed for a job with a wholesale chemist company.

I had seen the signboards for Shaw and Company lots of times in my travels, but had never really known what they did. Their office was in a four-storey building at the bottom of Albert Street close to everything; the post office, customs, the port, pubs, shipyards and a large number of clients' premises. The owner of the firm, Archie Shaw, was an avid rugby supporter and knew all about my modest career. He would be able to brag to his mates over lunch about his star employee. Either way, I wasn't going to knock it, a job was a job.

The head accountant, Albert Skinner, was a fastidious man, tall with balding hair, who wore a pince-nez on the end of his pointed nose. He walked around the office in his waistcoat with his shirt sleeves pulled up and clamped with elastic bands at his elbow.

The job turned out to be a doddle compared to the hard graft in the timber yard. Skinner would give me a bundle of receipts from the order clerk's desk and I would write them up in the journal and the ledger. The accounting staff were in a room of their own with a borrow light in the partition through which they could look out on the typing pool. I thought I had died and gone to heaven. After I had finished each batch, Skinner would come over and run his eye up and down the entries in the journal and ledger before picking up the pile of invoices and taking them away. Before long he would be back with another batch.

The office was just up the road from the Criterion Hotel and this became the hang-out for a lot of the younger staff after work. It was well known that the Shaws and Skinner were members of the Temperance Union, so we made sure that we entered the pub by the back door and departed the same way.

After about two weeks at the firm I ran into Suzanne Thompson in the street and we went to a tea shop in the Queen's Arcade to catch up. I hadn't seen her for several weeks.

"It's so good to see you," I said, pulling out her chair.

She didn't reply until I sat opposite her. Then she averted her gaze, making me feel like I had spilt my breakfast down my front or something. The waitress came over and we gave her our orders. When she departed Suzanne said, "I thought you would have known by now." I felt the accusatory edge of her comment cut me.

"Known what?"

"We've moved to Otahuhu," she said. I was so stunned it must have shown on my face because she said, "My father got a job at the Railway Workshops and Mum and Dad decided it was better to move house instead of all that travelling to and fro."

"That's all very well for them, but what about you? I mean you still have to come into town every day, don't you?"

We were interrupted by the waitress bringing our tea and scones. We remained silent while she placed these on the table. As soon as she had gone, Suzanne said, "I don't work in town. I just came in today to do some things for my mother. She's not well at the moment."

"I'm sorry to hear that," I said. It was an automatic response. It was only then dawning on me how much chance was involved in our meeting.

"I don't suppose we'll get to see much of each other from now on then?"

"I would like us to meet more, but it's all too hard now. It was nice to see you again. I mean that, but I have to go now or I'll be late for the train. Thanks for the tea."

I stared at her back as she left the tearoom. What she said made sense, but I couldn't help feeling there was something else to it. Maybe it was the old Prod-Catholic thing again. Whatever it was, it hurt. I really did like Suzanne, but that was long before I met your grandmother.

Chapter 9

I had been at Shaw's about three months before Skinner trusted me enough to do things other than entering data into the ledger. I had learned that most of our customers bought their products on tick and paid on invoice at the end of every month. Many people bought our products through our postal catalogue. Every day orders and money came in by post. One of my jobs was to record these orders and to enter the money received in the cash book and write out a dispatch docket for the warehouse. I began to see that in many cases the customer's scrawling copperplate handwriting was so difficult to read that it would be an easy matter to enter a similar looking amount into the cash book and to pocket the difference. The thought lodged in my mind and niggled away at my subconscious.

The bar room was thick with smoke as I came in from the alley off Fanshawe Street. Heavily embossed burgundy wallpaper covered the walls between the gloss of the dark stained timber mouldings. Nicco Piagni, the publican, was standing behind the bars directing people this way and that, like the conductor of an orchestra. As a new regular he gave me a nod and pulled the pump for my usual without my having to ask. His Italian extraction was evident in his small stature, olive skin and dark hair. Just to reinforce that he had a moustache that had been shaped into points at each end. Altogether, he was a debonair sort of chap and a good listener to boot.

"Where are your friends?" he asked.

"They've got an urgent consignment to get out. They should be here soon," I said, picking up my schooner from the bar. Nicco immediately whipped the white towel off his shoulder and polished the bar where my glass had been and pushed a coaster towards me to remind me to use one.

"I was hoping to have a private word with you sometime," he said.

I looked up in surprise. I only knew him by sight. He was watching me intently with his dark eyes as if assessing me.

"Oh, what about?" I asked.

"I've heard through the grapevine you're a dab hand at cards."

I took this in and turned it around several times in my head before coming up with a suitable retort. "Just casual stuff. I guess I've had my share of good luck."

"What do you play?"

"The usual; poker, euchre, five hundred, that sort of thing."

"Not bridge?"

"Nah! That's for the toffs and anyway, each game takes too long."

He then leaned forward across the top of the bar, a feat quite remarkable considering his short stature.

"How would you like to earn a bit on the side?"

"What would I have to do?"

"Work for me, just a few hours a night."

"I dunno. What's in it for me?"

"You could earn up to five quid a night."

"That much?" I said, looking up from my beer. "It's pretty tempting, I must admit."

"Well, think about it. We'll train you," he said, looking towards the door where the boys from the loading dock had just entered. "Here are your friends. Keep my offer to yourself and come back to me if you are interested."

"Right you are. Can I have three more draughts please?"

The others gravitated towards a table as soon as they saw me at the bar. It was taken for granted that I was shouting first. Not that I minded, it gave me more time to watch Nicco filling the glasses. I paid for them and picked them up without another word being said.

The following night, I told Ma I was meeting a friend in town and wouldn't be home for dinner. At work the next day, I made out I was working late and waited until the others had drifted off home to their families before leaving the office and walking around to the pub. Nicco told me to go upstairs to Room 10 and knock on the door. Someone would be waiting for me. The stairs to the rooms upstairs were next to the rear door that opened out onto the alley leading to Fanshawe Street.

It was with some trepidation that I approached Room 10. I really had no idea what to expect. I knocked twice and stood back. A voice from inside asked who was there and I gave my name. Immediately the door opened and a thin man in a waistcoat and bowler hat appeared.

"Come in, lad," he said, stepping to one side.

The room was still set up like a bedroom, but with the single bed pushed lengthwise against the wall. A baize-topped folding card table and two bentwood chairs had been placed in the centre of the room. He didn't introduce himself, merely pointing towards one of the chairs.

"Take a seat. We don't use names here. It's better that way," he said.

I nodded my head and slid into the chair. He put his eye to the peephole in the door, emitted a little huff, then sat opposite me.

For the next two hours he schooled me in the arts of at least ten games, some of which I knew. Poker was the game of choice for the big gamblers. My tutor schooled me in all the forms of the game; straight, stud and draw, two, five and seven hand, in all of their high and low forms. When it was over he put the cards away and walked across to the door. I hesitated for a second before realising he was expecting me to leave.

"Same time next week," he said before looking through the peephole, then opening the door. He poked his head around the jamb then motioned me out of the door and closed it behind me. It was all a bit bewildering at first. I had no idea there were so many variations to the game of poker.

Over the next three weeks the man, who I learned was Bert Chalcroft, schooled me on lots of tricks to do with dealing cards, how to know where a selected card was at all times and all the methods of cheating.

At the end of a month he took me along the hallway to their secret gambling room. From the hallway it looked just like another other bedroom. I had already figured that this room existed somewhere on the premises. It comprised two bedrooms with the dividing wall removed. Four card tables for up to six players each had been placed there. These were not the flimsy folding tables though. These were substantial pieces of furniture with heavy wooden surrounds on which to place your drink without needing to stain the green baize top. The tables were supported by a central post fixed to a large steel base. The chairs were parlour chairs with round backs, like my aunt Flo had. I took in the luxurious fittings, the divans, the rich upholstery and even the fancy wallpaper. Each of the former bedrooms still had a fireplace in which a gas heater had been installed.

I wondered if the moulded architraves and skirting boards were from Leyland-O'Connor. Maybe I had loaded these very boards onto a dray, but I doubted that. This room looked as though it had been like this for many years.

"I need you to take a look out here," said Bert.

I walked across the room to the window he was peering out of. He pulled one of the curtains aside and let me look out. There was a wooden fire escape directly outside the window that led down to the alley at the back. What I noticed was that a person could quite easily access the roof of the single storey building next door too. Internal doors from the room led to a separate toilet and washroom (for men only), and to a small room that served as a bar. Bert pointed to an electric buzzer located beside the bar, before saying, "Whenever there is a session on, the bar is always manned. If the police come in downstairs the barman pushes a button and the buzzer sounds up here. That's the time to skedaddle out the fire escape. Got it?"

"I've got it," I said, hoping that the occasion wouldn't arise. Even so, I was impressed by the set-up and couldn't wait to be part of it.

The next week I began my career as a card sharp. The patrons were mostly regulars. New clients had to have their bonafides checked to make sure they weren't the law. The regulars entered the bar room and ordered a drink from Nicco. He then put a coaster down on the bar before placing the glass of beer on it. A room number would be on the coaster, and as soon as the customer had finished his drink he would slip the coaster in his coat pocket and appear to head for the toilet before slipping up the rear stairs to the rooms. The gambling salons generally started around six o'clock and carried on till midnight.

My job was to get there as soon as I could after work and help set up the tables and then to man one of the poker tables. All sorts turned up to try their hand, from young lads barely old enough to buy a drink to old gentlemen in suits and ties. Patrons could buy a meal which was served in the salon at a side table so that the patrons did not have to leave the salon once they had entered. It also ensured anonymity to the patrons. Everything was done for their physical and mental well-being. We took their overcoats on their arrival and these were taken away.

Each patron was given his choice of drink and cigar before they commenced gambling at the tables. My table only took new patrons. I was schooled to let them come out about even on their first round and then let them win the second round. This usually encouraged them to try their luck at winning again. After a couple of wins for the house you might let them win another round. By then they would be getting reckless and you could fleece them of everything they had, often including gold fob watches and cuff links. A fine line was made between fleecing them and giving them the hope that they could reclaim their goods and pride the next time they came in. The regular gamblers, the ones that played for big odds, were placed at the other tables. In time, I would work my way up to hosting those tables where the big money was made.

Smoking was a good habit to have if you were a professional gambler. It gave you the opportunity to take your time to assess the odds and to study your opponents' facial expressions, especially their eyes. Many a time it was their eyes that gave them away. I had had the odd cigarette just to be social, but now I smoked cheroots when on the job. The trouble was that I got cravings to smoke outside of the job and soon found myself chain smoking cigarettes during the day. As Da had never smoked, Ma was quick to complain about the smell of smoke on my clothes. At work, Skinner made a comment about getting them cleaned more than once and I began to suspect that he might know about my secret life after work. To overcome this problem I took to carrying a change of clothing to work in a Gladstone bag which I kept below my desk. In it I kept a shirt and a spare jacket which I slipped on in the alley behind the pub.

Chapter 10

The curtain is suddenly pulled aside and a young nurse comes in. Her green eyes search mine, as though trying to determine my health before she holds out an envelope. It is a window envelope, the kind used for telegrams.

"Mr Bender?" she inquires.

"Yes," I say.

"Sister asked me to give you this."

"Ta," I reply, taking hold of the envelope.

I wait until she's pulled the curtain closed before opening the envelope. It is from my daughter, Libby. They are booked on a flight due to arrive in Auckland tomorrow morning. I fold the telegram up again and slip it back into its envelope before putting it into my pocket. I have until tomorrow to finish my story. My heart feels as though it is going to burst as I take in Steven lying inert in the bed with tubes going in and out of him. I had known him to be moody at times, but I had supposed that to be a teenage thing. I was never the same at his age, but then I suppose I was working. What do they say about idle hands? Now it occurs to me that Steven's problem might be more than that, perhaps some sort of mental illness like depression. Christ alone knows what he has to be depressed about. A vision of his father never home, too busy chasing money, and a mother too tied up in social events passes before me. I blink my eyes to remove the image. Who am I to judge? Anyway, where was I?

Yeah, that's right. I was eighteen when the rugby season started in 1914. I remember that year because we were halfway through the season when old Archduke Ferdinand was shot. Anyway, during that season I was elevated to the Ponsonby senior grade and played a few games for the club representative team. My dissolute lifestyle was playing hell with my physical condition. Rugby provided the only means for me to maintain any sort of fitness. Even so my smoking was beginning to affect my stamina.

It was a complete surprise to me therefore when I was called up to play for the Auckland representative team. It happened when the team's centre pulled up lame during practice with a torn hamstring. That night there was a knock on the door and Daniel opened it. There was a muffled conversation on the doorstep before Daniel let the visitor into the house.

"There's someone here to see you, George," said Daniel.

I rose from my chair at the dining table hesitantly, wondering who this person was and what I had done wrong. The visitor strode into the room ahead of Daniel. I didn't know the man, but felt relief when his face creased into a great beaming smile.

"I'm Rhys Jones, the coach of the College Rifles Senior Grade team and of the Auckland

Province rugby team. I've had my eye on you for quite a while."

"Uh, pleased to meet you," I uttered, not knowing what else to say. "Have a seat," I said, pulling out a chair. I eyed Ma who had remained sitting in her rocker by the fire darning socks. We exchanged a raised eyebrow before she looked down to her darning again, no doubt keeping her ears wide open.

Once Jones and I had sat down to the scraping of chair legs on bare boards we sat looking at each other waiting for someone to make the first move.

"I'll get down to business," said Jones, "you're probably wondering why I'm here."

When I made no reply he gave a slight cough before continuing in the same lilting voice that somehow reflected the hills and valleys of his homeland.

"Auckland's star centre, Phil Cooper, tore his hamstring at training this afternoon and will be out of action for several weeks. We've got our fixture against Wellington coming up in a fortnight's time and will need a replacement centre."

"What's that got to do with me?" I asked, not daring to think that I would even be considered. The best I could hope for was to be the bag carrier or the orange boy at half time.

"I know you haven't been playing premier rugby for very long, but the powers that be have been impressed by your speed and your side step. We feel you could be our secret weapon against Wellington."

"Are you saying you think my brother is good enough to play for Auckland?" asked Daniel, voicing the question I had dared not ask.

"Right," said Jones. "George, we'd like you to come to our training session at Eden Park at five this Thursday evening. Do you think you can manage that?"

"Yeah, I guess so," I replied.

"Right you are then. I'll be going now. I'll see you at training. Congratulations on making the team."

We stood up together and shook hands. Daniel jumped up to open the front door. Jones was about to put on his bowler hat and leave when I asked him, "This match against Wellington, is it here?"

"No, it's in Wellington," said Jones.

"Ah," I said. "Well, good night."

As soon as the front door closed Daniel let out a whoop and came and gave me a bear hug.

"Fantastic, George. You're going to Wellington. Your name will be in the papers."

"Maybe, I just hope I don't stuff it up."

"You'll be all right. Everyone else in the team will be as nervous as you, but when the whistle blows for the start of the game you'll forget all about that."

I looked at Daniel, wondering what experience he had in such things and whether he was right or not. He had matured a lot more than I had given him credit for. Anyway, time would tell whether he was right or wrong.

As it turned out the other members of the team were welcoming and keen to give me the benefit of their advice. After a couple of intensive training sessions I felt part of the team, albeit very much the junior member.

Auckland's railway station had changed a lot since Da had taken us out on the harbour to see the Great White Fleet. That seemed to have been only yesterday, but a lot had happened to both me and the town in the intervening years. Now it was full of volunteers off to training camp. The new Chief Post Office building, with its broad steps leading up to the entrance and its stone facings, had replaced the tatty old advertising hoardings at the end of the tracks. It seemed incredible that I hadn't been to this end of town for so long. Down the road, where there used to be a cluster of rusty sheds, steps and gangplanks, there was now a new Ferry Building with arches and a clock tower, from which spread several piers with canopies. The city was changing from a brash settler town into a semblance of a city. About the only thing that hadn't changed was the old station building which was still in Galway Street, but now overshadowed by the new CPO.

Daniel and I arrived at a quarter to seven to find the rest of the team already waiting for us. Rhys Jones promptly came forward and gave me my train ticket. He then shook Daniel's hand, an action that drew a large smile from Daniel. After the pleasantries were over, Jones told me to get on board. I shook hands with Daniel, who wished me luck also, then boarded the train with the rest of the team. I stood at the door watching Daniel walking back down the platform. It was then that I saw Suzanne Thompson come out of the station building.

For her to come down and see me off delighted me. The last time we met she had indicated that she wouldn't be seeing me again. I jumped back down onto the platform to meet her.

She gave me a huge smile and took me in her arms to give me a big kiss on the mouth. The other lads all jeered from the windows of the carriage. She wished me good luck and I thanked her for coming down. She had seen an article in the paper about the game and seen my name in the team list. No one outside the family had taken this sort of interest in me before and it felt fantastic. I climbed back on board wearing what must have been the most stupid grin ever seen.

There were six of us to each compartment and after stowing our gear in the overhead racks we sat down to watch late-comers race along the platform and listen to the slamming of doors and the shouts from people saying goodbye. Soon a whistle sounded and we began moving. The station buildings and platforms slid past followed by the shunting yards, then the brick warehouses fronting Custom Street. Before long we were climbing up a bush-clad gully below the Domain. Morrison, the full back, got out a pack of cards and put it on the pull-down table in front of him, just as we passed through a tunnel. When we emerged from the other end, we were still in the same positions. It was as if time had stood still in the interval.

"Who's playing then?" he asked. "Since there's six of us, I thought poker."

"Count me in," I said.

One person after another took out their packets of Craven A and tobacco and rolled their cigarettes and soon the compartment was wreathed in smoke. Fags hung off bottom lips, sleeves were rolled up, cards shuffled and dealt, hands swept up and hidden from others and the game was on. Nothing else was of concern as the carriage swayed from side to side and the engine driver sounded the hooter each time we approached a level crossing.

The few times I bothered to look out a window it was to see water towers, signal stands, green fields, fence posts, trees, rivers, mountains or ravines speeding by or the facade of some station while we waited for people to get off or board. The only time any of us left our seats was to have a leak or to have a break when we pulled into a station. These were invariably painted buff and brown and covered in soot. When we stopped one or other of us took turns to go and buy mugs of tea and pies. It was one of the longest card-playing sessions of my life. It went on for the full twelve hours. By the time we pulled into Wellington I had taken about five quid off each of my team mates. I had gone easy on them, but they still looked at me ruefully when we settled up. I mumbled that it must have been beginner's luck.

Chapter 11

Niccolò Piagni had at least five establishments around the town that I knew of. After more than a year working for him I felt I could take on anyone at cards and make some good money on my own account. The patrons there were ripe for the picking and I felt that if I could find another venue then I could fleece the patrons there as easily as I had at Nicco's. The difference was that I would be pocketing the money for me instead.

I found out about a gambling salon in Newmarket. It was in a warehouse next to the railway line and three doors down the road from the Exchange Tavern. It was out of my way and I didn't have that much spare time anymore to make more than one visit a week. I figured the Exchange was the key to getting into the gambling salon and it took almost two months before I finally managed to convince the publican I was a legitimate gambler.

As soon as I saw the inside of the salon I had to revise my description of the place. There was no way this deserved such a distinguished title. It was just a bare warehouse with the gambling area divided off by wooden crates. Instead of wealthy merchants for its patrons it had had a mixture of sailors, soldiers, bushmen and miners; men with dirt under their fingernails. They may once have had a sniff of making big money on the Coromandel only to see it dissolve in front of them. That sniff brought them back to gambling like moths to a flame. I was not a fancy dresser, but even I felt overdressed in such company.

The dealer was a bland sort of individual, of average height and build, the kind of man you would pass on the street and not give a moment's thought to. These could often be your most dangerous adversaries as you tended to misjudge them.

The first of my gambling companions was a man who worked with engines of some sort judging by the ingrained grease on his hands. I figured he worked in the railway workshops or some such place. He had a five o'clock shadow. The unhealthy grey skin of his face seemed to be set permanently in a grimace of pain. What looked at odds with this was that he kept his dark hair and mutton chops, both of which were flecked by grey, neatly trimmed by razor. He kept his cards close to his chest. Despite his furtive nature I could read in his eyes whenever he was dealt a good hand and when he was dealt a bad one.

The second man was the odd man out. He was taller than the rest of us and of slim build. I judged him to be a school teacher or some other underpaid professional gent. He always kept his eyes on his cards and rarely looked up at his opponents. If he did so it was just the merest of glances such that it was impossible to read his thoughts.

My other opponent had strong arms full of sinews and bulging muscle. His chest was like a barrel and I judged it to be every bit as hard. His face was almost genial in aspect, as though he had just remembered a good joke and was about to share it with you. His hair was pulled back and tied in a short pony tail similar to that of a seaman and this is what I called him in my mind.

None of us introduced ourselves by name, merely shaking hands before taking our seats. The terms of the game were agreed; it was to be five card stud.

At first I was put off by the crudeness and the intensity of these men, but as soon as I sat down at a table and concentrated on the task at hand I was all right. That task was to fleece these men for everything they had. I particularly watched the dealer as he shuffled and cut the cards before dealing them out. I quickly recognised him using the techniques I had been taught. I figured he would let one of us win the first round so I concentrated on making that person me.

I had saved up a stake of forty pounds which was a small fortune for me and I was keen to boost this at the first opportunity. Off we began, calling on the first two cards dealt. This was all a matter of bluff. After each round the dealer dealt out more cards until we each held a full hand. The school teacher won the first round so I had to be more patient for my turn to come. As expected the house won the second round, then it was 50-50 who might win the next round.

As the cards were dealt out I watched the small gleam of delight in the eyes of the railway worker and figured he had received some aces or maybe a straight. The school teacher picked up his cards and spread them into a fan without moving any of them around. Accordingly, I had no idea what he had. I had the three kings and two tens. I closed the cards into a stack inside my hand as the seaman picked up his last card. His amiable grin did not falter as he slid cards back and forward inside his fan. Once again he gave nothing away, but I thought the reshuffling of his cards to be amateurish.

The railway worker immediately pushed forward five chips and said he was in. The teacher met him and then it was my turn. I wouldn't get a hand this good too often, but didn't want to let on how good it was. I pushed forward five chips, apparently reluctantly, and said I was in.

"I fold," said the seaman.

This left the dealer to call. He raised the stakes by putting in six more chips. His eyes were on mine the whole time he slide the chips forward. It was between him and me; I couldn't fail.

"I'll raise you," I said, feeling confident with my hand.

He called me and I laid down my full house. For the first time I saw a faint twitch at the side of the mouth of the dealer as he laid down four sixes. I'd been beaten by four of a kind. I pushed my chips across the table and he scooped them up. I knew I had fallen straight into his trap and was mindful not to repeat the exercise.

I decided to sit out the next round and see if one of my companions could win. As it turned out the railwayman won the round. This surprised me somewhat and I began to wonder if he was also working for the house. If this was the case then I was up against it.

In the next round I picked up two fives, an ace, a ten and a three. I discarded the three only, not wanting to tell my opponents I had three rubbishy cards. My replacement card was another ten giving me two pairs. It was enough to try my luck. I felt the cards were low enough to slip under the attention of the dealer.

We began our bidding and I won the round. I was beginning to get the feel of the table and was emboldened to go for broke the next time I had a good hand. When I was dealt four queens I could barely hide my delight, but went through the charade of exchanging my fifth card which was an eight of clubs. The stakes had now risen to twenty pounds and I sensed a killing. Once again, I had underestimated the house; the dealer laid out a royal flush. I knew that I was in big trouble then. To keep in the game I had to sign a house IOU. I cursed the fact that I hadn't brought enough stake money even though it was all I had at the time.

With each hand now the stakes were doubled until they were a heady hundred pounds a round. This was a much faster escalation in the stakes to anything we had in Nicco's establishments. It wasn't as if anyone at the table looked to be a rich merchant or anything. We were all working blokes, apart maybe from the school teacher with those soft hands and long fingers. How could they afford stakes this high? I went for broke on two rounds and lost both. It was then that I knew the table was rigged against me. I quit the game in ignominy, feeling a right patsy. I was expected to pay the money I owed the next day. I had no way of gathering the hundred pounds owing and fretted all night about what I could do.

I didn't return to the establishment the next day or the next. I took to walking home by different routes, using the maze of streets through Freeman's Bay and Ponsonby to my advantage. I did this to evade the den's henchmen who I figured would be on the look-out for me.

That night I decided to catch the tramcar to the Jervois Road shops and cut through John Street to reach home. I hardly ever caught the tram so thought that the change in routine would be a good move. What I hadn't counted on was that my stalkers would have an automobile. I alighted from the tram and began to make my way through the backstreets of Ponsonby. A heavy shower passed over from the west as I was halfway down Ardmore Road and I cursed myself for taking such a convoluted way home. One of the men must have been dropped off at the shops to tag behind me while the driver turned around to head straight down John Street ahead of me. They were good. I had no idea they were on to me until I turned out of John Street into Richmond Road. He was standing there in the rain, wearing a navy blue two piece suit with brown brogues and a brown bowler hat.

"Hello, George," he said, greeting me like an old friend. The man was a brick shithouse of a man. I knew I was in deep shit myself. I didn't bother to reply, instead turning to flee back down the street. As I did so I saw his mate sprinting up the road to cut me off. He was almost on me when I turned to run up the road I used to live in, Lincoln Street, which also met at the intersection.

It was futile though. I felt my hamstring go and had to run in a loping style with a taut left leg. My follower was on me in a flash. I felt his great paw on my shoulder before I had barely covered fifty yards. As I was spun around a fist landed in my stomach, winding me. As I doubled over, my assailant held me against him in a bear hug, pinning my arms to my sides. The automobile slid alongside the kerb, sloshing rainwater over my trousers. I was propelled forward into the side of the car. My nose made the first contact. Pain rushed through my broken nose at it was pushed sideways by the impact. I felt blood erupt as my face was smashed into the top of the bodywork. My body followed suit, impacting with the rear door, rocking the car on its springs.

Before I knew what was happening, I was hauled back and the rear door was opened from the inside. Next thing I was flung inside to sprawl across the velour upholstery. My subconscious registered the vast width of the seat. I was sprawled full length and only my fingertips touched the far door. With a crash the door slammed shut behind me, and a weight kept me pinned to the seat. The car leapt forward with a roar of its engine. That was the last thing I remembered before something hit me on the back of the head.

Chapter 12

I awoke to cold water being thrown over my face. I shook my head to shake off the water and immediately wished I hadn't. My head throbbed and my nose ached. When I crossed my eyes to look at it, my nose seemed enormous. It reminded me of the proboscis of a sea elephant. I was in a warehouse with brick boundary walls and timber floors supported by timber posts. My arms were tied behind my back around one of these posts. Looking down I saw thick ropes wrapped around my ankles. Wool bales were stacked all around from floor to ceiling. It occurred to me that they provided the perfect sound insulation.

I knew then that things were not going to go well for me. The two goons were sitting in bentwood chairs staring at me. One was smoking a cigarette while the other was slapping a rubber hose in his hand.

"Well George, you've led us quite a dance, haven't you," said the one with the bowler hat, cigarette in hand. It occurred to me they might use that to torture me.

"You owe our boss a hundred and twenty quid. I hope you are going to tell us that you have it nice and safe and are going to hand it over to us," he said.

It had only been a hundred quid two days ago, but I didn't think this was the time to argue the finer points of how much I owed. "I'm putting it together, but I need more time."

"That's disappointing George. We were hoping that we wouldn't have to do this. In our business it's all a matter of trust. You sign a chit saying you owe the house such and such money and we expect it to be redeemed. You can consider us debt collectors, I suppose, just balancing the books so to speak."

I remained silent during this little speech while my brain ran through all the possible means of coming up with the money. Short of robbing a bank I could see no earthly means of obtaining it in a hurry.

"It's a great inconvenience when people don't pay their debts," droned on the man in the hat. "Our boss loses interest on his investments. We've invited you here to remind you of your obligations. There's one thing that we want to impress upon you, George. From now on we are charging you interest on what you owe at the rate of twenty per cent per month. The sooner you pay the less the interest is. It's an incentive if you like. Now then, have you the money?"

"Some."

"That's really not good enough," said my inquisitor, who then nodded his head to the other thug.

He stood up and slowly advanced towards me slapping the rubber hose in his hand. The first blow struck my right knee sending tears to my eyes. The next was my other knee. My knees wouldn't support me then, leaving me hanging from my bindings. I worried that I wouldn't be able to play rugby again. That thought was fleeting; in a few minutes I might not even be alive.

The next blow struck me across my right arm followed by one to my left arm. My elbows were next. This was excruciating and I thought I might black out, but that was not to be my escape just yet. By now my eyes were closed, praying for the punishment to end. A fist slammed into my right cheek snapping my head to one side. I had barely recovered my senses before another fist smashed into my other cheek snapping my head flying in the opposite direction. Fearful of them hitting my still throbbing nose I opened my eyes to see my assailant slam the hose into my right knee again. It registered somewhere inside my head that they had commenced on round two. I thought I now knew what was coming next. It wasn't much satisfaction being right when more pain erupted from my left knee. It was excruciating the way the pain was so centred on the point of impact before it then rippled through the rest of your body.

By then I had slumped further down the post. Through the slits of my eyes I looked down at the floor expecting the blow to my arm when a blurred image of a boot passed before my eyes. It came into contact with my scrotum sending a burst of pain through me. That was when I blacked out.

I awoke to the sound of leaves rustling and branches clacking in the wind. Strangely, I had no sense of smell. I felt as though I had done ten rounds in the ring with Jack Johnstone. It was some time before I mustered the will to open my eyes. When I did I saw vapid moonlight filtering through the branches and leaves above me. I quickly shut them again when a stabbing pain in my head sent a starburst of colours across my vision. I waited for the pain to subside before attempting to get up by first rolling onto my side. I was lying against an iron railing on a thick bed of dry leaves. When I reopened my eyes I had to blink to make out what I was looking at.

An angel was staring down at me. For an instant I thought I had died and gone to heaven, but the pains and aches that racked my body reminded me that I was still in the land of the living and wondering how that could be. I put my hands up to touch my nose, only for more pain to shoot through my head. I was amazed the goons hadn't hit me on the nose at least once since it was broken against the side of the car. It wouldn't have been out of kindness. A shiver ran through me at the very thought of them smashing a fist into the sorry mess I now called my nose.

The angel's wings threw a shadow over me. Its hands were clasped together in prayer. The white marble gave off an effulgent gleam in the moonlight. Dark shapes completed the background. The angel was comforting to me at that moment. A great wave of peace passed over me and I closed my eyes, hoping to rest a little bit longer before getting up.

I must have dozed off because when I next awoke, dawn had broken. I staggered to my knees and saw I was in a graveyard, a very dilapidated one at that. A blackbird above me in the trees called out in alarm. All around me lay broken graves. The retaining walls that surrounded them lay cracked and broken, rent apart by tree roots or land subsidence. The slabs covering them had suffered similar fates, broken into irregular shaped pieces lying at different angles to their neighbours. I knew how they felt.

The few slabs not broken had sunk inside the walls that surrounded them, to act as basins now filled with dead leaves. Young seedlings grew in happy abandon amongst the leaf mould. Large trees grew out of the remains of other graves. I leaned on the wrought iron railing against which I had rolled. The vertical railings, now bent and twisted by the heaving of the ground, were topped by cast iron fleur-de-lys. I staggered and crawled my way uphill through the fallen leaves and broken branches. I looked up to see the obelisk had fallen off the next grave and rolled down the hill. Only the truncated pedestal still remained, its smooth marble surface now pitted and cracked. The squeak and rumble of a streetcar high up the slope told me I must be in the Symonds Street cemetery, the only one within the limits of the tramcar network. My assailants must have tossed me over the wall at the top after beating me up. It wouldn't have mattered a damn to them if I was dead or alive at the time.

I came to a well-worn path, possibly used by the shady inhabitants of the graveyard. I lurched forward, bent over and holding my knees in my hands. My knees threatened to give way at any minute. After pushing through scrub for a time I came out on a gravel path. Gravestones and monuments leaned at drunken angles in all directions, but as I shuffled my way further along I came to a newer section of the cemetery. Here the gravestones stood in straight rows and erect, like soldiers on parade. From the names on the epitaphs it seemed that I was now in the gentry's section, either Church of England or Wesleyan. The more elaborate graves had obelisks supported on little colonnades over their bases or gothic arches around them. All were in good order despite being covered in lichen and moss.

My recollections of the previous evening were sketchy at best. I remembered being smashed into the side of the car because that was when they broke my nose. After that it was all a blur which may have been a mercy. I felt in my pockets to see if I had my wallet or any money to get home with. My hands came up out empty; even my hankie was gone.

I paused as a wave of dizziness overwhelmed me. Once it had passed, I went over to the side of the path and sat down again. I was more aware now of the birds in the trees above me and the hum of the city about me. I lurched to my feet to stagger up the path some more before leaning against a trunk of a tree. I looked up past the smooth bark of the trunk into the dark interior of the canopy above me. It was a matai, one of the giants of the forest. It was a living thing, a thing that held no malice towards me. For that I was thankful. In return for its support I fertilised its roots by throwing up all over them and my boots. I muttered my apologies to the tree and staggered onward up the path.

Somewhere I heard the sound of trickling water and I set out to look for its source. The sound was coming from the bottom of a small gully full of brambles and scrub below the path. I began climbing down through the tangle of vines and branches. The deeper I went, the darker it got with the boughs of trees meeting together overhead to cut out the light. I groped my way forward, slithering and sliding, all the time afraid of falling into a grave.

Enough religious training had been pumped into me as a child to scare the bejeezus out of anyone. Now all of my fears came back to bite me. I looked around the whole time, looking left and right and behind me, to make sure there was no one out there watching me. Of course, as soon as you think someone is watching you, you become convinced of it. Sinister figures loomed out of the gloom only to materialise into yet another grave monument.

Suddenly the ground vanished from under me and I fell forward to land in water. The idea of a semi-submerged grave flooded through me, making me panic. I slithered about trying to get purchase to lift myself out. While doing this, it dawned on me that there were no vertical sides about me and that I was in a small stream. I automatically lifted a cupped hand full of water to my lips before thinking about all the decomposing corpses the water had flowed past or through to get there. Instead I threw it over my face. It felt good and I sat there washing my face in the water.

Just then the sun broke out from behind the clouds. Through the canopy of the trees I saw one of the massive abutments supporting the arch of Grafton Bridge. The sight of a familiar object gave me hope. I was definitely in Symonds Street cemetery and it was just a matter of walking along Karangahape Road and then Ponsonby Road to get home. What I didn't know was whether my battered body would get me there.

It began as a long and painful walk, with stops anywhere I could sit down. Passers-by gave me strange looks and then hurried away quickly. I guess I didn't look too good, but there was little that could be done about that. The thing that preyed on my mind was that if I didn't get some money and fast, then I was a dead man.

The only source of quick money available to me was at Shaw and Company.

Chapter 13

I arrived at work early on Monday, determined to be seated at my desk first, so that as few people as possible would notice the bandages over my face. Every bit of my body ached and it had taken all my physical effort to get there. My ribs hurt and my breathing rattled in my ears each time I took a breath. Making my way slowly along the footpath I had felt like a cripple. Now I self-consciously waited for the others to arrive.

I was thankful that the long sleeves of my shirt and my trousers covered up the damage inflicted to my body, arms and legs. I kept my shirt collar buttoned up to the top, to present as good an aspect as I could. However, there was nothing much I could do to cover up the damage to my face. It wasn't long before word had got around that I'd been beaten up. You could tell this by the furtive glances thrown my way and by the urgent whispering. When Skinner arrived he took one look at me and walked straight into his office. A little later one of the secretaries was called into his office and then came out to walk across to me.

"Mr Skinner wants to see you," she said.

"Thanks," I said, standing up too suddenly. A shower of fireworks went off in my head. I had been wracking my brain all morning for an excuse that would explain my injuries and it was only as I entered Skinner's office that a credible excuse came to me.

He didn't invite me to sit down, as he usually did, but kept me standing in front of his desk while he checked some figures in a ledger. Without even looking up he said, "You need to know that the Shaws will not stand for any of their staff brawling in the street or elsewhere. I hope that you have a good excuse for your disgraceful appearance."

It was only as he finished his sentence that he looked up at me and took in my broken nose and the bruising over my face.

"I apologise for my appearance. I can assure you that it was an accident and not a brawl."

"Really?" he said, clearly unconvinced.

"I was dragged under the wheels of a dray on College Hill. I was lucky to come out of it alive," I said.

"Can you corroborate this?"

"It'll probably be in the papers, I should imagine. There were a lot of witnesses. It was coming down the hill and the horse got spooked by a motorcar backfiring beside it. The horse bolted towards the footpath bowling me over. That was when the dray ran over me."

Even I was impressed by how well this sounded. A man as desperate as me had no place for scruples. Skinner looked as though he might have swallowed the story when he asked, "Did you go to hospital?"

"No, my GP sorted out most of it. My broken nose makes me look far worse than it is."

Skinner eyed me for an unsettling period of time, weighing up whether to believe my story or not. There was a real risk of his giving me the sack.

If he did, all my plans for getting enough money to repay the bookie would come to nothing and my life would be forfeit. It was a relief when he put down the pen he had been jabbing into his blotter pad during the interview.

"Well," he said, "if you feel up to it you had better get back to your duties. I would appreciate it if you kept a low profile until your nose has healed and the bruising has gone down. It doesn't do the firm's reputation much good having one of its employees looking like a pub brawler."

"I understand. You have my promise. Thank you."

Every eye in the office was directed towards me as I left his office. I gave a sick grin to them all as I walked back to my desk. I could tell that I had lost any goodwill they had for me up till then. I was tainted now. None of the girls would want to know me.

The two goons had a habit of turning up on a street corner every time I went home. I never knew where or when they might appear and they never said a word, just looked me in the eye with a grim smile across their mugs. I knew that I had to pass over money to them, but couldn't take too big a risk in my nefarious fiddling of the books. I took just a fiver, or so, a day so as not to raise the alarm with the head bookkeeper. My usual ploy was to substitute twos and threes for sevens and eights when entering the amount into the journal and pocketing whatever the difference might be from the money enclosed with the order.

By the first Friday I had cobbled together twenty-five pounds and added a tenner of my own money to give to the goons. The problem was I didn't see them that night when I went home. Now I had all this money I was fearful of losing it or someone stealing it. I began to get an inkling of what it must be like for rich people trying to protect their money from thieves. My biggest fear was that Ma or Daniel would discover it so I kept it on my person at all times and put in in my pillow slip and slept on it at night.

Another of my worries was that I might spend it if I went to the pub after work. This anxiety led me to bypass it and head straight home each night. I had to make excuses up for why I hadn't been going to the pub with the other blokes from Shaw's. These were lame at first and even I didn't think they sounded believable until I came up with the excuse of helping my uncle reblock his foundations each night. By the third week I had become bolder and began pocketing both the money order and the money without entering anything into the journal. I figured that the customer would complain after a few weeks that they had not received their order, but if it was only one or two a week then it could be put down to the order getting lost in the mail. When I look back on it now I can see that the people around me must have noticed my nervousness and the stress that I was under.

The game was up the day Skinner sat down to go through the journal entries with me. He pulled a chair across from the adjoining desk and eased himself down like a slow leak in a bicycle tyre. In his hand he held a pile of order forms.

"I've been going over these orders," he said. "I'm having difficulty reconciling some of these with what has been entered in the journal."

I tried to put on a brave face and act nonchalant, but I couldn't manage it. Instead I was silent while he sifted through one order after another. Some of the discrepancies could legitimately be put down to misinterpretations of the handwriting which at times was over florid and at others barely readable. Those orders he put to one side, evidently giving me the benefit of the doubt. At those moments I felt a wave of hope pass through me. The next instant this hope would be dashed when he peered at an order form where the amount or maybe the number of items had been altered by a different pen from the original. In those days we used dip pens with ink from an inkwell. The thickness of the nib and style could be copied, but it was hard to get the shade of ink the same.

"This looks like it has been tampered with. What have you got to say?" he asked. His warm breath wafted across my face each time he did this, reminding me of what he had had for breakfast. I felt it bring out the colour in my cheeks and I wondered if my embarrassment was showing. I'd glance up to see his cold eyes boring into me. My feeble protestations failed to move him. He had the bit between his teeth now.

On and on he went from one entry to the next. As the litany of entry errors mounted my silence deepened. It must have been an hour or more before he finished. When he did so, he stood up and pushed his chair back to its original position. Skinner then drew himself up to his full height before turning to me. He stared at me with contempt in his eyes. You could have cut the air with a knife. Then he spoke the words that sealed my fate.

"I have given you every chance to explain these irregularities. It is deeply regrettable that you have been unable to provide any reasonable explanation for them. I can only presume that you have falsified these records for some pecuniary gain. I have no alternative but to advise Mr Shaw of this matter."

At the time I had no idea what the word 'pecuniary' meant, but it didn't sound in any way hopeful to me. With a little huff he collected the invoices and the journal and headed for Mr Shaw office. He knocked on the door, then went in, closing the door behind him. I then watched the shut door waiting for the inevitable.

Lunch hour arrived and still no one had come out of Mr Shaw's office so I decided to go out for my lunch. There was always the small chance that Mr O'Connor would give me the benefit of the doubt when it came to interpreting the order forms. I bought some sandwiches and walked around to St Patrick's Square where I ate them sitting on a low wall. It felt as though my whole world was about to collapse. It was a strange feeling, a bit like being in shock. I had no appetite and spent most of the time in a daze breaking up the sandwiches in my hands and feeding the crumbs to the pigeons, the sparrows and the gulls. The presence of the cathedral so near to me also weighed on my mind. Even though I often had my lunch in the square it seemed on that day that I could not ignore its bulk so close to me.

After the last of my lunch had been distributed to feed the birdlife of the city I stood up and walked towards the cathedral entry. Once inside, all the sounds of the city vanished; the car horns, the rumble of traffic, the shouts of newspaper vendors.

Everything was quiet in that closed atmosphere of candlewax and stone. I stood inside the entry looking at the banks of candles filling the air with a warm fug of spiralling smoke that blackened the stonework all around them. A few women were at prayer in the pews near the front. The door of a confessional banged open and a woman came out.

The teachings of my youth pulled me inwards. Perhaps my hatred of Father O'Riorden had overridden my faith. Many times had I questioned whether it meant anything to me, but now I felt a great need for help from above. I hovered by the entrance. The communists said it was all cant, superstition, and fairy stories. Perhaps they were right. I was a fool to think that some divine intervention was going to get me out of this hole. I shook my head and turned on my heels. As far as I could see I had two choices. To go back to work and hope that nothing would come of it, or go to the pub for the afternoon. Let me tell you, going to the pub was very tempting then, but it would also be deemed to be an admission of guilt. With a weary heart I made my way back to work and whatever the fates had decided for me.

Mr Shaw's door was standing open when I re-entered the office. There was no sign of Skinner either. I sat back down at my desk and resumed my work, more diligently that I had for several weeks. I guess this was my way of attempting to make amends. At five past three Mr Shaw and Mr Skinner returned to the office with a man in a long overcoat and large black shoes. They all went into Mr Shaw's office and the door was shut once again. A few minutes later the phone on Mr Shaw's secretary's desk rang shrilly and she answered it. While listening to her instructions she looked across at me. When she put the phone down she got up and came over to my desk.

"Mr Shaw wants to see you in his office," she said. In the old days there might have been a bit of banter, but since the episode with my broken nose, the rest of the staff had kept distant from me. I dare say there had been all sorts of rumours circulating about my activities.

"Did he say what it was about?" I asked, contriving to sound innocent.

"You'll find out," she replied over her shoulder, heading back to her desk.

With an air of resignation I stood up and walked towards that fateful door. I remembered another door that had impressed itself on my mind. What was it about doors? In my life that which was beyond the door did not always bode a new future blessed with good fortune. I knew that my future was now in the balance. I rapped my knuckles against the woodwork.

Someone called out "Come in" and I turned the handle to enter. Mr Shaw sat behind his desk looking up at me. Standing behind his right shoulder was Mr Skinner. On the desk in front of Mr Skinner was the incriminating evidence. I took all this in at a glance before looking at the stranger standing to one side. His eyes were on me as soon I entered the room, weighing me and judging me.

"You wanted to see me," I said in a faltering voice that I immediately despised myself for.

Mr Shaw was what was called a self-made man. Probably from some bog-hole in Ireland originally, he had come to New Zealand to do better for himself and had now amassed a small fortune. Good luck to him I thought, as I looked at him and he looked at me. There were so many men like that about the town. Had I missed my chance? Was it too late for me to make my fortune in this rambunctious colony? Now that we were a Dominion, it probably was. We had grown respectable. In my heart of hearts I still longed for the main chance to come my way. Well, it wasn't coming my way that day, of that I could be certain. Mr Shaw should have been a poker player. I could read nothing in his face as he sat there in his expensive suit with his paisley tie.

"Sit down, lad," he said. I was surprised at his conciliatory tone and immediately sat down in the chair placed in front of his desk. Was he going to show he was a man of understanding and merely admonish me?

"Mr Skinner has found a number of discrepancies in the books. I have been through them with him and have come to the conclusion that Mr Skinner's suspicions are correct," he said. "It is our contention that you have been deliberately falsifying the amounts put into the ledger and pocketing postal notes and monies sent in with the orders. Do you deny this?"

I was on the point of denying it all when I saw in all their eyes that I wouldn't be believed if I tried. The best thing I could do was plead extenuating circumstances.

"Mr Skinner's right. I have been fiddling the books and taking money to pay my gambling debts. I'm sorry that I have broken your trust in me. My only defence is that if I hadn't repaid these debts my life was forfeit."

"Are you saying that the broken nose you had last month was the result of a beating?" asked Skinner.

"Yes," I replied.

An uncomfortable silence descended on the room as Mr Shaw took in the import of this. No one else moved. Mr Shaw clasped his hands before him on his desk before clearing his throat.

"It is my painful duty to inform you that we have placed this matter before the police. We have given you the chance to clear yourself of this matter, however you have now confessed in front of witnesses so I have no other option than to press charges against you. Chief Detective O'Donnell, if you would now do your duty."

The other man stepped forward. A heavy hand descended onto my left shoulder, keeping me firmly in the chair.

"George Cyril Bender, you are hereby charged with embezzling ninety-six pounds, eight shillings and four pence from your employer, Shaw and Company, wholesale chemists. This money was embezzled between October 19, 1914 and April 17, 1915. Anything you say will be taken down and may be used in evidence against you."

All eyes in the room were on me, Mr Shaw's the only ones that showed any mercy. Perhaps he had been in similar straits once in his life. Skinner's were hard, showing no compassion at all. Well, I had made him look a bit of a chump, I suppose. He had a right to be pissed off.

"Right lad, we'll best be going now," said the detective, taking off the pressure of his hand from my shoulder. I had half risen from my chair when I realised that Ma would be expecting me home for supper. I looked straight at Mr Shaw before saying, "I'm truly sorry, Mr Shaw. It would never have happened if I had not been in such a fix."

"I can see that lad. But it doesn't take away the fact that you have broken the law and our trust in you."

"Will you get word to my mother about what has happened? She will worry when I don't come home tonight."

"Aye lad. We'll take care of that."

"Thank you."

Chapter 14

I spent the night in the police cells under the police station on the corner of Princes Street and O'Rourke Street. I was given a meal of hot spuds, cabbage and beef slices and a mug of cold tea in the evening. I didn't feel like talking to anyone and curled up on the hard bench that was to serve as my bed for the night.

About eleven I was disturbed in my self-pity by the arrival of a religious nutter in my cell. He raved on about men being all sinners and that the end of the world was nigh. I couldn't contradict what he was saying, but wished he would shut up. By the time morning came around he was curled up in the corner fast asleep. I was amazed that I had slept at all, but I must have because I felt quite good, just a little chilled. Outside birds chirped in the trees and the rumble of a city waking up could be heard. The clank of keys and the murmuring of voices drifted along the corridor as the drunks of the night before were let out to stagger off home.

At nine in the morning all those facing the magistrate were let out of the cells and lined up before being placed in paddy wagons for the short trip down the hill to the recently built magistrate's court. On arrival there we were herded into a room to wait our turn at being called up. When mine came I was escorted up the steps into the dock. The magistrate was sitting in his bench above me, dressed in his black robe and white wig. A court clerk sat below him while in front of the bench the barristers and their assistants sat in their ranks to try and defend their clients or otherwise. I was heartened to see Ma and Daniel sitting at the back and we exchanged smiles from afar. Behind Ma, I was surprised to see Niccolò Piagni and some of my former colleagues from the Criterion Hotel. After the general murmuring settled down the court clerk stood up.

"Please state your full name, marital details and address."

"George Cyril Bender, single, 74 Lincoln Street, Ponsonby."

"George Cyril Bender, you are charged with stealing the sum of ninety-six pounds, eight shillings and four pence, the property of Shaw and Company, wholesale chemists, the money having been embezzled between the 9th of October 1914 and the 17th of April 1915. How do you plead?"

"Guilty."

The magistrate seemed to be distracted, looking at some documents on the desk in front of him before looking straight at me and saying, "It is noted that you have pleaded guilty to the charge. In view of the fact that you have an unblemished record until now I'm willing to place you on bail until such time as your trial is scheduled. I set the bail at one hundred pounds. You are to be bound over until such time as the bail is paid. Next case."

The constable bustled me back down the stairs to let the next defendant take the stand. He then escorted me through to a holding room where I joined several others waiting to be bailed. I didn't have much hope in this regard knowing my Ma didn't have that kind of money. My only chance was that Ma's brother might front up. I was surprised therefore when after only twenty minutes or so I was called out of the room to see Nicco Piagni's beaming face. He was the last person I expected to see, pumping my hand for all it was worth, before declaring that he had paid the bail money. This shocked me. I should have thanked him on the spot, but I could see immediately that it was a two-edged sword. His paying it put me in his debt and he was part of the reason I was in that mess. I mumbled my thanks to him, wondering what he was going to demand in return.

On the day of my court appearance, we caught the tram into Queen Street and walked up Durham Street to the courtroom. Waiting for us outside the courthouse was Ma's brother, Declan. We shook hands and he wished me luck, as though I was betting on a horse. The only sure thing here was that I was going to prison. Inside the building Ma gave me a hug and Daniel shook my hand. Ma didn't say a word; she had been expecting this day all her life. Self-pity flooded though my veins when I realised that I had fulfilled her prophesy. All I could do was say I was sorry and that I loved her.

She released me from her arms and looked me in the face before saying, "Look to the Lord, son. I know you don't have a lot of time for the faith, but it really can help in times of trouble."

"I'll keep that in mind, Ma," I said.

I turned and nodded my head towards Uncle Declan and Daniel, before walking over to the desk clerk to report in. A constable led me to a small room and told me to wait. After what seemed an eternity the door opened and a constable asked if I was George Bender. When I said yes, he asked me to follow him. We walked along a corridor and then down some stairs to the lower level where we walked along another corridor until we came to a lobby with another stair. There we waited while listening to muffled voices above drifting down to us. My name was called out and a policeman put his head around the corner at the top of the stairs and repeated my name.

"C'mon my lad," said the constable sitting next to me. He was barely older than me and I wondered if the police trained them to call everyone 'lad'. I mounted the stairs ahead of him and emerged at the top inside the dock. The policeman already there took station on my left shoulder while the one who followed me up took station on my right. It was a daunting experience facing that crowded room, where every eye was on you, most prejudiced against you, others blank and a few sympathetic towards you.

The woodwork all around the room gleamed, whether it was the panelled walls or the intricately carved benches, docks and rails. The opulence of it all seemed to state this was the preserve of the rich and that justice was theirs. I knew in that moment, that by embezzling from my employer, I had performed, in their eyes, a more dastardly act than murder.

The magistrate, dressed in a red robe and a white wig, sat hunched like a vulture waiting to swoop down on me from his elevated perch. The barristers dressed in their wigs and black robes looked like so many crows waiting to make their obeisance to their leader perched on high. The magistrate cast his beady eye about the room until the general murmuring and shuffling of chairs and papers died down, then the clerk stood up to read the charges.

"George Cyril Bender, you are charged with embezzling from your employer the amount of ninety-six pounds, eight shillings and four pence between October 1914 and April 1915. How do you plead?"

"Guilty," I replied.

An eerie silence fell over the courtroom after I made my plea. I wasn't sure whether they all despised me, thought I was mad, or whether they were disappointed I had taken away their sport by not allowing them to drag out the case and humiliate me more than I was already. The magistrate pushed up his spectacles from the end of his nose and peered down at me.

"You have pleaded guilty to the charges. The trust between an employer and an employee must be held sacrosanct. As you are young and this is your first offence, I am prepared to be lenient. You are sentenced to two years hard labour. I hope that this serves as a warning to you. Take him away."

Before I knew what was happening I was bustled down the stairs and led along a corridor to a door. One of the constables unlocked the door and I was pushed through to the outside. I sucked in the clean air of freedom for a few seconds before being told to mount the steps at the back of a paddy wagon.

The paddy wagon was still that: a closed wagon drawn by two horses. It was painted a glossy navy blue with gold pinstripes painted around the doors and along the sides where the word 'Police' was painted. A constable got in after me and sat in the corner by the door to look at the opposite wall.

I sat in the middle of the bench and closed my eyes as the driver clicked his cheeks and called out to the horses.

With a slight lurch the wagon moved forward, the steel rims rumbling over the cobblestones and the wagon swaying from side to side. I listened to the clip-clop of the horses hooves on the road and the sounds of the street outside. We were making our way to my incarceration. The motion dulled my senses and I was falling into a doze when we suddenly stopped. I had to put my arm out to brace myself from falling sideways. A chain and keys rattled from outside the door before it swung open and the constable motioned me to get out.

The sunlight was blinding after the darkness inside the paddy wagon. Climbing down the steps at the back of the wagon, I squinted. The second my feet hit the ground my right arm was gripped by the great paw of a sergeant who looked as if he could lift me off the ground single-handed. The constable climbed down and saluted his superior before grabbing my left arm and together they frog-marched me though the door of the prison. The door, and its larger brother in which it was located, were painted in the same glossy paint as the paddy wagon. That was the last shiny surface I was to see.

Inside everything was bare stone: grey rock covered in millions of tiny holes. It looked like the place was infested with some sort of borer. They called it bluestone, but there was no blue that I could see, just a bleak greyness which matched my spirit. I was bundled across the courtyard and through a door where the sergeant and constable let go of me. A man in a white coat stood in front of me. His badge of office in the form of a stethoscope hung from his neck and down his front.

"Oh, shit," I thought as the sergeant told me to undress.

When I hesitated he said, "C'mon, we haven't all day, we've seen it all before."

"Not me you haven't," I thought. "What about the cuffs?" I said out loud.

"Get your trousers down around your ankles and then we'll remove the cuffs."

I did as he asked. As soon as the cuffs were off I was able to take off my jacket and shirt and pull my singlet over my head. I stood there with my hands over my privates while the doctor inspected the now dull bruising all over my body, my still swollen joints, looked into the orifices at both ends of my body by asking me to bend forward and then to open my mouth. Finally he inspected my hair for nits. He walked across to a table where he picked up a clipboard and began filling in a form and writing notes at the bottom of the sheet. I could see that it was at least in triplicate by the number of carbon pages inserted between the sheets.

"Step out of your pants," ordered the sergeant.

As soon as I had stepped forward the doctor picked up my pants with a pair of tongs and threw them into a bin, to join my jacket, shirt and singlet.

"You can have all those back when you leave. I shouldn't think you'll be putting on too much weight in here," said the sergeant with a grin. "Now put these on."

The constable put a pile of folded clothes in my arms. These were my prison gear. A singlet, a rough jacket and a pair of loose pants tied at the waist by a short cord sewn in at the front. Not long enough to take out and hang yourself, just long enough to keep your pants up. Both the jacket and the pants were striped in black and white. A pair of woollen socks fell to the floor when I unfolded the pants. Even these were striped, horizontally this time.

Chapter 15

There were two things you could do in prison in those days. One was to work in the basalt quarry and the other was to make mail bags. The latter was reserved for those who were disabled in some way or too old to work in the quarry. Having been sentenced to hard labour I was put to work in the quarry.

There was a basalt flow next to the prison which had been quarried by the inmates for many years. The quarry face rose about a hundred feet above the quarry bed. It had formed into columns when it cooled from red hot lava and now presented a smooth grey face. The first time I saw it any confidence I had in getting through my time unscathed pretty much collapsed. It seemed ridiculous that we would break up a wall of solid rock. We were nothing more than slaves so far as the system went. I soon found out that they used explosives to bring down the huge basalt columns. My relief at this was short lived when I was told that these were broken up by the prisoners using sledgehammers, chisels and picks.

We worked on the quarry bed in all weathers. This was the flat area formed after the face had been cut away. When it rained we were issued with long oilskin jackets, enough to protect the top half of you, but not enough to protect your lower legs. As a result the bottom half of our pants were more often than not sodden. Whenever there was blasting we were given a rest and waited well back from the quarry face to watch the big bang. Just having that moment's respite was like a holiday. We looked forward to that.

On that first day I was handed a sledgehammer and told to break up the rock. The first time I struck one of those rocks the shockwave went right up my arms and through my body like a runaway train. My swollen elbows and knees really felt it. I realised pretty quickly that I was going to have to have a strategy otherwise I was going to break before the rock. What you had to do was just put enough energy into it for the stone chisels to do the work. You learned to work as a team with the other guy.

Swapping places during the day cut down the jarring from wielding a sledgehammer. The guys on picks were generally the older prisoners. It wasn't too bad for them since they were just picking away at small stones. It was a wretched existence, like something from the middle ages. I felt a deep and bitter resentment with the world each time one of those shockwaves rattled through me. I cursed all those involved in the justice system. However, with the days and weeks that passed, you gave up all these thoughts; you needed all your energy simply to survive. You became a machine, working without conscious thought, repeating what you did the minute before. The only thought left was that your body ached. There was nowhere it didn't ache.

Each day they brought water around at smoko time and at lunch time we went back to into the prison to the dining hall. On Sundays we had the day off. The only time you returned to being human again was at night or on Sundays when you weren't working. I missed Ma and Daniel on those occasions a lot to start with, but even they faded into strangers after a while. You knew they were out there, but they could do nothing for you. Thinking about them enjoying all the freedoms you had lost only gave you more grief.

Sundays were the days I dreaded most. On week days everyone was working and at night everyone was too tired to bother with any shenanigans. Sundays were different. In the morning we had church parade which was always Church of England, never Catholic, not that it was a lot different. After church parade there were always do-gooders coming round trying to get you to join one church or the other, always trying to put you on the right path away from evil, whether crime or booze or both. With little else to occupy their minds Sundays was the day when the more basic urges of the men manifested themselves. I learned to see the warning signs and kept to myself at these times. That was when I dreamt of Suzanne Thompson and the life that might have been.

The funny thing about those church parades was that they classified you. As soon as you entered the gates of prison the old lags would know everything about you. They would know your name, age, where you were from, what level of society you came from and what your sentence was. What the church parade did was to fill in the unknowns, such as whether you were religious, an agnostic, an atheist, a communist or whatever. In other words, they typecast you into one of the tribes within the prison walls.

You could not escape these tribes. Anyone who tried to go it alone was quickly set upon. Belonging to a tribe protected you. I was an Irish Catholic whether I liked it or not. Someone had known I went to the Catholic Boys' School in Summer Street. The network seemed incredible, but then again the town wasn't such a big place back then. All the Christian denominations, the C. of E., Wesleyans, Presbyterians and Baptists, Unitarians and the Catholics were again divided into Irish, English, French, Chinamen and South American to name a just few. Tattoo-faced Maori renegades and foreigners made up the other groups that stuck together. Then there were the political affiliations, if you could call them that. These included the communists, the socialists, the nihilists, Hauhau, and all those who resented the present system of government.

It was a good breeding ground for hatred. You had to take it out on someone and your fellow inmates were the easy target. I think they went out of their way to be as obnoxious as they could. Some would hate you for what you were and you returned the venom. Fights were fast and vicious. People died. Within a week whoever had done it would also be dead. You learnt not to look anyone in the face. Keeping your head down and minding your own business became a way of life. If someone gave you some grief you took it and moved on.

I had been in prison for a fortnight before I had my first visitor. That was my Ma. She had given up an afternoon working at the laundry in order to come. The visitors' room was about twenty feet by sixteen feet. The walls and floor

116

were made of bluestone. It would have been a dreary place if it hadn't been for the sunbeams slanting across the room from the windows placed high up on the north wall. I was staring up at the dust motes dancing in these beams when the visitors were escorted into the room. A waft of new scents followed them in, a lingering memory of what it meant to be on the outside. We all secretly relished the female scent as something rare and precious after our regular diet of male body odour.

It was a stilted affair that first time. She looked tired. She asked how I was coping, that sort of thing. I tried to put a brave face on things. She had enough problems of her own. I felt that she had a low opinion of me. In her mind anyone that fell for the demon drink was damned. My gambling only made that worse. I promised to make amends when I got out, but even that seemed inadequate when there was a good chance I wouldn't survive anyway. When time was up I told her I loved her. A tremor caught one side of her lips and then she was gone.

After that she came every week. I had been inside for almost a year before Daniel got up the gumption to accompany her. I couldn't blame him for not wanting to come into the prison. It had that effect, like it was contagious. No one wanted anything to do with it if it could be helped. I can still see him as he accompanied Ma across to my table and sat down. Ma had on her blue mid-length coat with the fur collar and the floral dress she so often wore. What surprised me was her blue hat made of woven cane with a band of white lace around it. It was new and the first new thing I could remember her buying for a long time.

The only contact we were allowed was to touch hands. Ma clasped mine in hers, inspecting me, no doubt to check whether I was all right. I gave her a smile.

"Nice hat," I said.

"Oh that, I bought it at St Vincent de Paul's," she replied, taking off some of the gloss from her buying a new hat.

"This is quite something to have the whole family here," I remarked. "What's the occasion?"

"It's been a while since my last visit. I'm sorry for not coming more regularly. It's hard getting the time now that I have to work every day. I brought you some biscuits. The guard took them and told us he would give them to you after we leave."

"Not much chance of seeing them then. The guards will be having them with their tea, no doubt."

"Never mind that then, Daniel has some news to tell you."

"Oh, what's that?" I asked, turning to my brother. He looked taller and stronger than the last time I saw him. His face had filled out and there was the hint of a five o'clock shadow. "Are you getting married?" I asked.

He leaned forward, eager to tell me his news.

"Well, almost. I'm engaged."

"Anyone I know?" I asked.

"I don't think so. Her name's Beth Drummond."

"Well, congratulations are in order then, good on you." The best I could do was to shake his hand. He looked so happy at that moment. I wanted to give him a manly hug, but that was out of the question in the circumstances.

"There's something else," ventured Daniel. He seemed to be loath to broach whatever he was about to say and looked at Ma who gave him an imperceptible nod of her head. He then looked back at me. "I've enlisted in the army."

If he had told me anything else, I would not have been more taken aback. I hardly thought him old enough to get engaged, but now I knew the real reason for his getting engaged. I had heard of many men getting engaged before marching off to war only to leave their wives widows at the end of it. It was not something I approved of, but I maintained a straight face. It then struck me how absorbed in my own existence I had been; I was oblivious to what was going on in the outside world.

The war in Europe had been waged for years by then. Initially it had all seemed a long way off and only those brought up on a diet of gung-ho Boy's Own stories had volunteered to fight. Each time Ma had visited she had told me of the growing carnage and the mounting casualty lists. Reports of the battles had circulated around the prison. Fights had broken out over these reports between those supporting the war and those against it. The Hauhaus, the Irish Catholics and the German speakers had formed an unlikely alliance against it. It surprised me that Daniel had volunteered for this bloodbath. He was seventeen, old enough to enlist.

"You mean you volunteered?" I asked.

"No, they've brought in conscription now. They've done away with the ballot system. Everyone is getting their papers now. I'm joining the Auckland Regiment."

He sounded proud of the fact. Ma couldn't have been happy about it, but she remained silent. "When do you start?" I asked.

"I'm doing my basic training in Trentham, then taking a troopship out of Wellington."

"Is this the last time I'll be seeing you then?"

"Yeah, that's why I came. I'm off on Monday."

The futility of our existence then overwhelmed me. Here was I in prison. My Ma was working herself to the bone just to survive and now my brother was being sent off to fight in a war on the other side of the world. Not one of us seemed to have any control over our destinies. "Well, look after yourself," I said, somewhat lamely before remembering something and looking at him more cheerfully. "You know what they say about the army. Don't volunteer for anything."

"I'll be all right," he said. "In fact, I'm looking forward to it. Just think I'll be able to see London and Paris and all those places you only read about."

There was nothing more I could say. Those in the navy said they only ever saw the sea. What is a soldier stuck in a trench going to see other than mud or the sharp end of a bayonet? It made me sick to my stomach, but I couldn't voice those thoughts. He was going to need all of his naïve enthusiasm just to survive. All I could do was shake his hand.

"Good luck and look after yourself," I said. "Ma will pray for you."

"It wouldn't do you any harm to pray for him," said Ma.

"Perhaps I will. Have you got any other news?"

"Only that I've found a smaller place down Richmond Road by Cox's Creek," she said, like it was the most natural thing in the world. "I've put our house on the market and hope to move in a fortnight's time."

I looked at her. Had I heard her right? We'd been in the house in Lincoln Street my whole life.

"That's a bit sudden, isn't it?" I said, not knowing what else to say.

"Not really. With both you and Daniel no longer there, it seemed silly having a house with five bedrooms and I can do with the money."

"I suppose it makes sense. How big is this place you're looking at?"

"It's a cottage with two bedrooms, but there is another room next to the washhouse that can double as a bedroom."

"What, you mean it's in the outhouse?"

"Yes."

"I suppose that's all right," I replied, wondering which one of her sons was going to have to sleep there. You didn't need three guesses for that one.

Just then the bell rang for the end of visiting hour. Ma and Daniel stood up to go.

"Good luck," I called to Daniel.

He turned and gave me a grin before vanishing through the door.

A screw arrived to stand over me, signalling it was time for me to return to my cell. I stood up and looked him in the eye.

"Did my Ma bring in something for me?" I asked.

"Wouldn't you be so lucky," he replied. "The only thing you'll be getting from me is a hurry-along."

Chapter 16

One day I was called to the visitor's room. I joined the queue in the corridor outside the room, waiting for the visitors to arrive and be seated. The rules were explained once again by the guard before he opened the door and we burst into the room. In the melee of bodies rushing this way and that I couldn't see Ma at first. Then I saw her sitting by herself in the corner. She had on a long navy blue duster coat over a white blouse and full length navy skirt and a pin in her hair. Her formidable purse was on the table in front of her leaving me wondering how long it took for the screws to go through it. When I thought about the straits she was in I had to admire the way she dressed when she went out.

I slid into the chair opposite her and her hand immediately covered mine for a brief second before she withdrew it again.

"No hat today?" I asked.

"It blew off when I got off the tram," she replied, seeming to be amused by the event. "Anyway, it was getting old and tatty."

"Didn't someone run after it?"

"They did. A street urchin ran after it and got it, but he didn't bring it back to me. He made off with it."

"Well, I guess his mother is getting a present tonight."

"I'll probably see it for sale at the market tomorrow."

I was pleased Ma was able to smile about it. When she stopped smiling the sun went behind a cloud once again and I was made aware of her grey skin and the bags under her eyes. Underneath the trappings she was just skin and bones.

"How are you coping?" she asked.

"Me? I'm all right. I was going to ask you the same question."

"I get by. I've taken in another lodger and made him a space in the washhouse."

"That'll help make ends meet," I said, wondering whether there would be anywhere for me when I got out. It seemed to me that the only way there would be room for me was if I paid rent. I didn't voice these thoughts though; it would be a while before that bridge had to be crossed.

"I've a letter from Daniel here. Would you like me to read it?"

"No, you rest your eyes. I'll read it. You'll have to wave it in the air so the screw can approve your giving it to me."

After a nod from the screw walking around between the tables, Ma handed me the letter. It was in a special envelope, the sort you might get a Christmas card in, but this was headed On His Majesty's Service. Inside there was just a single sheet of paper so I knew it wasn't going to take long to read. I unfolded the thin paper to find that Daniel had written as small as possible to cram as much writing as he could on the single piece of paper. It was amazing how he could write so much and yet say so little. It was evident he missed home and gave his love to Ma and me. I handed the letter and envelope back to Ma.

"At least he's alive and well. Let's hope he stays that way."

Ma looked cross at me for saying these words, as if I was tempting fate. You could be as Catholic as you like, but the old superstitions were still there.

"Is there anything happening outside I should know about?"

"The war goes on. There have been some terrible battles. The papers are full of page after page of casualties. I don't know anyone not affected in some way. They say there's a shortage of labour everywhere. I suppose that's not surprising now all the men are overseas fighting. Prices of everything are going up. It's hard to make ends meet. Even fish is in short supply now."

"The war can't go on much longer now," I said, hoping to placate her fears.

She gave a thin smile at this.

"How are you really coping?" I asked.

"It's hard. I've now got two jobs. I work in the laundry down in Freeman's Bay three days a week and clean an office building on Friday and Saturday. The pay is pitiful, but it keeps the wolf from the door."

"I'm sorry I can't help. I should be out soon, then I can help."

"Like you did before?"

"I've changed. You wait and see."

Ma looked at me with an air of resignation that I interpreted as; 'Seeing is believing.' I couldn't blame her for this attitude. I had let her down in more ways than I could count, but I was still resolved to do better once I got out.

"The other news you might be interested in is that the government has bought in six o'clock closing for bars," said Ma. She looked me in the eye, no doubt hopeful inside that this might curb my drinking when I got out.

"That's going to put a damper on a lot of lives," I said, thinking of how Nicco Piagni's little enterprises would survive.

The day finally came when my sentence was complete. A lot had been going on outside the grim walls of the prison while I had been incarcerated. The war in Europe was still raging. There was a good chance I would be dragged into it against my will, but that bridge had to be crossed when I came to it. All I wanted to do was taste clean air, see Ma and smell the scent of a woman.

Early the next morning I was taken from my cell to the same room where I had first been introduced to the prison. There they gave me back my clothes and few possessions. Taking off my prison garb and throwing it in the laundry bag marked a significant victory for me. I could now put that part of my life behind me.

When the warder opened the little side gate a wave of relief passed through me. My sentence was over and the light flooding through that little door seemed to promise a new life as I stepped through it, ducking my head. I looked about for Ma, but my new sense of well-being plummeted to my bootstraps when I realised she wasn't there waiting for me. The road was devoid of both people and solace. I stood outside the grim walls at a loss for several minutes, not quite believing in the freedom I now had or that no one was there to greet me. I breathed in the sweet air of freedom, hyperventilating to clear my lungs of the foul prison air I had endured for two years, before setting off down the road.

A fine misty rain had begun to fall and I lifted my face up to the sky to let it wash over me. It felt good, anything to wash away the taint of incarceration in that bleak place. As quickly as it had started it stopped, and the sun came out again. At the intersection of the roads I turned right and headed up the hill towards Symonds Street. A smell of burnt wood permeated the air. The source of the smell was to my right. The tall smokestack of Henderson and Pollard's board mill belched forth pollutants into the air. The skeletal framework of the Colonial Ammunition Company's shot tower stood over to one side. With a war on now they would be working around the clock.

The road wound around in a long left-hand curve to reach the Symonds Street ridge. From there it was not too far to walk down Newton Gully and up the other side to Ponsonby Road. I'd be home in less than an hour. Not that I knew this home. I had never been there before.

Ma's new house was on the edge of town in Richmond Road. I tried to picture in my mind what the house might look like. It had to be smaller and less grand than the old house in Lincoln Street. This wouldn't be a kauri villa, more of a workman's cottage, if what Ma had told me was right. I passed by the houses along the road with the fields across from them. The formed road then gave way to a dirt track fit only for bullocks. It wound down to Cox's Creek where it crossed the estuary on a rickety looking timber bridge to climb back up the other side.

Once the road stopped so did the houses. From then on the track was surrounded by fields full of sheep, cattle and horses. Still I hadn't found number 175a. For a moment I thought I must have gone past the house and turned to check the numbers. It was soon evident that I had not gone far enough so walked out into the middle of the dirt track and continued on my way, wondering what sort of shack Ma had bought.

At the bridge I caught sight of a little cottage built by the bank of the creek and surrounded by kahikatea trees. The original owner must have reached it by boat up the creek from the harbour. Ma met me at the front door and gave me a hug. I clung to her, soaking in her smells: smells of cooking, baking, detergents, face powder and woman. I never had a better welcome home.

Chapter 17

One day I noticed that someone had left an Auckland Star in a tram shelter. It felt a real treat to have a newspaper to read. It was the second edition for Thursday, 20th of September 1918. Looking at the first couple of pages you wouldn't have known there was a war on. Both were full of classified advertisements. Things like 'Shipping', 'Wanted to Buy', 'Lost and Found', 'Situations Vacant', 'Domestics Wanted', 'Houses and Land for Sale'. I trolled through the classifieds. There were few jobs. I tossed up whether to apply for those that I stood a chance on, but a sense of unworthiness had come across me since leaving prison. I needed more time to find myself before plunging into employment. Instead I scanned the news which wasn't at all encouraging.

On a following page there was a heading 'Dominion's Heroes' with a list of the dead and wounded. I began to look for Daniel's name, but when I realised the list went on for three columns I couldn't look any longer. I wanted to be sick. That's when I saw the article on an epidemic breaking out on a troopship. Men were dying without being near the fighting. Below that was a list of people in Auckland Hospital with bronchitis and influenza. That was the first time I had seen the word 'influenza'. It was soon to leave a bitter harvest. I remember reading on another page a bold headline stating 'Nine Thousand Prisoners in the New Offensive' and another article on the New Zealander's assault on Trescault Ridge, wherever that was. Somewhere on the Somme front line no doubt.

I breathed a sigh of relief when I saw the next page was devoted to sport. The Cup Final for the Auckland Rugby Union was to take place on the next day between College Rifles and Ponsonby. It was to be at the Domain. With nothing else to do and a desire to pick up my life where I had left off, I decided to go.

Crowds streamed into the ground from all sides. I paid the shilling entry charge and joined the throngs standing ten deep all around the ground. It felt good to be among the boisterous crowd where people were there to enjoy themselves, giving one another a bit of stick, mates meeting mates. I had missed that sort of thing. What struck me most was the unrestrained rowdiness of the speech, no longer the tight-lipped mutterings of prison. Discarded beer bottles were dropped at people's feet to get kicked around or tripped over. I pulled the collar of my jacket up to protect me from the spray of beer directed at me from behind and kept myself to myself, still not comfortable at being back in real society.

In the middle of the pitch a brass band was going through its paces, marching up and down. When the band finished playing they marched off the field with the bandmaster throwing his staff up into the air and twirling it around, much to the appreciation of the crowd. The loudspeaker then burst into life to make a garbled announcement.

Evidently enough of the crowd understood it and there was a buzz around the ground.

A few minutes later some ball boys ran on to the field followed by the two teams. The crowd roared their approval that the game was about to commence. The jerseys of neither side had changed. When I saw the Ponsonby strip I felt a glow of pride sweep through me and I looked to see if I recognised any of the players. Billy Laidlaw, Jim Sykes and Bert Cummings were still there in the forwards, but the only back I knew was Charlie Hanson, still playing at centre. He was now playing for Auckland and there were those who thought he was good enough to make the national team.

The ref blew his whistle and the game was underway. Nothing had changed in the game since I had last played. The high up and under was still in vogue, with the backs trading kicks much to the chagrin of the poor old forwards forced to run up and down the field with almost no chance of touching the ball.

At half time the two teams congregated in two groups to either side of the field to have their oranges and a drink while their coaches ranted and railed at them. I joined the queues outside the toilets to have a slash before the game recommenced. As I was walking back to my place a bloke beside me who I had never seen in my life kept looking sideways at me.

"You're George Bender, aren't you?" he suddenly blurted out.

Several heads turned around in front of me as the bloke said this. For a second I was tempted to say no, but the look in his eyes told me he was a true aficionado of the game.

"Yeah, that's me."

"My God, let me shake your hand. You were one of the best centres Auckland ever had."

A ripple of affirmation ran through those standing around and I was soon shaking hands with strangers. I was someone again. It felt good.

By the time I got back to my place everyone around me seemed to know who I was and wanted to talk to me. Bottles of beer were put in my hands. After Ponsonby lost the game 9-6, the crowd filtered towards the exits. I made my way down to the front and climbed over the rope to walk across the field towards the grandstand with the changing rooms underneath.

As I entered I sensed the familiar air of despondency one always gets after losing a big game. The team members were sitting on the slat benches with heads down, mostly leaning forward, resting their elbows on their thighs while the coach ran through their failures. The coach was no longer Bert O'Hearn, but his long-time critic, Jock McAlister, a raw-boned ascetic from the Scottish borders, known to be an anti-Papist and a teetotaller, altogether a hard and uncompromising man. In an instant I knew that I would not enjoy playing under his tutelage. I could have tried at another club, but that seemed to be disloyal to my old mates and to the club.

Jock paused in his tirade to turn and look at me.

"Well, look who the cat's dragged in? Bender isn't it?"

"Jock McAlister, I presume?" I replied, in an attempt to pre-empt his inevitable sarcasm.

"Mister McAlister, to the likes of you."

"Right, I was at the game and thought of seeing if any of my old team mates were still here."

By now the heads of the team members had lifted and all eyes were on me. Several of them grinned at seeing me, some remained impassive, not knowing who I was and others pulled faces behind the coach's back.

"Well, you're not in the team now," said McAlister, clearly annoyed his grip over the minds of his team had been broken. With a dismissive gesture he said, "Wait outside."

Charlie Hanson was the first out of the door and he pumped my hand for all it was worth before exclaiming, "Christ, George, it's good to see you. You've lost weight."

"Yeah, well, that's hardly a surprise is it?"

"Nah, I don't suppose prison food is too flash. Are you coming back to the team?"

"I suppose I was hoping to have a training run. My knees aren't what they were anymore so I'm not sure if I can run or sidestep as well as I used to. Anyway, it's a waste of time now that McAlister is coach. What happened there?"

"They rolled old O'Hearn after he lost the championship two years in a row."

Charlie turned as two other players emerged from the changing room to join us.

"George, meet Terry Donald and Billy Sinclair. Billy plays in your old position."

I shook hands with them. They looked good lads though both seemed incredibly young.

"You were my idol when I was at school," said Billy. "I was sorry about what happened."

"You and me both," I replied, feeling old all of a sudden.

"The lads usually go on up to the local after a game. Do you want to join us?"

"Is McAlister going to be there?"

"Yeah, all the club officials come along."

"Well, in that case I would feel like I was in the way. It was good seeing you again Charlie. Perhaps, we can have a quiet beer sometime and catch up on what has been happening at Leyland-O'Connor."

"I wouldn't know. I'm at Parker Lamb's now."

That caught me by surprise. I had figured Charlie would be there for the duration. I wondered if he had left as a result of what had happened to my Da. I was about to ask him why he left and then thought better of it. Leyland-O'Connor was ancient history. We both looked down at our shoes and scuffed the dirt about, before I decided to break the impasse.

"I don't suppose any of you know of any work going. I'm in need of a job."

They all nodded their heads, looking pensive, but I sensed this was just being polite. Once I had said I wouldn't be joining them I sensed they had quickly lost interest in me.

"Yeah, well, if any of you hear of anything can you get in touch?"

There were a few grunts at this and the group broke up. Charlie put out his hand and said, "I'll let you know if I hear of anything."

"Thanks Charlie, I'll be seeing you, then," I said. As I walked away I felt as though the whole world had moved on, leaving me two years behind.

Leaving the ground a pall of despondency fell over me. Any hope I had of renewing old acquaintance now seemed a forlorn hope. They all had new lives and new hopes. For all I knew, Charlie might have married with kids by now. I hadn't even asked. What sort of mate was that?

The only thing left for me was to find employment and start my own life from scratch.

I arrived home to find a letter for me on the table. It was in a brown window envelope with a blue cross stamped across and headed On His Majesty's Service. I tore the envelope open and pulled out a card. It was a standard card headed New Zealand Military Forces – Notice to Attend for Medical Examination. I was warned to attend a medical examination at the Drill Hall, Rutland Street, Auckland on Wednesday 15 October 1918 at 10:30 am. That was a couple of weeks away. I wondered at the warning bit? The inference was that if you didn't attend they would put out an arrest warrant for you. It seemed that any chance I had of leading my own life had been snatched away once more.

I sat down in the armchair to think through my options. I could do a runner to one of the bush camps. I knew where some of them were, but then I'd just be slaving away from morning till night just like any other navvy. That life didn't appeal to me and if caught then there was the chance of being sent back to prison. I couldn't even claim to be working in an essential industry. It seemed that they had me by the short and curlies. There was nothing for it but to front up for the medical and hope that I was turned down on health grounds.

The army drill hall in Rutland Street was easy enough to find. A hand-painted sign hung over the door leading to the medical rooms. Inside, everything apart from the floorboards, was painted white. Even the army personnel were dressed in white coats. I walked up to the desk and gave my name. After confirming my full name, age, address and next of kin, the orderly ripped off a carbon copy and handed it to me.

"Wait over there," he said, nodding towards a bench seat against the wall where several others were waiting. Some of them couldn't have been more than fifteen. I had heard that a lot of the lads lied about their age, but to see these boys so eager to go to war depressed me. I sat down to stare at the opposite wall. Every so often the door to the next room would open and a name would be called out. One of those waiting would stand up and go through the door which was then closed. We all shuffled along the bench seat to make room for others arriving behind us.

When my name was called out I stood up and went through the door. There were two men standing beside a desk. The only other things in the room were a bentwood chair and a set of scales. One of the men had a stethoscope hanging down his chest so I presumed he must be the doctor. He was a short man with a pointy nose and dark hair. He looked impatient to get the consultation over with, a sentiment I agreed with entirely. The other man was the taller of the two. I sensed he was a military man by the way he held himself ram-rod straight, looking ahead unless spoken to. I imagined he could stand like that for hours. The doctor put out his hand to take my sheet of paper. He looked at it for a moment. "Right, take your clothes off."

After prison I had no modesty left and soon divested myself of my duds. The doctor came across and listened to my chest through his stethoscope while at the same time tapping my chest. He repeated this on my back before examining every part of me, as though I was a show horse, beginning with my teeth and ending with my goolies, for which I gave the usual cough when asked. He then bent lower to look at my knees. I watched while he put out his hand to touch one before deciding against it. That was when he looked up at me and asked, "How long have you had these swollen knees?"

My hopes soared when I realised that my knees might rule me out of being shot at. I then wondered if the army had access to my prison medical records. It was highly unlikely. The civil service wasn't known to be that efficient.

"A couple of years now. I got them playing rugby," I said.

"Funny looking rugby injuries," he said, looking up at me quizzically. When I remained silent he asked, "Do they cause you any problem?"

"Only when I run, then they give twinges. That's when I stop."

"I see," he replied, writing up his notes on his form. "Right, you can get dressed now. The army will be getting in touch with you."

"Thanks doc," I replied, reaching down to pick my clothes up from the floor.

Chapter 18

There seemed no point looking for permanent work. I expected to receive my call-up papers at any time. By then the little money I had been given on leaving prison had vanished. I still had a small amount put away in a savings account that I could draw on, but that was about it. With nothing else to do I just wandered about the town looking up old mates. I convinced myself that one of them would help me find a job, but it seemed that I had 'ex-con' stamped across my forehead. I guess what I was really craving for was their acceptance. Of course, what I ended up doing was asking them for money. The few willing to have a drink with me couldn't or wouldn't help on the job front. They all looked at me in a piteous manner. It hadn't occurred to me then that I was slipping down the path towards drunkenness.

On my way home one night I passed a sign outside the city destructor stating, Men Wanted. I paused in my travels and then went back to check. It wasn't the sort of work I would have taken on in normal circumstances, but right then it suited me. It was close to home, it was casual labour and I needed the cash.

I began work on the tip site at the back of the destructor. Each day horses and drays brought the city's rubbish in an endless stream. I would help the drivers manoeuvre their drays into position and then help them tip the dray up to unleash their load on top of the fetid and often steaming heap. The wheels of the drays were plastered with all manner of filth which we tried to scrap off before they returned to the city's streets, but all too often this was a half-hearted attempt at cleaning them, resulting in a trail of paper, mud and ordure lining the streets all around the destructor.

The drays were high-sided affairs built of robust timbers and wooden wheels having heavy steel bands around them. They were built to allow them to be tipped back without having to unhitch the poor horse that waited stoically in his traces between the heavy wooden drawbars. The only good thing from the horse's point of view was that the destructor was at the bottom of a hill, which meant he always brought his heavy load down the hill and only had to haul an empty wagon back up. Every time we emptied a dray, a great cloud of dust would erupt as soon as it slid off onto the mound of steaming rubbish that caked the ground we walked on.

Most of the time I worked without a shirt and tied it around my neck as a kind of neckerchief with which to wipe my face periodically or to pull up over my mouth and nose when the dust was more than a person could bear. Rats ran here and there through the mounds of rubbish. I wore leather boots and made sure that my work socks always covered the legs of my pants.

Smouldering fires were always springing up in the piles of rubbish either from broken bottles focussing the sun's rays on paper or from the embers of a cigarette butt carelessly tossed onto the rubbish. When this happened we had to run around with buckets of water to put it out before it took hold. If it did there was little we could do except get out of the way. Fires could burn for days in the mounds of rubbish. No one really cared when this happened since it got rid of a lot of rubbish in one foul swoop. The only people to complain were the inhabitants of Freeman's Bay who had to put up with palls of stinking smoke for days on end.

Ma made me take off my clothes in the washhouse and wash myself all over with a flannel and bucket of cold water and don clean ones before I could enter the house. Each night I expected to see a brown On His Majesty's Service envelope sitting on the table.

A week went by and then on the next Friday there it was. I sat down in the armchair and stared at the envelope. My life was shit at that moment, but I still had freedom of action. I could quit my job. I could even work my way around the country. There were plenty of things I hadn't done. If I was going to do a runner it had to be now. With a sigh, I reached forward, knowing I didn't have the courage to run. I tore the top off the envelope and pulled out the letter.

'George Bender (No Mr. or Dear there!)

You are to report to the Drill Hall, Rutland Street, Auckland at 8:00am on Tuesday, the 12th of November 1918 to pick up your rail ticket. You are then to proceed to Auckland Railway Station for embarkation to Trentham Camp. Your regiment will the Auckland Regiment and your regimental number is 12521. Please remember this number, as it will be used for all correspondence and orders from now on. You will be issued with a uniform on arrival at Trentham Camp. Bring only clean underclothes and what you need for personal hygiene.

Signed by Captain W.R. Copeland

Well, I hadn't managed to get out of it on medical grounds. The war had now reached that point of desperation where they took anyone. I'd have to tell them at the city destructor that I wasn't going to be at work next week. It was Friday night and the office staff wouldn't be there on the Saturday. It would have to wait until Monday before I could tell them.

I can't say I was looking forward to reporting in. No one could ignore the casualty lists in the paper. God alone knew if Daniel was all right. We had had no word from him for over a month. The best thing I could do was go to work and keep busy. Lolling about home only made the waiting worse.

On the Monday I reported to the office and told them I would be finishing up that night. The clerk said he would have my pay packet ready to collect at five o'clock. That day I was put on receiving the rubbish carts. Just after eleven the hooter sounded. Then every hooter, siren and bell in the city began sounding or ringing, creating a cacophony of noise. We all looked at each other wondering what was going on when one of the office workers came running out shouting the war was over. I stood there dumbfounded. Did that mean I didn't have to report in the next day? I couldn't be certain. Everyone stopped work and moved off the rubbish heap to throw their arms around the nearest person. We all had our own motives for the exuberance. Some were relieved that loved ones would be coming home. Others, like me, were relieved they wouldn't have to join the carnage. The drivers unhitched their carts to leave them partly tipped back at the edge of the heap and all work stopped for the day.

The Auckland Star that night had banner headlines stating 'Armistice'. For once I read it from front to back looking for anything about the next intake, but there was nothing.

The following morning I packed my toothbrush, shaving gear and changes of underclothes into a small haversack and threw it over one shoulder before leaving the house. Ma gave me a peck on the cheek. It took just over half an hour to reach the central city and the Drill Hall. It was a fine spring day and Queen Street was its usual bustle of tramcars, cars, horse drawn drays and people enjoying the sunshine. I was particularly attentive to all the little things that day, as it felt as though it might be the last time I saw my home town. I walked in to what seemed like an empty building. The front desk was unmanned so I banged on the bell. I was about to bang it again when I sensed a presence behind me and turned to find an officer standing there.

"What are you doing here?" he asked.

"I've come to report in," I said.

"Christ, haven't you heard? The war's over."

"I know, but no one told me I didn't need to come."

The officer gave a little sigh of resignation at the inefficiencies of the War Office and the world

141

in general. He put out his hand. "Give me your papers."

I handed over the envelope and he took out the contents before flipping up a hinged section of the counter and going into the office behind. I heard a drawer open and shut then a thump before he reappeared with my orders.

"There you are. You have an honourable discharge."

"Is that it then?" I asked.

"Yes, you can go home. The last thing we want is more men in the army now. It's going to take all our organisational powers to get our men home."

I took the papers, checked what he said was right and then folded them and put them in my pocket. Finally, something was going right in my life! I walked all the way home grinning from ear to ear.

I could now plan my life, but the thought of those tens of thousands of soldiers coming home looking for work worried me more than I liked to say. Instead of looking for a permanent job I grasped at the only straw I could see and went back to work at the city destructor. Even though I detested the work I soon found that I had the dubious honour of being transferred from the rubbish pile unloading the drays to working inside the incinerator building.

I don't know whether it was a promotion or a demotion really, because life inside the building was like hell on earth. All of the stories of purgatory that Father O'Riorden had ever preached came back to haunt me. It seemed as if I was one of those wretched creatures consigned to damnation for the rest of eternity. Not only was the heat and dust bad, the smell was enough to make you wretch and then there were the vermin. The smell was a potent mix of rotting vegetables and human waste. Of course, in time the smell became part of us and we found ourselves ostracised by normal folk. We were pariahs who had to steer away from genteel company, walking everywhere and giving other people wide berths in case we offended them. It was as if you had a cloud of flies buzzing around you that announced to one and all that you were one of the untouchables, a leper in your own society. Even a night cart collector was a better occupation. At least with them everything was done at night when no one was about to recognise you.

When I say I was in the incinerator building I was not actually in a covered area, but in a pit open to the sky into which mounds of rubbish was tipped. It was our job to rake the rubbish, spreading it out so that it would fall through the grille floor into chutes which took it down into the incinerator. Any larger matter that would not fit through the grilles had to be broken up with spades and hammers until it was small enough. Sweat dripped off me the whole time from the heat rising up from the furnaces below. Coupled with the heat and the smell was the dust, which stuck to your sweat until you ended up with a veneer of caked dust all over your skin. The rubbish all over the floor and the open grilles was a constant hazard, causing me to watch each footfall lest I put my foot through the grille or sprained my ankle. If you couldn't work you didn't get paid. It was that simple. I certainly had no loyalty to the Council over the job, I hated every minute of it, but I needed the money.

Each time we unloaded a new batch of rubbish there would inevitably be some extra passengers, in the shape of rats. These would run across the piles of rubbish with us chasing them with our shovels and our rakes. Most fell to their certain deaths through the grilles, but some also escaped to hide in the rubbish and startle us each time we disturbed their lair.

In my time there I saw everything from dead animals, human limbs to dead infants. I could handle all of it except the babies. The first time I found one of these I was raking the piles of rubbish up to the grille when the newspaper used to cover it fell open to expose the poor little thing. It wasn't the result of an abortion. This one had reached full term and been born. It may have been a still birth, but somehow I didn't think so. I knelt down in the muck and scooped it up in my arms. There's nothing more poignant in life than to hold a dead baby. I suppose it is because they look so innocent. Someone must have smothered it and thrown it out like so much household rubbish. I was pretty shaken up the first time. After that I found dozens. Each time I found a dead foetus or child, maybe as old as five or six, I picked it up with one of broad mouth shovels and placed it to one side for the police. Nothing was allowed to stop the destructor operating twenty-four hours a day, six days a week.

Most of the time, it was a junior constable that came to look at the dead infant. He would record its particulars before it was bagged and taken away to the mortuary for a post mortem. We would give brief statements about when it arrived and on which driver's dray we thought it came on. From this they could narrow down the likely place it was dumped. None of that was any concern of ours. I was surprised one day therefore, after I had put aside yet another foetus, that our supervisor called me into his office. I leant my rake against the wall, wiped my face and upper body before pulling on my shirt. I left this hanging out over my trousers as I entered the supervisor's office.

I hadn't seen him since the trial, but there he was as large as life and just as threatening.

"George," said my supervisor, "this is Detective Inspector O'Donnell. He would like a word with you."

He had been promoted since I last saw him. That was hardly surprising considering the time that had passed by. He was still a big bloke, His bowler was perched slightly askew on his head and he was dressed in a neat suit and brown leather shoes, all shiny on top, but I noticed, with secret mirth, the paper and rubbish adhering to their soles. I looked into his dark eyes. A smirk creased his clean shaven jaw.

"Yeah, we go back a long way, don't we George," he said.

"I'll take my leave then" said the foreman. You two can have the office in the interim. I don't want to know about your past connections."

Both O'Donnell and I waited in silence while the supervisor picked up his hat and went through the door, closing it quietly behind him.

"I saw your name come up on one of our reports and thought I might see how you were getting on," said O'Donnell.

"Is that a fact? I didn't know the police went in for the pastoral care of old villains."

"Well, you had got yourself into a bit of a bind, last time. It could happen to anyone, I suppose. It's good to see that you are trying to get your life back together."

"You can hardly call this getting my life back together. The only reason I'm working here is that no one else in town will employ me. I'm barely subsisting on the pittance I get here and most decent people I meet in the street give me a wide berth when passing."

"Aye, I know that."

I was surprised at his response. It was almost as if he had some sympathy for me. My normal cynicism then took hold, so I asked, "What do you really want?"

"Just to give you a friendly warning. Now that we know where you are we'll be keeping an eye on you."

"I wouldn't be wasting my time if I was you. I won't be going back to prison, if that's what you think."

"Now where have I heard that before?" he said, tipping his hat towards me, as he took his leave.

I was left in the empty room staring at the door, knowing that the full force of His Majesty's Police would now be looking at every opportunity to make my life hell.

"And up yours too," I muttered under my breath.

It was after that interview that I decided it was time to move on. I didn't enjoy being a pariah in my own society and there had to be a better way of making a living.

Chapter 19

I was twenty-two as I trudged the streets, going from interview to interview. What became evident was how many bosses about the town followed rugby. After two years in jail, I thought my brief period of fame as a five-eights for Ponsonby and for Auckland would be forgotten. However, they did remember that, plus my fall from grace for embezzling funds from Shaw and Co. The fact that I did it to support my Ma and brother in a time of need cut no ice. Each time I applied for a job, I came up against the same chilly reception. It became apparent that I was not going to get an office job where there was even a sniff of trust required.

Even my old mate, Niccolò Piagni, had decided I was a bad risk. To have my old mentor afraid I might run off with the takings from one of his gambling dens, when it was partly his fault that I ended up a gambler, was a bitter pill to swallow. My options were limited to working in the port, crewing on one of the coastal sailing scows that brought firewood, timber, sand or shingle into Auckland, joining the broader merchant marine as a deckhand, or working in a milling camp in the bush somewhere. They all meant a life of hard physical work, something I still thought of as a mug's game, but I hadn't any choice in the matter. The unions had the port jobs all sealed up for their own and their dependents, so there was nothing there. The first options at least had the advantage of getting me out of town and away from the beady eyes of the law.

Working on a scow was my first choice and I asked around where one might find a skipper of one of these craft. I was directed to several city pubs, the closest of which was Gleeson's Hotel above the Western Wall in Freeman's Bay. The pub was a pretty dodgy sort of place, even for the likes of me. It was frequented by lightermen, sailors, ferrymen, watersiders, stevedores, wharfingers, warehousemen, shipwrights, carpenters, coopers, and the entire flotsam one would expect around a busy port. I took the Friday off from work on the pretence of having to attend a funeral, and hoping two days of bathing and swimming in the sea might remove the worst of the smell that usually enveloped me like a shroud.

When I arrived in the evening, I looked around the smoke-filled atmosphere for something that might indicate one of its occupants was the skipper of a scow, but everyone looked much the same in working gear. He was hardly going to be dressed in a uniform with brass buttons and wearing a captain's cap, was he? I ordered a jug of draught and sat at one of the bar stools to sup my ale while keeping a sharp ear open to the conversations going on around me. Since the pub's opening at ten that morning the base of the cigarette smoke had gradually drifted down from the ceiling, now tinged yellow, to a point a mere two feet above the floor, not that anyone seemed to mind or even notice. I hoped that the smell of cigarettes would mask the lingering malodour that hung about me.

Not seeing anyone I recognised, I remained by the bar keeping my eyes firmly fixed on a spot on the opposite wall, so as not to offend anyone. This wasn't the sort of place you wanted to cause offence. Fights were a regular occurrence here and even the police gave it a wide berth.

My jug was nearly empty and I still had not heard anyone mention anything that might lead me to believe they were crew on a scow. By then I was dying for a pee and looked around for the toilet. I couldn't see any signs or even doors through the thick smoke so I leaned forward and asked the barmen, "Excuse me mate, where are the bogs?"

He turned his bald head and bull neck to look at me. I could tell that he had already decided that I wasn't a regular of the establishment. With a flick of his towel over his shoulder he gave a sneer, which I was charitable enough to think of as a sniff, before saying, "The head's out the back door, where'd you expect?" With a nod of his head he pointed me in the right direction so I gave him a nod of thanks and slid off my stool to thread my way through the crowd. The rear door was flung open just as I reached it and three men the size of oxen came through it. A blast of fresh air hit me at the same time and I moved aside to suck in the fresh air before making a bolt through the open door.

I was in a yard stacked with crates and kegs and surrounded by high brick and rendered wall to both Custom Street West and Hobson Street and a corrugated iron wall to the rear. The toilet was in a lean-to tacked onto the rear wall. Inside there was a section of eave gutter nailed to the wall which emptied straight into a gully trap.

When I re-entered the pub I sensed the mood had changed. Men were no longer jawing away to each other in groups as they leaned against their little tables. They were now pushing and shoving to get to windows and doors to peer outside. Jugs of ale sat forgotten on tables all around the room. Even the barman had abandoned his post to stand by the front door. Obviously something major was happening outside the pub, but I couldn't see what it was. With no way of getting through the throng, I went back out through the back door and climbed over the corrugated iron fence into the adjacent yard. This also was full of crates and when a guard dog came bounding out with lips curled up I climbed up some more crates and leapt down onto the footpath in Custom Street West, right in front of some startled men who grabbed me by the arms and lifted me up.

"You all right mate?" said one.

I thought I might have sprained my ankle, but not wishing to sound like a girl I replied, "Na, she's right. I was trying to see what all the kerfuffle was about."

"You can see for yourself. Just look over there," said another.

Immediately, I could see what was causing all the commotion. A red glow in the sky and the pall of smoke above it spoke eloquently of a major fire down by Victoria Park. From its direction I figured it must be coming either from Leyland-O'Connor's or from The Kauri Timber Company directly behind it. The only way of finding out for sure was to hike it down the road.

Despite the contents of several jugs of ale slopping around in my gut I hobbled my way quickly towards the blaze. My ankle hurt like blazes. Another fire engine passed me as I made my way past Bailey and Lowe's shipyard. I was all hot and clammy and felt a great upwelling from deep inside me. I staggered to a standstill by a lamp post and leaned against it to let the contents of my stomach erupt forth. A bead of cold sweat cloaked my forehead. A second and then a third eruption spewed over the ground in front of me. The hot flush that had gripped me just before being sick passed and I began to feel better. I wiped the spittle and drool from the corner of my mouth and looked towards the fire. The wind had driven the plume of smoke back down in a swirling spiral to the ground, obliterating the end of the road. I straightened up, looked myself over for any splatter and then walked further along the road.

Thick smoke covered the entire area and I was forced to take out my handkerchief and hold it over my nose as I made my way forward. A crowd had congregated on the footpath outside Leyland-O'Connor's mill. The orange glow of the fire reflected off their enthralled faces as they stared up at the blaze. This had now taken hold of the entire saw shed and two-storied office building. I remembered the time I had gone up those stairs with my father for my first job interview. It was also where my father had died. A sense of justice washed over me when I saw the fire take hold of the office building. The windows soon blew out causing the crowd to draw in their collective breath. Firemen were damping down the piles of sawn timber in the yard in an attempt to stop the fire spreading. It was pretty apparent that they had given up on the main buildings. The roof of the offices collapsed in a shower of sparks and cinders. Everyone gasped at the sight.

Police arrived and began to push the crowd back to the far side of the road. I was enthralled by the blaze. All my resentment at the way the company had treated my family seemed to be avenged in one foul swoop. I wondered why I hadn't thought of this solution myself. It was then that I wondered if this was indeed arson, and if so, by whom. The sight of so many constables arriving made me nervous so I turned around to return to the pub, only to find Detective Inspector O'Donnell standing there. His face was even ruddier than usual in the light of the fire. His unruly hair and sideburns looked like they were alight, so red were they. An evil leer came over it at the sight of me.

"Well, well, if it isn't young Bender. Enjoying the spectacle are you?"

"I was up at Gleesons when I heard."

"Is that so? It occurred to me that you might have had something to do with this," he said, waving his arm towards the conflagration. His eyes never left mine as he said this. I held his gaze knowing that to look away now would be as good as an admission of guilt. "That was a long time ago. I've moved on," I said.

"Yes, well don't be surprised if you get a knock on the door one of these mornings. You're a no-good piece of shite and I've got my eye on you."

"Bully for you," I replied. "You have a nice day too." I turned and walked away aware of his eyes boring into my back.

When I got back to Gleeson's Hotel it had emptied out appreciably. A good half of the patrons had rushed off to enjoy the pyrotechnic display down the road. The same barman was back behind the bar and he greeted me more warmly than on the first occasion. With a full jug in my hand I looked around the room at the small groups scattered about and decided to try my arm. After all, I had nothing to lose except maybe a broken jaw. In order to prevent that happening I had to time my approach so as not to break into someone's conversation. The first group I approached stopped talking and looked at me with a malevolent air wondering who had the audacity to break into their discussion. I decided to jump in first before one of them took too much offence.

"Sorry to interrupt you, but I'm looking for work. Are any of you working on the scows?"

They all shook their heads in unison as a sign of their commiseration for my being unemployed.

"Sorry, we all work at Henderson and Spraggon's. There were a couple of men off the Herald in here before," said one of them. "If its work you're looking for you might do worse than see Joe Williams over there."

"Is he a scow skipper?" I asked.

"Nah, he's a fisherman. He owns a couple of mullet boats."

"Right, thanks for your help," I said.

The man they had pointed to was sitting alone at the bar drinking a whisky. I walked up beside him and put my now half-empty jug down on the bar before sitting on the bar stool next to him. The man barely acknowledged my existence. He sat quietly supping his whisky and looking straight ahead. I left him to his thoughts for some time before deciding to make the first move.

"Are you Joe Williams?"

"Yeah, and who might you be?"

"The name's George Bender. I was told you might be looking for crew for your fishing boats."

"Is that right? I might be and then again I might not. Have you any experience?"

"I don't know much about boats, but would like to learn. I've worked in a saw mill and an office, but that job fell through when the company went into receivership. I'm currently labouring."

For the first time, Joe Williams swivelled around in his chair to give me the once over.

"Are you married?"

"No."

"Good, married men find the hours difficult. It so happens I do have a spare berth. I'll take you out on trial. If you shape up, I'll take you on full-time, if not, you're back on the street."

"Thanks, when and where do I start?"

"Be down at Queen's Wharf at four o'clock tomorrow afternoon. Report on board the Milly. She's a 28-foot mulletty. Have you got any oilskins?"

"No, I've nothing like that."

"Right, wear heavy duty trousers, boots and an old woollen jumper. I'll provide you with the oilskins. There's not much point in your buying anything until you decide whether it's the life for you or not."

"I can't thank you enough," I said. I slid off my stool and put out my hand. Williams looked at my hand for a second before gripping it hard with his right hand.

"Don't be late. We sail with the tide. We won't wait for you."

"I'll be there, don't worry."

Chapter 20

Queen's Wharf was a hive of activity with the fleet of fishing boats being prepared to go out. The Milly was easy enough to find with her name painted in bold script across her counter. Five other boats were going out with her. Men were loading trays on board and stowing these under the half deck near the bow. Joe gave me a nod and indicated that I should help the others load the trays, which I did. The crew were dressed in gumboots, oilskin dungarees and flannel shirts. Once the boat was loaded the sails were hauled up and then the lines were pulled aboard. The boat slid out from the dock and swung around with the tide.

The sails filled and we canted over, causing me to grab hold of the coaming much to the silent mirth of the rest of the crew. The men had taken off their gumboots now and pulled on their oilskin jackets. Joe pulled out a set of oilskins from a locker under the half deck at the bow of the boat and passed them to me. My attempts to put these on must have caused a great deal of amusement amongst the other members of the crew. It isn't easy putting over-trousers on in a boat canted over twenty degrees while rolling and yawing about in a cross sea. Several times my feet shot out from under me forcing me to make a desperate lunge for a halyard or the coaming. I think that in the end my antics were what endeared me to the rest of the crew.

That was the first sailing boat I had been on and I soon fell in love with the boat as it surged along with its great bowsprit pointing the way. We sailed in close to North Head before gybing for the run up the channel. Sunlight glittered off the water and seabirds dipped and soared around us. The sandstone cliffs of the North Shore stretched off to our left while the silent sentinel of Rangitoto Island guarded the harbour entrance to our right. It took me a while to get used to saying port or larboard and starboard.

Apart from me, the rest of the crew were old hands and no words were needed as each went about his duty by rote. I sat to one side of the cockpit while they pulled in sails, dodged the swinging boom or ran up front to pull around the headsail. I guess Joe Williams was letting me get the feel of the boat and how she was run before letting me get involved. For this I was grateful to him. The last thing I wanted to do was stuff something up.

The ebbing tide and the sou-westerly wind sped us down the channel and out into the wide gulf. So far there had been a light chop which the boat easily cut through, but now we were in the Gulf proper the boat began to move in time to the big swells rolling in. My stomach began to perform somersaults and I had to gulp down the bile that rose in my gorge. Joe Williams looked at me and must have seen the change of colour.

"Don't try and hold it down," he advised. "It's better to let it go. Just make sure you throw up to

157

leeward. The rest of the crew doesn't want to wear it."

They were all grinning from ear to ear as I sidled to the lee rail. I hung there emptying my insides while wind and spray hit my face. They served to refresh me and I felt better. The green swathes of Motutapu and Rakino Islands came into view on our right while off in the distance Tiritiri Matangi Island was a yellowish-green smudge on the horizon. One of the other crew members, Albie Clark, pointed these out to me and gave me their names.

By nightfall we were well out to sea. The only land we could see jutting out above the horizon was the peaks of Coromandel and the tops of Rangitoto and of Little and Great Barrier Islands. With the setting of the sun came the cold.

The skipper rigged up a kerosene lantern on the mast which lit up the sail so that we could be seen from a long way off. The other boats in our little flotilla did the same and we could all see each other widely spaced about the sea.

"Right, George," said Joe Williams. "You've been initiated to the sea, now it's time to initiate you to commercial fishing. The reason we came out on the ebbing tide was so that we would be in the fishing grounds on the turn. We fish on the incoming tide and make our run home to make it in time for the opening of the markets. It just so happened on this trip that the ebbing tide means we'll be out all night. Once we've finished fishing you can catch up on a bit of sleep on the run home. Have you got any questions?"

"No."

"Good, Mattie there will show you how to tie the knots for the hooks."

There were plenty of fish out there and I was baiting lines and throwing them back in the water as fast as I was pulling them out. The bottom of the boat was soon awash in flapping fish, shining silver in the moonlight. No one showed any sign of stopping so I kept on even though it must have been well past midnight. Dark shapes drifted across the stars and the moon sending shadows across the water. For someone like me who had never been to sea before apart from a couple of harbour ferry trips, the variety and size of the fish we caught was staggering. Some of the snapper were huge and when brought aboard their experienced eye would fasten on mine, as if to ask what I was doing in their world.

To be at sea alone at night, bobbing up and down in the swell, quickly makes you realise how fragile and insignificant human existence can be. The late hour and the cold took hold of me and my eyelids began to droop. I guess I wasn't returning the line to the water or bringing in the catch as fast as I had been because the skipper called back to me, "Don't fall asleep now."

I then got a new charge of energy, but it didn't last long. I was soon dozing with the line wrapped around my hand. I was jolted back to the land of the living by something big pulling the line through my fingers. I gripped the line and pulled against my unseen enemy. The line cut deep into the quick of my palms as the fish dashed this way and that then under the boat. Suddenly, the line went slack and I fell backwards onto the piles of bodies now lying inert in the bottom of the boat. I sensed the mirth of my crewmates, but they had the decency to look the other way when I stood up to re-hook my line and start all over again.

It must have been two in the morning before the skipper called it quits. We hauled in our lines and carefully wound them up and stowed them under the half deck at the bow before sorting the piles of still or still-thrashing bodies lying in the bottom of the boat. The skipper close-hauled the mainsail and one of the others joined him to sail the boat back to port while the rest of us sorted the fish by type and by size into the various trays. As soon as we had finished that we all found somewhere to curl up and go to sleep.

We got into port in the dark around five to unload our catch which was taken off to the fish market. Afterwards, Joe came up to me and said, "You did all right. Do you reckon you could get used to the life?"

"Yeah, it was great. It sure beats working at the destructor."

"Right, well I'm willing to take you on, but I have to have your assurance that you'll turn up each time we are going out. I can't risk sailing short-handed. Do you reckon you can manage that?"

"You can count on it," I said.

Joe stood there silently watching me for any sign of evasion.

"All right, here's your wages for last night. Be down here again at 6 o'clock tomorrow night. You can take your gear home and give it a wash in fresh water. I expect you to look after your gear. In a couple of weeks you can buy your own."

"Thanks, Joe. I really appreciate this."

"Just don't let me down."

I staggered off home with a snapper poking out of each pocket of my jacket and money in the pocket of my pants. I knew I stunk of fish, but with food and money in my pockets, I felt that my life had turned around. I could now help maintain the household and I wouldn't have to return to the destructor.

Over the weeks and months that followed I settled into a regular routine of sailing on the outgoing tide and sleeping when I got back, whether that was in the day or night. There was something very comforting in this; we were in complete harmony with nature. I grew to like the life. There was an inherent bond among the crew, where little needed to be said, where each and every one of us had a duty to perform and could rely on the others to do it. The solitude of being at sea in the middle of the night with sea birds at work around you and the occasional call of whales also grew on me. I found this almost spiritual.

When Joe announced he was entering Milly into the Auckland Anniversary Regatta everyone on board hoped they would be picked for the race crew. Each boat was only allowed three crew members for the race. One would be the skipper, Joe Williams. Albie Clark was probably going to be on the winches. That left open the position of for'ard hand. By then I had been a regular up for'ard sorting out the headsail and putting up the spinnaker. The first time we had put this up I had been amazed at how the hull straightened up, no longer canted over with the leeward rail under water. With the spinnaker up the bow lifted right out of the water and we just took off. It always gave me a thrill and I desperately wanted to be the third team member.

In order to pick which one of us was going to be the for'ard hand he put Mattie and me through our paces putting up the spinnaker and taking it down again. Mattie made an absolute hash of pulling in the spinnaker on one of his turns, letting it drag under the boat during a gybe. Joe immediately came into the wind while we all hung over the side trying to retrieve the sail. I should have been elated at Mattie's misfortune, but knew it could easily have been me.

In the event Joe chose me as the for'ard hand for the race with Albie on the winch. Once this was settled all fishing stopped three days out from the big race so that we could practice. It was a big thing, this race. A lot of money changed hands on the outcome of the boat races and winning earned huge kudos around the town. If your mullet boat won you were the uncrowned king of the fleet for the following year.

On the day of the big race we took the boat out early for a spin around the harbour and out into the channel, checking all our sails and making sure the rig was secure before sailing back up the harbour to Watchman Island. The other mulleties were sailing around by then, waiting for the starting time. Some of the big boats surged past, their leeside coaming under water and crew stacked out on the windward side to give the boat extra ballast.

As the time for the starting gun approached at nine o'clock, the other boats began to converge on the start line off the Ponsonby Cruising Club clubhouse in St Mary's Bay. I counted ten boats, recognising at least six of the others as ones we had gone out fishing with. The others had come from far and wide for the event. The beach and cliff tops were lined with people, and so too was the deck to the clubhouse. We jockeyed for position, watching for signals. Boats came close together and then veered off. Insults and catcalls were shouted across the water, as sails flapped and cracked about us with each boat trying to keep behind the starting line.

A flag went up from the clubhouse, signalling we had three minutes before the gun. The wind vane at the top of the mast was flicking around this way and that in the fluky winds in the lee of Point Erin. I knew from our harbour runs that the wind was steady from the southwest at about ten knots. We would want the spinnaker up as soon as possible once the race started and I had the sail ready to hoist and clipped onto its pole.

The boom of the cannon resounded across the water and Joe immediately steered the boat straight out from the cliff. The hull canted over as it filled, the bowsprit pointing straight towards O'Neill's Point. I waited, crouched down beside the mast for the gybe. The boats were already scattered with only two others following us.

"Prepare to gybe," called Joe.

The boat pivoted about on its axis, crashing over onto its opposite side as the boom swung over with a solid thwack behind me. I let go of the mast to step forward to grab the forestay and pull the headsail around while Albie pulled in the sheet and madly winched the mainsail tight. I then began hauling on the downhaul to raise the spinnaker. Albie came dashing forward to lift the pole up. In seconds the sail had filled and set and the familiar surge took over the boat. We fair flew up the harbour towards North Head.

A quick glance around told me the other boats weren't far behind, though the crew on Myra had

163

fluffed their spinnaker lift and they had fallen back. We managed to stay ahead of the rest on the downwind leg, but the others were all thereabouts and caught us on the upwind leg. By then we were scattered all over the place as each skipper tried to find a bit of extra wind off the shore. Joe was a canny old fox though. He took us far out to the right of the course and picked up enough wind to ease us ahead of our rivals to cross the line first.

We sailed Milly into St Mary's Bay beach and jumped out to haul her further up from the water. The beach was littered with people and boats of all sorts, some with sails still flapping loosely at their masts and others with their sails already folded and stashed away.

Chapter 21

The clubhouse was a seething mass of sunburnt faces, grizzled hair full of salt, beaming faces, clinking bottles and booming voices. Many of those there had been imbibing for some time and would be until late that night. I knew every pub and clubhouse around the harbour would be the same after the regatta. Joe shouted us each a bottle of beer and we found a spot in a corner where we could all stand together. There we could avoid getting beer spilled over us, poked in the ribs or shoved in the back.

Joe raised his bottle and we touched bottles. "Here's to Milly and a win," he said.

"To Milly," we chorused, before downing our first gulp.

"By crikey," I said. "Venus gave us a run for our money coming back up Tamaki Strait. I thought she was going to beat us for a while there."

Joe smiled to himself, knowing he'd always had the measure of the other boat. "Well, she didn't, that's all that counts," he said.

Of course, he knew the traits of every boat and its skipper in the fleet. Every time we went out he assessed the other boats. Joe was a skipper you could put your faith in. I knew then that I would stick with him through thick and thin, so long as he would have me.

Around ten o'clock in the evening a girl with a sunny smile pushed her way through the crowd towards us. She wore a light pastel pink sundress and white cardigan. With her suntanned skin she looked a picture of health itself. She stopped beside us and said to Joe, "Mom sent me down to take you home."

Joe was by then a few sheets to the wind, as were most of us. He looked at his daughter and gave her a big smile.

"Thanks love. It's time is it?"

"Yes, Dad."

"You haven't met the latest addition to the crew, have you?"

She turned to look at us one at a time. She gave Albie a nod of recognition, then looked directly at me. Our eyes locked and I had to stop a gulp in my throat.

"This is George Bender, our latest for'ard hand. George, this is my eldest daughter, Lydia."

"Nice to meet you, George," she said, holding out her hand. I noticed in passing there were no rings on her fingers. I took her hand in mine and gave it a gentle shake.

"The pleasure's all mine," I replied, to the lecherous grins of my companions.

"Right then, I'm off," said Joe. "Give us a hand will you, love."

Albie and I watched Joe walking arm in arm with Lydia back through the crowd. The sight made me realise how long it had been since I had been in a woman's company. After prison I hadn't given myself a ghost of a chance of striking up a relationship, but now everything had changed.

"Where's old Joe live, anyway?" I asked. I tried to look as nonchalant as I could when asking this, but I don't think Albie was fooled for a second. He took his time answering, all the time watching the growing expectation in my face.

"They live in Hackett Street," he eventually informed me.

That was just up the road from where we were. No wonder Joe's wife had sent one of the girls down to fetch him before he was too legless to make it home. My mind quickly ran through the distance between where I lived and Hackett Street. What excuses could I have for loitering around the house? Perhaps she worked in town? I took another sip from my bottle before putting it down again. Albie would probably know. What the hell?

"Does Lydia have a job?" I asked.

"I thought you would never ask," he replied, wearing a smirk from one ear to the other.

"Go on then?"

"She works at Cashmore's."

"Where, in Cox's Bay?"

"Yeah, she's a secretary down there."

My mind was racing now. Cashmore's mill was not far from our house, as the crow flies, but for that you needed a boat. By land it was a tortuous journey around the top end of the muddy estuaries. I figured my best bet was to intercept her between her home and her work.

"I don't know whether Joe would approve of your seeing her, but best of luck anyway," said Albie.

"Wha—" I began before stopping myself saying something I might later regret. I had initially assumed that Joe might know I was an ex-con, but then it occurred to me that he might not want me hanging around his daughter because I was a Catholic. I might not be a church-goer anymore, but my Irish ancestry was as good as having a brand across my forehead. The idea of pretending to be a Presbyterian flitted through my mind, but that seemed a betrayal of everything I stood for. I could imagine Ma's reaction if she found out about that. Still, Joe seemed a decent sort of bloke. It had to be worth a shot.

On the mornings we didn't have to be on the boat I took to hanging around the tram terminus at the end of Jervois Road. Even if she did catch the tramcar from the top of Shelley Beach Road she still had a reasonable walk from the terminus down the hill to Cox's Bay. What I didn't know was that it was Lydia's job to go to the Chief Post Office each morning and collect the mail. This meant that she didn't get off the tramcar until about 9:30 in the morning.

On the first morning I hung around for an hour and a half in the wind and rain before returning home in the belief that I had missed her. A male doesn't really know why he does these things. It seemed strange to go off and hang around a tram terminus in the hope of seeing a girl get off, but those are the crazy things a smitten fellow does. Anyway, my luck changed for the better the third time I waited for her. I had been waiting only half an hour when off she stepped down from the tramcar, dressed in a woollen coat, cloche hat and brown calf length boots. As soon as she saw me her face lit up, making me smile too.

"What are you doing here?" she asked.

"Waiting for you?"

"Oh! What for?"

"I wanted to see you again."

"Are you always this bold?"

"Lord no. I'm usually as meek as a mouse around a girl."

"Well then, you can accompany me down to the mill if you like."

"That would be grand," I said, instantly rueing those Irish sayings my mother had implanted in my head. As we walked down the hill she kept looking sideways at me and a small smile appeared at the corner of her mouth.

"It's George, isn't it?"

"Yes, George Bender's the name."

"Well George, are you going to ask me out?"

"Nothing would please me more. Would you like to go to the flicks?"

"All right. What about Friday night? Kathlyn Williams is in 'Redeeming Love' at the Queen's or Pauline Frederick is in 'The Woman in the Case' at the Tivoli."

"Do you know everything that's on?" I asked, impressed by her knowledge.

"I saw they were on in the Herald this morning," she said, the corner of her lip curling up ever so slightly to indicate she had scored one up on me. Neither sounded much like anything that I might want to see, but I had to choose one or my mission would fail.

"Well, 'The Woman in the Case' sounds good to me," I said, hoping it was a detective story. "But I'll need to check whether we'll be out fishing then."

"Well, if you're not, I'll meet you outside the Tivoli at seven o'clock."

"Done."

By then we had reached Cashmore's. She gave me a smile and disappeared through the door leaving me grinning like an imbecile. Suddenly she reappeared and called out, "Bring a friend."

I was about to ask why, but she had disappeared again. Now I was in a real tizz. Why did she ask that? Was she planning a foursome? Perhaps she was coming with a girlfriend so she could get out without her parents learning who she was going out with. Either way, I was stuck. I had no one else to bring.

The Tivoli Theatre was near the corner of Symonds Street and Karangahape Road. A pub had the prime location on the corner. Both buildings were next to the tramline and much of their patronage came from tramcar passengers. The area was all right in the daytime, but at night it became a bit dodgy. That was when the alcoholics living in the Symonds Street cemetery came out of their holes to top up their supplies from the corner pub and then wander the streets with their red eyes, sallow skin and white hair sticking out of their heads, as though they'd received an electric shock. As soon as there was a hint of dawn approaching this army of lost souls would vanish back to their lairs in the cemetery under Grafton Bridge like so many vampires.

That was the reason I wanted to get there early so that Lydia wasn't molested by any of these creatures of the night. Of course, I knew I was a hypocrite thinking this way because I secretly wished to molest her myself. The difference, I hoped, was that she might approve of me doing it.

I'd been waiting outside the theatre for a quarter of an hour, all the while resisting the temptation to join the rowdy throng inside the bar, when a tram drew to a stop in the middle of the road. Several passengers alighted, but it wasn't until the tramcar had moved off before I could see who had alighted. The first person to come into view was a middle-aged man in a three-piece suit and bowler hat. He was helping a middle-aged woman, presumably his wife, across the road to the footpath. Behind them was Lydia, looking like a film star in a velour dress buckled at the waist and wearing a fascinator in her hair. She gave me a beaming smile when she saw me and then turned to say something to her companion. My heart sank when I saw another girl about the same age. She too was a beauty. I felt gauche for not bringing a companion. By then they had reached the footpath and Lydia, in her high heeled shoes, looked me in the eye.

"Hello George, this is Emily," she said, all the while looking around for my companion.

"Pleased to meet you, Emily," I said, shaking her hand formally, fearful of appearing too forward yet wanting to be more relaxed than I felt. I inwardly cursed my upbringing at all the terrors and tribulations associated with dealing with the opposite sex.

"Didn't you bring anyone with you?" asked Lydia.

"Sorry. I had someone arranged, but he pulled out on me at the last minute," I replied, feeling relieved that my white lie sounded believable.

"Oh well, we may as well go in then," she said.

"Ladies first," I replied, wishing I had the style to take each lady by the arm and escort them in. Like the mug that I was I ended up buying both their tickets, not that I really minded. When the usherette showed us to our seats I found that Emma was sitting between us. I couldn't believe it. When we stood for 'God Save the King' I looked sideways at the girl's faces in the flickering light from the screen to see amusement etched on their faces. I was pretty sure that they had arranged it all to make me feel like an idiot. In that they had succeeded.

We all sat down again once the anthem had finished and watched a newsreel showing starving people and ruined villages. Fortunately this was followed by some slapstick giving the audience some relief from the morbid newsreel images. At half time we went out into the foyer to buy ice creams.

When the main feature came on Emma surreptitiously placed her hand on my thigh. I was so surprised I almost leapt up and yelled, "What are you doing?" Shit! What was a man to do? If I did anything to encourage her, she would tell Lydia and that would be the end of any chance I had in that department. If I did nothing, they would think I was a really cold fish. I let her hand stay where it was while my frenzied brain tried to sort out what to do. In the end, I decided that the two of them had planned this all along to embarrass me. Well, two could play at that game.

I placed my hand over hers and lifted it off my thigh to rest it on my straining manhood. I was grinning to myself, expecting Emma to recoil in horror. Instead she began gently kneading it with her fingers. It was not what I had expected and soon I was suffering a paroxysm of anguish. My eyes watered and I had to bite my lips to stop crying out. Even so, a soft mewing escaped my lips. I looked around hoping nobody had heard it. By

172

then, I was slouched down in my seat trying not to make a noise. Although my mind told me to thrust her hand away I remained curiously inactive. Why shouldn't I enjoy it? Before I knew it, it was all over. Emma took away her hand and I felt wetness spread through my underpants and run down my thigh. Tears came to my eyes and a red flush of shame washed over me. I looked down to see if there was any sign showing on my trousers, but couldn't be sure in the darkness. I just hoped that when I stood up nothing would show. Both girls were looking at the screen, as if nothing had happened.

When the movie finished I got up and led the way out of the theatre keeping my back to the girls as much as possible. That was when I wished I had a hat to hold in front of me. Then girls both pecked me on the cheek before boarding their tramcar. I waited until it vanished around the corner before setting off down the footpath towards home. If this was how genteel ladies acted then I had been misinformed. I was bloody sure it kept them in fits for weeks.

Chapter 22

The next time we went out fishing we came back to port late in the afternoon. We were running before a storm coming in from the nor-east. The sky behind us was full of roiling black clouds climbing one on top of the other to see how high they could go. The wind was gusting, threatening to carry away the mast at times. To make matters worse, the wind and the ebbing tide had combined to churn the sea up into a series of small mountain ranges. I was near drowned in flying spray standing there on the half deck in front of the mast, hanging on desperately to the spinnaker pole to stop myself being swept overboard. With so much sail up there was the constant threat of broaching each time we hit a deep trough, but Joe was an old hand and kept us out of trouble, seeming to anticipate every trough and every wind gust.

We were all on the lookout of the tell-tale ruffles coming across the surface of the water. These forewarned us that another gust was about to hit us. Joe and Albie huddled together in the cockpit with their oilskins on. Spray and waves covered them every time we hit a trough. Mattie and Bill were also huddled together behind the coping of the half deck. It was reckless to have the spinnaker up in such conditions, but Joe was anxious to get back into port ahead of the storm. He was the skipper and far more wise to the ways of the sea than I was, so I did what he asked.

We were all right until we tried to round North Head. There we were forced to gybe so we could head up the harbour. At that moment a gust caught us and the boat heeled over alarmingly. Joe yelled out from the tiller, "We're going to broach. Let everything out!"

By then we were heeling about thirty-five degrees and it took all my time to remain standing. Once Albie slackened off the lines holding the boom and the sheet to the jib, the boat righted, but then began wallowing about like a cork in a bottle. In such conditions bringing in the spinnaker single-handed requires the dexterity of a four-armed monkey. As I was freeing the downhaul the spinnaker was caught in a gust only to disappear over the side, pulling the pole with it. It then acted like a giant sea anchor, pulling the boat side-on to the wind.

I called out to Mattie and Bill to give me a hand. They sprang up and helped me pull in the sail, but it was as heavy as lead with the ebbing tide filling it. All the while it kept dragging us towards the rocks. The next minute, Joe was beside me, muttering oaths under his breath about all the incompetent bastards he had seen in his life. In the circumstances, I didn't think it wise to argue the point.

The wind and tide carried us inexorably towards the Bean Rock lighthouse where the spray danced and broke all around the edge of the reef. With four of us at the task, we managed to drag the spinnaker back on board, but just as we accomplished this another gust hit us from abeam and drove us onto the rocks. I was thrown off balance by the impact and only prevented myself going over the side by grabbing hold of a halyard at the last minute. That was when I saw the bottom planks had sprung and water was pouring into the hull.

When I told Joe this he yelled back, "Plug the hole with the spinnaker and sit on it while I try to get some leeway. As soon as we're off the rock we'll drag the storm main under the hull and tie it up tight. One of you will have to go over the side to fix it."

I plugged the gaping hole with the spinnaker and both Mattie and I sat on it while Albie pulled out the storm main. At Albie's signal, Joe winched in the mainsail. The wind caught and the hull ground its way along the edge of the reef before popping off like a cork. Water was now pouring into the hull, making it settle lower in the water with every passing second. Albie was over the side in an instant dragging a rope under the hull. His head popped up on the other side where he passed the rope across. His head bobbed down along the side and around the stern before ending up where he'd started. With another line he vanished once more under the hull.

By now we were semi-submerged. Joe kept looking up at the mast, no doubt expecting it to go anytime. He then let go of the boom, letting it dip in and out of the water with each passing wave, relying on the headsail to give us headway. Albie climbed back on board and he and Bill pulled the mainsail through under the hull and pulled it taut to the shape of the hull. As soon as they had finished Joe ordered everyone to start bailing.

By then, several other boats had come to our assistance. A line was thrown from a steam launch and the risk of running back up on the reef was averted. Even so, with the boat full of water and the tide still on the ebb our progress up the harbour must have been barely more than a knot in true terms. With the concerted effort of everyone on board we managed to get the water level in the boat down. Then, after a couple of hours the ebb tide began to wane and we began to pick up speed.

It was near midnight by the time Joe ran Milly up on the ramp below Collings and Bell in St Mary's Bay. It had been a near thing saving the boat. Joe didn't say a word to any of us except to issue a curt command here and there. It would be all around the harbour by morning. Joe's name would the butt of jokes doing the rounds. I didn't think that it was totally my fault, yet I sensed his ire directed at me in particular.

Once the boat was secure, we began unloading the gear and the catch. The sails were all brought ashore first, followed by the fish in their trays. These were piled up at the top of the ramp while Joe stormed off to his house to organise a truck to deliver the catch to the market and get Collings and Bell to repair the boat. We hung about, not looking at each other, waiting for him to return. By then, we had taken off our oilskins and folded these into piles which we stacked with the sails.

When Joe returned we waited until the truck arrived from the fish market. Once that was loaded, we helped carry the sail bags and our wet-gear up to Joe's place. It was about three in the morning when we finished and I was shivering with cold. Albie must have really been feeling it after his dip in the water. He had donned a heavy fisherman's sweater and oilskin pants afterwards, but had never really had a chance to dry himself properly or get warm. It was usual for Joe to pay us off after each trip, but none of us wanted to be the first to ask. Joe merely told us to all go home and meet him at the Britomart at ten the next morning, when we hoped he would have our wages.

The crew met on the footpath outside the Britomart, all looking sheepish about the events of the previous day. Albie seemed to be acting as our intermediary and led us into the pub where we found Joe leaning against the bar with a seven-ounce glass in front of him. It looked as though he hadn't tasted a drop. He looked up as we entered, then looked back to stare at his reflection in the mirror behind the bar. No one said a word. We watched him take a long drag on his cigarette before stubbing out the butt in the ashtray on the bar.

"Right, let's go and sit in the corner and we can sort this out," he said, turning and leading us into the corner of the bar room where a leather chesterfield and a couple of worn armchairs were arranged around a low table. Once we had sat down, the barman came over with a tray full of seven-ounce glasses full of draught beer. We each picked up a glass and sipped at its rim. This left a bead of foam on our upper lips. It looked funny, but not one of us felt it was the time and place to comment.

"I don't need to tell you that I was pretty mad last night," said Joe. "I have made it a policy not to go off half cock in those situations, but to sleep on it before blaming anyone. For your information, it's not all bad. We saved the catch and got it to market. We saved all our sails and gear and the boat can be repaired. The yard reckons it will take them a week. What it's all going to cost me is the cost of repairs to the boat, a new spinnaker and a week's lost revenue in catches. Have any of you got anything to say on the matter?"

I took a long time drinking my beer at that point, not trusting myself to say anything. A heavy silence followed. No one else was any better than me. When it was evident that none of us was going to say anything, Joe continued.

"I realise that it was a tricky situation making a gybe with a storm running behind us, but we've done it many times before. It shouldn't have led to the near-disaster that it did. I've thought about this a lot during the night. I've come to the conclusion that the cause of the accident was the fact that George here lost control of the situation when pulling in the spinnaker. That was the root cause of the problem. Because of that, I'm going to have to let you go, George. I can't have someone on the crew I can't trust to do his job."

I looked Joe in the eye. In my heart I knew he was right. I had stuffed up. He pulled out an envelope and passed it over the table to me. I took it, knowing I then had to say something.

"I'm sorry for what happened. It was one of those things whereby you can look back at it and say you could have done better. In those conditions I should have asked Mattie or Bill to be up there with me, but I thought that I could handle it. I've enjoyed being on the boat and enjoyed all your company. I understand that the skipper has to have total trust in his crew and I know I let you down. I won't ask for a second chance from you Joe, I know that you don't work that way. What I will ask though is for you to see if you can get me on another boat."

"You don't think that I can recommend the bloke who almost lost me my boat to another skipper, do you?"

"You know there were extenuating circumstances."

Joe looked down at the table and the seven-ounce glass which he had not touched since he sat down. "I can't promise anything, but I could ask some of the scow skippers if they have a berth."

"Thanks," I said, leaning forward to shake his hand which I was pleased to see that he accepted.

I then shook hands with the rest of the crew before standing up. "I hope to see you around then," I said, turning towards the door.

Chapter 23

It was still before noon and I had a full pay packet
in my pocket. I didn't feel like going home, but
didn't know what else to do. I felt pretty down.
Once more the fates had come together to thwart
me. Working on the mullet boat had been the first
positive thing to happen to me since coming out of
prison. The thought of returning to work in the city
destructor depressed me more than I could say.
Joe's comment about asking around the skippers of
the coastal scows fixated in my mind. I didn't need
Joe for that. I knew where to find the scow
skippers. With a skip in my step, I set off for
Gleeson's Hotel.

I walked through its portal only to find the bar
empty. The barman gave me a nod. I ordered a
schooner before looking at the blackboard with the
lunch menu. After ordering fish and chips I took
my schooner and sat on one of only two sofas in
the establishment. You had to be early to nab a seat
in one of these and today I was the early bird.

A quarter of an hour later a girl brought out
my fish and chips. By then I'd drunk half the
schooner and had that leaden feeling seeping over
me. The hot food and the salt revived me
somewhat so I got up and went to the bar to order
another schooner. When I returned from the toilets

I saw my plate had been taken away and the new schooner full of draught beer was sitting on the table.

Around two in the afternoon the pub began to fill as crews came back into port. High tide that day wasn't until six o'clock so these weren't fishermen. I drained the schooner in four gulps and went up to the bar to order another, at the same time listening in on their conversations to get a hint as to which boat they were off. It was apparent that they were from a trading schooner that had just returned from the islands. That got me thinking about palm trees and sandy beaches with dusky maidens. I hadn't thought of crewing on anything that went so far, but it had its merits. I returned to my seat with my refilled schooner to watch the group.

There were eight of them, seven of whom were wearing cotton shirts and pants cut off below the knees. The eighth wore a black pea coat and a captain's cap. This was battered and well weathered. It wouldn't have surprised me if it hadn't been blown overboard and rescued a few times. The face under the cap was sunburnt and his hair grey. The captain was smoking a pipe, the style of which I had not seen before. He was holding forth about something, gesticulating with his arms at the sky or something up an imaginary mast. One of the others joined in every so often, also waving his arms about. The others listened slavishly to the pair of them while grinning at the yarn. Every so often they would break into guffaws. The captain paused for breath and looked around the near-empty room.

It was then that his eyes rested on mine. I must have cut a lonely figure, sitting there by myself, drowning my sorrows. It was a fleeting look before he charged back into his story or possibly began a new one. I felt a pang of regret at not being part of a crew anymore. That bond between men was something I cherished. Chancing my arm I stood up and went across to them. The worst thing that could happen was for them to tell me to clear off. The captain paused in his narrative as I approached him, and once again, I found myself looking into his pale grey eyes.

"Excuse me, but I'm looking for a crew position. I don't suppose you have one on your boat?"

He looked at me intently for several seconds before taking his pipe from his mouth.

"Have you any experience?"

"I've been crewing on mullet boats and was looking for something on a larger vessel."

"Is that right? I heard that a mullet boat almost swamped in the harbour last evening."

Several of the crew members gave a soft chuckle at this. It was evident that word had spread far and wide about the mishap.

"So I heard. That was the Milly I believe," I said.

"Was it now? Well, we've just returned to port and won't be sailing again for a fortnight. We don't have a crew position free at the moment, but you never can tell. Give us your name and address. If we need someone at the last minute we'll get in touch."

"The name's George Bender and I live at 279 Richmond Road," I replied. I was pleased to see the captain take a small notebook from his pocket and write my details in it with a blunt pencil.

Probably nothing would come of it, but just the fact that he did that perked up my spirits.

After returning to my sofa I lost track of time. I don't even remember how many drinks I ordered. I was roused from my stupor by someone sitting down heavily beside me. I looked up to see Mattie sitting next to me, grinning from ear to ear.

"I thought I might find you here," he said.

"Wha' are you doin' here?" I asked, aware that my speech was slurred.

"Looking for you. I've been around the other boats to see if there are any berths available."

"And?"

"Sorry, word's got out about what happened yesterday. Joe's the laughing stock of the fishing fleet and your name is mud."

"Gee, thanks for that. I needed jollying along."

"Cheer up, something will come along."

"Yeah sure. With my luck it will be a crew position on the Mary Celeste."

"I'll keep looking, but I've got to get back to the missus now. See ya."

He heaved his heavy frame out of the couch, making it rise like a wave. His figure became a blur as he headed towards the door. By then my gut was performing a jig with the fish and chips and the ale slopping around inside it. Just then the publican called. "Time, gentlemen please. Last orders!"

I still hadn't got used to pubs closing at six o'clock and blamed the wowsers for this situation. How was a man to relax when he's turfed out of the pub? I reeled my way back out to the lavatory. A wave of peace overcame me as my bladder released at least three full schooners of draught beer into the channel. So at peace did I feel that I stood there propped off the wall for some time before taking my leave.

When I re-entered the bar room the publican was going around telling his patrons it was time to leave, giving the more unruly a helping hand towards the door. I didn't even get a chance to sit down again before his beefy arms swept me forth into the street.

From being warm and fuzzy I now found myself in the path of a cool south-westerly breeze. The first spots of rain landed on the ground around me. As I put my hands in my pockets and bent my head into the wind my thoughts went to Lydia. It was bad enough losing Joe's trust, but now it seemed as though I wouldn't be able to see her anymore. There was no way Joe would put up with me courting his daughter now. Once again, I was my own worst enemy, but this time I had to say that I had not seen it coming.

"Stuff them all," I thought. I still had money in my pocket, not as much as before, but some and I knew where to find after-hours drinks. Nicco Piagni would let me drown my sorrows at one of his places and I knew of one just around the corner.

I was running towards a door painted in glossy red paint. It had a brass latch with a Union lock above it. I paused, sensing a slight disturbance in the air – a tremor only. The door suddenly blasted out of its frame and the wall around it disintegrated into a fusillade of broken bricks and mortar. After the initial battering, a blast of hot air and boiling water hit me with the force of a steam train. I was flung me backward through the air to smash into a stack of rough sawn 6 x 1s. I rebounded off them to land on the ground. A timber-slide of planks rained down on me. Then, something hit me on the head and I lost consciousness.

When I awoke everything looked weird. My boots were smouldering, and so were the socks inside them. My shirt, singlet and trousers had vanished. My bare pale skin was splattered with some sort of dark matter. Fine dust fell all around covering everything in a brown shroud. I took all this in, but what held my attention was my belly which had split open like a ripe tomato. Projecting out of it was a strange worm-like creature. As I stared at it, mouth agape, it continued to ooze out and slide down my belly. It was then that I realised the dark matter was blood and the thing I was looking at was my intestines.

Bile rose in my gorge at the same time as a flush of heat passed over me. I rolled to one side and threw up. A pool of brown liquid erupted over the ground, splattering me in the face. Drool hung off my lower lip as another spasm racked my body and I threw up again. I wiped the drool off my lip with the back of my hand and took in my surroundings. It was night time and I was in a doorway. It had been the same recurring nightmare I had had before, though the puddle of vomit beside my head looked real enough. I could smell it. It was real all right.

I dragged myself away from the foul odour of bile and stale beer. When I pushed myself up off the doorstep my head swirled and I thought I was going to pass out. When I stood, I had to lean against a brick wall for support. Thankfully I was still fully clothed. For an instant I thought I was back in my dream. A tight band tightened around my head, threatening to split my skull. I waited until the worst of the pain had passed before venturing out of the doorway.

I was in an alleyway. Blank brick walls ran down both sides. I had been out of work for over six weeks now. My last wages were gone and I had taken to asking people on the street for change. I recognised the alley as Fort Lane. The dim glow of a gas lamp lit up the end of the alley.

I was about to walk towards it when the silhouette of a policeman, with baton in hand, walked past the end of the alley. I pressed myself against the nearest wall and stood still until he had passed, before venturing out on to Custom Street. There I looked up and down it. The footpath was empty. A sole horse and dray was making its way along the far side of the road away from me. Thankfully, there were few passers-by to see me staggering along the road towards home. Every time I saw a passing cart or car, I sought the anonymity of a darkened doorway until it had passed.

At the Queen Street intersection I crossed over tramlines shining in the glow of gas lamps high up on the cast-iron poles that supported the overhead wires. The terminus was bereft of cars and people. Black shapes lay scattered about on the Chief Post Office's steps. Others, like me, sleeping off a binge. I smiled to myself, gratified that I was not the only soul in Auckland that night a little the worst for wear.

A little bit past the Tepid Baths I came across a horse trough and sat down on the edge of it to wash my face. By then, my throat was dry and my mouth tasted sour. I reckon I could have lit a match at five paces with my breath. Without really looking, I cupped my hands and took a drink. It tasted vile and I immediately spat it out. When I peered down at the water I saw a layer of green slime covering its surface. That accounted for the vile taste, but what made me recoil in disgust were the white tendrils of horse slobber floating about on the surface. I tried to spit out any residue left in my mouth and wiped the back of my hand back and forth across my lips. I then stumbled away from the trough full of self-loathing. Even so, it had served to remove the acid residue from my mouth.

Chapter 24

I have little memory of wending my way through Freeman's Bay and up Hepburn Street. I have confused memories of people taunting me and making comments as I passed. That may have been on another occasion, who would know? I felt in a fighting mood that night and may even have taken a swing at some of my detractors. Echoes of laughter reverberated in my head. It was only when I reached Ponsonby Road and the cold south-westerly wind hit me that I sobered up enough to take in my surroundings.

By then, headed down Richmond Road, I was on the home straight. After Lincoln Street the row of workers' cottages ran out. Ahead of me was total darkness. I sensed more than saw the dark shape of beasts in the field beyond the fence on the far side of the road. The dark outlines of trees looked sinister in the darkness. My ears strained to listen for any danger. All I heard were some shorebirds flying overhead calling out 'pip pip' to one another and the rustle of the wind in the trees. The footpath I was on came to an abrupt stop. I muttered an oath each time my foot slithered on the mud or I tripped over a broken branch hidden in the grass. At the bottom of the valley, near Cox's Creek, there was more protection from the biting wind and I began to warm up a little. This in turn began to make me feel seedy again. I thought I was going to throw up and a little man in my head was doing lazy circuits beating on a drum.

The cottage was in total darkness. I had no idea what the time was. Only God knew how long I had been asleep or how long it had taken for me to stagger home from town, resting here and there along the way. At the front porch my foot caught on the edge of the decking and I sprawled forward to crash into the wall next to the door. An oath shattered the still of the night as my shoulder rebounded off the weatherboards and my legs gave way beneath me. I hit the porch decking like a sack of potatoes and lay there dazed for several minutes before pushing myself upright again. I rattled the front door handle only to find someone had locked it. Mumbling to myself in the darkness I groped about in my coat pockets for my house key but came up with nothing.

Cursing, I leaned my head against the door jamb. Another wave of nausea passed over me before I tried searching my trouser pockets. When my fingers wrapped around the cold shaft of the key and I pulled it out I gave a little cry of triumph. Finding the keyhole and getting the key into it became an immense task, but eventually the key slid into the slot and I turned it to open the door.

A smell of burning wax and roast beef greeted me the minute I stepped across the threshold. I was about to take a second step when an arm clamped itself across my windpipe and a knee rammed into my back. Frustration with everything exploded in me. I jabbed back with my elbow, but only managed a glancing blow to the side of my assailant who gave me an almighty shove from behind to propel me out through the door. For the second time that night I felt myself flying through the air, only this time it was real. My arms windmilled about in the air in an attempt to fend off whatever I was about to land in. When I hit the ground the wind was knocked out of me and I slid forward across grass and dirt and finally perennials to end up in a heap against the picket fence. I raised myself onto my hands and knees, thinking that this is a fine welcome home when someone kicked me hard in my rump. My head crashed into a fencepost sending a blast of pain though my head.

"Geeze," I yelled. "Whasamatta with you? I live here, ya stupid bugger. I'm not a thief."

"Yes you are," said my assailant. I immediately recognized that clipped Scottish accent typical of Aberdeen. It was Ma's lodger, Angus Mac-somebody or other. I had never bothered to catch his last name. He was seldom home when I was. We came and went in the night, as the saying goes. For some reason, I recalled he was a teetotaller, one of those holier-than-thou-Temperance-Movement nutters. Trust him to get on his high bloody horse about my drinking.

"It's George you stupid Scottish git. Don't you recognise me?"

"Aye, I recognise you, a'right. You're a drunken wastrel. All you do is bludge off your mother's goodwill and hard work. Your brother's been awa' fighting for King and Country. Noo look at you! You're an affront to the God and the human race. All you contribute towards this household is grief. Well, take it from me sonny, she's had enough. You're oot! Don't darken this doorway ever again or you'll have me to answer to."

"Who the hell do you think you are? This is my house. You're just the bloody lodger!"

"Aye, I'm the lodger and I pay good money every week to your mother for the privilege. When was the last time you gave her any money for board? Not only are you a drunkard and a blasphemer, you're a complete waste of time and space. Your mother doesn't need any more aggravation or worry from you in her life."

A little light went on in my head as he said this, and despite everything that had happened to me, a sly grin crossed my face.

"You sanctimonious prick. You're in my Ma's bed, aren't you?"

My grin was wiped off my face when a size twelve boot hit the side of my head. The impact sent me flying to one side, but I had barely hit the ground before he picked me up bodily by the collar. His hot breath passed over my face and I was thinking of poking my thumbs in his eyes when he kneed me in the groin. Immediately, pain radiated through my body and what little fight I had in me fizzled out as he dropped me. I landed with a thump and rolled into a ball on my side with my hands cupping my genitals.

"I'll get you for this, you bastard," I cried, somewhat feebly I must admit.

The only thing I heard was the door shutting quietly and the tumblers of the lock clicking into place. Christ, the bastard even had the consideration not to wake Ma by slamming the door.

I must have crawled across the road and into the scrub lining the creek for I awoke flat on my back looking up at the stars. Scudding clouds passed over them from time to time, but the bank of cloud that had made it so dark when I went home had broken up. Thinking about going home brought back what had happened to me. Aches and pains from the pummelling I had received now made themselves manifest. I rolled on to my side and put out an arm to lever myself up only for my hand to slide in slimy mud. Before I knew what had happened I was sliding down the bank into the water.

My befuddled brain registered it was saltwater as I went under briefly before sputtering back to the surface. I struggled to get a purchase along the bank until I reached an overhanging tree and used its branches to haul myself ashore again. I lay there exhausted, cold and wet. Never had I felt so wretched. I knew then that I had to sort myself out. Then I was going to take on the Scottish prick again, only this time I wasn't going to let him get the better of me; fancy kicking a man when he was down. I curled myself into the foetal position on my side and sought to stop shivering. After a time my eyes closed and sleep overcame me.

I woke up cold and still wet. Grey clouds were sweeping in from the west and the air had the damp feel of rain about it. The first thing I needed to do was get into some dry clothes. A brass band was playing in my head with special attention being given to the man on the big bass drum. I staggered to my feet and put my hands to my head in an attempt to prevent it splitting in two. I didn't think

Ma would really throw me out. It was just unfortunate I had met that bastard lodger.

I could see the gable of our house with its finial sticking up through the plumes of toitoi and forest sedge. I pushed my way back out to the road and up to the front gate. The hinges of the gate gave their customary squeak when I pushed it open. At the same time, I thought I saw a movement in the blind in the front room. When I tried the front door again I found it was still locked. The house was hardly ever locked and I took this as a bad sign. I then began knocking on the door and calling out, "Ma, are you there?"

"Go away, you can't come in," she called from the other side of the door.

"I'm your son!"

"I'm sorry, but I'll not have a drunkard in the house. You're not welcome until you can prove to me you've given up the bottle and can bring home an honest wage."

"I'm soaked. At least give me my belongings."

"You'll find your things in the wash house."

I couldn't believe it, Ma had locked me out. As I made my way round to the back of the house it was to the accompaniment of sashes being pulled down and bolted ahead of me. The old girl seemed quite determined about it. I could see I wasn't going to change her mind, that day at least.

True to her word my paltry belongings were sitting on the scrubbing board on top of the copper. I used a shirt to dry myself and changed into dry clothes. Ma hung up her spare bags on a hook behind the door and I took one of these down and stuffed my spare clothes inside. I looked at my other possessions; my brush and comb, cut throat razor, shaving brush, a pencil sharpener, a couple of books, pocket knife and my cigarette card collection from when I was a kid. I had a wry chuckle at the last item before throwing them all on top. I might be able to sell them, you never knew.

The only two people I could think of who might be able to help me were Nicco Piagni and Charlie Hanson. I headed back to Freeman's Bay hoping to catch Charlie at work. The gatekeeper at Parker Lamb's let me sit in his shed while he sent a boy with a message to Charlie. It was a long wait before their lunch break when he could come to see me, but I didn't mind sitting there getting my thoughts together. There was also an outside chance that Mattie or Bill from the Milly might be able to put me up. My problem was that I didn't know where either of them lived. I could try the Britomart, but I didn't have a farthing to my name and I had been thrown out of there a couple of times by now. The other option was to go to the library and look up their addresses in the provincial directory.

Charlie gave a double take when he saw me. I stood up, and he came over and we shook hands.

"Gidday George," he said.

I detected the cautious nature of his greeting and decided to put it all on the line.

"Hello Charlie. Thanks for seeing me. I'm in a bit of a bind and was hoping that you might be able to help me out."

"What can I do to help?" he asked.

"I've been out of work for a while and I've no money to pay for my board. I was hoping you might be able to put me up for a while until I'm back on my feet."

195

"Geeze George. I've got a wife and a bairn now. I'm sorry, but it's a no go."

"Fair enough. What about a job? Is there anything going here?"

"I don't know. I can ask if you like."

"I'd appreciate that."

"All right, you wait here and I'll go up to the office and ask."

I watched him walk off with a feeling of envy. I could have been like him, but the fates had decided that was not to be. He came back within ten minutes shaking his head.

"Sorry George. There are no vacancies at the moment."

"Right you are then. Can you let me know if anything comes up?"

"Sure, how can I get in touch with you?"

I didn't know how to answer that one. I was a man of no fixed abode. Then, on an inspiration, I said, "I'll drop a note to your gatekeeper to pass on to you when I have somewhere to stay."

As I said that the hooter went and I realised that I had kept Charlie from his lunch.

"I'd better get back to work," said Charlie. "I hope things work out for you."

"Thanks Charlie," I replied, hoping earnestly that would be the case.

I walked along to Queen's Wharf to see if the boats were in or out. The Milly was tied up to the pier, but there was no one about. I stood on the dock and looked down at her. Apart from new paint you wouldn't have known that her bottom had been ripped apart. Even though the boat was an inanimate object I felt a surge of love for the vessel. She had been a good and trusty travelling companion. Just looking at the boat filled me with renewed hope and I decided that was the turning point for me. I was going to get a job and I was going to find somewhere to sleep. From now on I was going to lay off the booze and make it all up to Ma.

I still needed somewhere to stay. It was a risky business going into the Criterion, but Nicco Piagni was my best hope of getting a roof over my head. I needed that if I was going to get my life together. The best of intentions can come to nought. He saw me the minute I walked through the door and watched me every second that it took me to walk up to the bar.

"What can I get you, George?" he asked.

"I need a place to stay for a while. I can't pay you now, but will pay you back when I can."

He looked at me in silence while still drying some glasses with his towel. I could tell he was weighing up the chances of his ever seeing any return. He then put the glasses down and flung his towel back over his shoulder.

"You don't want a drink?" he asked.

"No, I'm trying to dry out. Can you help me?"

For an answer he opened a drawer and took out a key. "Room 16 on the second floor. Keep it as long as you like."

"Thanks, I owe you."

"I know."

I stayed there for three weeks. Word filtered back to me through friends and the odd neighbour I met on the street that Ma was still attending church on Sundays. I figured that she was praying for Daniel and for some escape from the cycle of poverty she was trapped in. I sometimes wondered if I figured in her prayers. I certainly had no right to expect so. One of Ma's favourite sayings was 'God helps those who help themselves'. I had always thought this funny in that I imagined it meant He turned a blind eye if He saw you nicking something. Now I knew what she really meant. It was time for me to start believing.

Chapter 25

A large crowd filled the road between the tram
terminus and the railway station. It overflowed
from Queen Street all the way down Galway Street
to the station house. Once I joined it, I was jostled
from all sides, prodded with handbags and
umbrellas and thumped in the back. It all made it
very difficult to keep my temper. The railway
station had not been designed for such a large
crowd. It was one of those permanent 'temporary
public amenities' the public had got used to in this
sea of brick warehouses and corrugated iron shacks
that some people had, in their more ambitious
moments, labelled a city.

Despite the discomfort of being pummelled by
all and sundry an expectant buzz filled the air.
Uniforms of every type filled the crowd: nurses,
tram conductors, Salvation Army workers, matrons
and personnel from the three armed services. In
front of me the dead eyes on a fox stole stared
back. I stood on my tiptoes to see over the heads
of those in front. The woman with the fox fur had
on a hat like Ma's. For a minute I thought it was
Ma, but then Ma had no furs and was unlikely to
ever have any. Looking over the sea of hats, I
realized there was not a bare head in sight.
Working men wore their cloth or felt caps, while

the toffs wore bowlers. Those in between wore anything with a rim, from smart trilbies to battered fedoras. The women wore such a range as to defy the imagination, wearing fascinators, little pill boxes decorated with ostrich feathers or large piled-up creations that looked like multi-tiered wedding cakes stuck to their heads.

It was impossible to see over the plethora of millinery that people wore. I dropped back down off my toes wondering how I was going to get anywhere near the platform. That was when my natural street cunning took me further down the street to the opening in the hoardings that was the gateway to the No. 4 platform. A small trickle of men and youths were making their way through this opening and crossing the tracks to the main platform. I followed them and was soon clambering up the side of No. 1 Platform behind them. Thick soot and grime covered the wrought ironwork supporting the platform canopy. The bricks of the main building, once a beige colour, were now black, as were the once-white picket fences and wooden kiosks. A uniformed ticket collector stood by each kiosk.

The western end of the platform was packed with people and it was evident the guards and police were letting no more people enter. Already the police had moved to seal off the gate to No. 4 Platform from Queen Street. A cordon of police and army personnel was keeping anyone from the eastern end of the platform where the troop train would disembark its passengers. I once again gave a silent prayer for the fact that the war had ended before I was shipped off to become another statistic.

Not that it had been easy remaining behind. There were always those thin-lipped women who would come out of the crowd to thrust a white feather at you. At first I was embarrassed and tried to talk to these women, but soon realised they had nothing to say except bitter words for some private loss of their own. The best policy was to turn away when you saw one coming your way. From force of habit when waiting, I took from my trouser pocket my tobacco and a packet of rice paper to roll a cigarette. My fingers deftly drew out the tobacco and twisted it into the length of a cigarette before placing it on the paper. I lifted the paper to my lips and wet the edge with my tongue before rolling it into a cylinder ready to smoke. The cigarette dangled from my bottom lip while my hands strayed back down to my pockets, searching for a box of matches. Just as my fingers groped around in an empty pocket I was suddenly elbowed in the ribs from behind. The cigarette was in danger of flying out of my mouth, but I managed to grab it.

"Bloody hell!" I turned to see who had elbowed me. From the corner of my eye I caught sight of a dark serge uniform and was about to turn away when I realised it was that of a tram driver with the Auckland Transport Board.

"Sorry about that," he said. "It wasn't deliberate. Someone pushed me from behind," said the driver. His eyes looked amused by the incident, as though he had recognised my aversion to the law.

"That's all right," I muttered.

"At least let me give you a light."

"Thanks."

The flare of a lighter appeared in front of my face. The heat from the flame brushed against my skin as he leaned forward to light the cigarette in my cupped hands. The end papers caught with a line of red before turning black.

"Thanks mate."

"Who are you waiting for?"

"My brother. He's been away three years."

"I guess we're both lucky to have someone come home at all. There are plenty of poor devils that didn't."

"You're telling me."

"When did you get home?" he asked.

"I never went. They wouldn't have me. Said I had flat feet," I lied. It didn't pay to go around telling people you had been inside. "I was pretty pissed off. I've got to say now though that I'm glad they didn't take me."

The tram driver turned silent, as though I had suddenly let out a bad fart. I had seen it all before. I could tell he didn't think highly of me, but what the hell. I shrugged my shoulders and turned back towards the platforms.

A toot down the line stifled all of the surrounding conversation as everyone craned forward expectantly. Bags and elbows poked into sides and backs as the crowd surged forward. I was surprised to see the tram driver come level with me once again. He turned towards me and gave me a grin. Perhaps he didn't hold it against me after all for not going off to war.

"Well, I'll be seeing ya. Best of luck."

"You too, mate."

The black locomotive hissed and wheezed into the station. Steam enveloped the platform and drifted through to the concourse. Soot drifted down over people's heads and shoulders like ice crystals. Lace handkerchiefs appeared in women's hands as they held them up in front of their faces, the pure whiteness of the handkerchiefs turning grey in the swirling steam and soot. Some of the men held hands over their faces, but most stood there resolutely, while they were engulfed by the acrid fumes.

The bang and crash of doors opening signalled the first of the passengers to disembark. Uniformed guards began pushing into the crowd. "Clear a path – step back," they called. The people were compressed even further as a path was cleared though the unwilling throng.

Soldiers began to stream down the platform. Each held a kitbag on his shoulder and began to scan the crowd. I saw trepidation in their eyes. Would they be strangers to their families now? Cries rang out from the crowd when sons and brothers were recognised. The men seemed startled at their names being called and made their way, some hesitantly, towards those who had shouted out. People coalesced and split up to depart in groups. Still there was no sign of Daniel. The last of the able-bodied men passed by, leaving a hiatus for those left standing on the platform.

Then, a group of nurses descended from one of the carriages. My eyes were at once locked onto their uniforms, the bodies under those uniforms and then to their faces. All wore white wimples with a red cross emblazoned on their foreheads. Their faces, though pretty, were now grey with fatigue. The red made a rare splash of colour amid the khaki uniforms of the soldiers, the sombre blacks, navy blues and browns of the onlookers' clothes, and the dreary station with its covering of soot and grime. A sense of purpose came from the movement of these nurses as they helped the wounded down onto the platform.

What remained of the crowd was now silent. They took in the wreckage of war being unloaded and about to be delivered to them. Men on crutches, disdainful of help, hobbled along the platform first. Behind them, the nurses helped men into wicker bath chairs. Then the prone were brought out on stretchers.

By then, the men on crutches had passed me by, some of their faces evoking a determination to return to their loved ones and families, despite everything that had happened. Up until then I'd managed to feel no shame at not having joined my mates in battle. But standing on that platform in full health and civvies gave me no cheer. A phalanx of men in bath chairs now came through. All were being pushed by nurses, but it wasn't the nurses that my eyes were drawn to now, it was the men in the chairs. Plaster cast legs poked forward of some, while in others the empty blankets indicated lost limbs. Some had arms missing, but the worst were those whose faces had been shot away, making a pitiful horror for their families to look at each day.

I wondered how these men could face life in such a state. I tried to imagine what it would be like, but there was no way I could get halfway to what those wrecks of humanity must have been thinking. Despite all the horror, people came forward out of the crowd to plant kisses on the unbroken bits and to embrace them. These men were then led off, leaving the nurses to return to the rear of the train.

There was now just a spattering of people waiting. A silence descended on the platform. The dozen or so people left stared fearfully down the length of the platform. The steam had now dispersed up into the rafters where starlings went about building their nests. An officer with a swagger stick tucked under his arm descended from the very last carriage and spoke to one of the nurses. More nurses and some medical orderlies then stepped down from the carriage assisting soldiers between them.

These were not listed among the injured. These were the ones who had suffered the unseen wounds of the mind; those who had lost their wits in a bedlam of noise and terror. All were the silent victims of mankind's drive to improve the weapons of war, the casualties of the industrial madness that had gripped the world. They came shambling down the platform in fits and starts, their legs not fully co-ordinated, their faces blank and their eyes dead. The officer gave a command and the nurses and orderlies rounded them up and brought them into a regimented file, three men wide with a nurse or orderly holding the arm of each. In this manner, they moved slowly down the platform towards us.

I recognised Daniel and stepped forward to claim him. The officer leading the group, a young lieutenant, looked up at my approach.

"Do you know any of these men?" he asked.

There was a lump in my throat and I could not immediately give voice to reply. I could have said no and walked away, but even that act would have been too low, even for me. I pointed at Daniel. "He's my brother."

"Right, we'll need you to sign for him as the next of kin. You realise that in his current state he's not capable of looking after himself. He'll need constant nursing and must not be left alone until he has recovered?"

"How long will that take?" I asked.

"Nobody knows. It might be just a few weeks and then again it might take years."

I envisaged poor Ma lumbered with a vegetable for the rest of her days.

"Don't worry," I said. "We'll look after him, one way or the other."

The lieutenant gave me a baleful look, as though doubting my word before looking down at his polished boots.

"What is your brother's name?"

"Daniel Bender."

"Do you know his rank?"

"No. He was a private when he left."

"I see," said the lieutenant, examining a clipboard brought to him by a nurse. He then turned the clipboard around and presented it to me. "If you will sign here and then print underneath your full name, address and relationship with the patient, the army medical corps can then hand your brother over to your keeping."

After filling in the required information, I handed back the clipboard and shook hands with the officer. He gave a wry smile and said, "Good luck." Then he turned and gave instructions for Daniel to be brought forward.

"Gidday, Squirt. Welcome home," I said, stepping forward to embrace him. Some sixth sense made me hesitate as Daniel gave no acknowledgment. It was as if he didn't know me. "Come on, Daniel, its George, your big brother."

He stared unblinking at a point somewhere past my right shoulder. The eyes were blank, like a veil of rain had fallen across them.

"I'm afraid he's mute and has been since the last action he was in. It's a common enough symptom. He may start to recover his voice as he begins to recognise things from his past life. You will need to be patient with him," said the lieutenant. "Even when he recovers he may still have a speech impediment."

"Is there anything else I should know?" I asked.

The lieutenant looked down at his boots, seeming to decide whether he should tell me more. I could tell that there was more, but I didn't know whether I wanted to hear it.

"I suppose you're entitled to know the worst. After all, you will be the ones looking after him. We don't know a lot about shell shock victims yet. There are some doctors in England doing studies on it. What we do know is that the symptoms can be varied. Mutism or general speech impediments are the most common symptoms. Others include nightmares, insomnia and heart palpitations, dizziness, depression and general disorientation."

"Christ," I replied.

"You shouldn't assume because your brother is mute that he has amnesia. Many people make this assumption just because the patient doesn't speak and shows no response to anything around them. Anyway, good luck. We've others to take care of so I'll leave Private Bender in your care."

I put an arm under Daniel's to support him and felt for the first time his dead weight. It was then that I wondered how on earth I was going to get him home. A feeling of dread passed over me. Meanwhile the shambling procession continued on its way through the concourse, stopping and starting each time a patient was taken into a family's care.

"Sweet Jesus," I muttered. "How many blokes like you are there out there who are limbless or addled in the head?"

As the last of the sorry procession disappeared through the station doors out onto the street the station became silent apart from the chirpings of the starlings and sparrows up in the roof. A few pigeons had flown back in to strut about on the platform looking for crumbs. Outside I was aware once more of the dull roar of traffic and the ding of tram bells from the tram terminus.

Ma would get in a state when she saw him, I just knew. We had only just received a telegram saying he would be on the train. It said that he was wounded, but gave no more information. Perhaps it was better that she hadn't come to the station to meet him. She had said she couldn't risk taking time off her work and I had believed her. Had she had one of her premonitions about him? I put my hand around Daniel's waist and lifted him half onto my shoulder and half carried and half walked him out of the station.

We had barely got to the line of hoardings fronting Queen Street when a woman called out his name. I looked around the crowd to see Beth pushing her way towards us. I had only met her when I had gone to her place to tell her. Ma had insisted that she had to know. She had struck me as pale and thin, one of those pensive types. I had felt her scrutiny of me as I stood in her doorway, perhaps comparing me to Daniel, perhaps judging me, who knows? When I had told her Daniel had been wounded, I saw the sudden reluctance in her

208

to face the man she once loved and possibly still did.

Now there she was again, panting slightly, her eyes quickly taking in the state of Daniel before they turned back to me.

"I tried to get here earlier, but missed the tram and had to wait for another."

I knew this to be just an excuse, but could feel no animosity towards the woman who had become engaged to my brother a couple of days before he had been shipped out. She must have scanned the lists of dead and wounded with mounting dread every day since then.

"How is he?" she asked, looking from me to Daniel and back again.

"He's mute," I replied not wishing to say that he was scrambled in the head. "I don't know how long he'll be like this. Do you want to hold him? He's a dead weight."

In answer she leaned forward and placed a kiss on Daniel's cheek. Daniel showed no emotion from this act.

"What are you going to do with him?" she asked.

"Take him home and look after him. What else can we do?"

She looked from him back to me, her eyes filled with anguish. "I don't think that I can face him like that," she said, barely suppressing her emotions.

"Christ Beth, you and he are engaged."

"I know. I'm sorry. I just can't do it."

She stood their looking at me with a pleading look in her eyes. I guess I always was a soft touch. All of my own muddled emotions raced around in my head. I understood perfectly the way she felt.

Looking after Daniel was going to be both physically and emotionally draining. I let out a little sigh of resignation before saying, "It's a bit of a shock for us all, I guess. Ma and me will manage, at least till he gets his wits about him again. Perhaps you can call around and visit him."

Her eyes flickered for an instant over Daniel before coming to rest on me. I could see the doubt in her face, but she seemed to be relieved anyway.

"Thanks George, I won't forget this," said Beth, stepping forward to kiss Daniel on the forehead this time before turning and fleeing down the steps towards the tram terminus. I couldn't see her face, but knew instinctively that she was crying.

"Me neither," I muttered. "Come on Squirt, how about we share a jar or two before going home to Ma?"

Chapter 26

It was dark when I carried Daniel up to the veranda. The heady mixture of raw emotion and alcohol had left my head spinning and my legs barely able to support either of us. I leant against the door jamb while I freed a hand to push down on the front door latch. My shoulder slipped off the jamb and the pair of us fell through the opening to land in a heap on the floor. I looked up into the empty eyes of my brother. He had a stupid grin on his dial, as though he was enjoying himself. Perhaps there was a little spark inside his head after all, a pilot light waiting to be ignited.

"You've bin drinking again," cried Ma. "Will you look at the state of the pair of you? Both as legless as pot-bellied snakes. What sort of homecoming is this for Daniel?"

"Stop asking daft questions and help get him off me," I replied, unable to move.

"Don't talk to me like that! You know I won't have drunken men in me house."

"It was a special occasion."

"Aye well, I'll concede that, but don't give me any of your lip. You're not that big that I can't give you a good clip about the ears."

With Ma's help I extricated myself from under my brother and was stood up. She and I were then able to hoist Daniel to his feet.

"I don't like to tell you this Ma, but he's not really with us," I said.

"What do you mean? He's right here, isn't he?"

"In a manner of speaking. Look into his eyes and ask him who you are."

Ma's face turned the colour of chalk when she took a hard look at Daniel. "Oh, lawdy! Has Beth seen him like this?" she asked.

"Yes. She met us outside the station. She couldn't face him the way he was and asked us to give her more time."

Ma's lips set in a thin line and she looked me in the eyes. I didn't need to be a mind reader to divine what she thought of Beth, but at least she hadn't given vent to her opinions on the matter.

"I guess he's had a long day even if he can't remember much of it. Best we get him to bed," I said, glad to deflect Ma's spite towards Beth.

"Do you think he's continent?" asked Ma.

"What do ya mean?" I replied, wondering what Europe had to do with anything.

"I mean does he have control of his bladder."

"Christ, you don't want me to hold his thing, do you?"

"Better you than me."

"Jeez, thanks for nothing."

"That's enough of that blaspheming too."

I caught Ma's grin from the corner of my eye as I bundled Daniel through the kitchen and out the back door. It was funny how people sometimes revert to humour when faced with adversity. I thanked God it was dark as I unbuttoned Daniel's fly and rummaged around for his dick. The last thing I wanted was the neighbours to see us. A veritable torrent emerged from Daniel, which I directed onto the lemon tree. The thought of his dick being called 'Adversity.' brought a smile to my lips for the first time since the train station. At least the lemons would be good next season. I just hoped that Daniel would be well enough to appreciate them.

Collecting Daniel from the Railway Station had broken some of the frostiness that had existed between Ma and me. She still didn't let me move back into the house, but she did let me visit and sit with Daniel. On those occasions she brought me a cup of tea and a biscuit, even making me lunch sometimes. I could tell she still didn't approve of my life. No doubt the parish spy network kept her well informed. Still, it was a beginning and I was thankful for it.

There was no way of knowing what was going on in Daniel's head. I often wondered whether he was aware of his condition. If he was, he should surely be depressed, but there was no sign of it. He certainly seemed to be disorientated most of the time. When I was there I tried to do little things about the house to help, like chop the firewood or light a fire, but even in these tasks I failed. Her lodger, old Macwhatshisname, would have already cut up the firewood and each time I tried to light the fire with the wet wood, I would lose patience trying to draw the fire. Ma always ended up getting it going.

She let slip one day that she was often woken up in the middle of the night by Daniel banging on the wall or crashing about in his room. When she went in he would be slumped down on the floor bathed in sweat with his bed clothes strewn all over the place. Whenever this happened she would put him put him back into bed and place a cold compress on his forehead. I figured the constant stress of looking after Daniel was taking its toll on her, but I hadn't realised her sleep had been broken on such a regular basis.

Since being kicked out of home, I had been staying in a number of places. At first I slept rough because it was summer and the weather was kind. With the onset of autumn I managed to stay with friends and friends of friends for about a month until my welcome had worn out. Nicco put me up once or twice but I only approached him when I was desperate. Since then I'd been living in a boarding house in Vincent Street. I had my own room with a sturdy lock on it.

At first, the smell of the place made me gag each time I went in, but I soon became used to it. For so many people all living in one place it was surprisingly quiet. The street itself had little traffic and the house was surrounded by private dwellings, the owners of which no doubt would rather have had the lodging house somewhere else. We shared the kitchen, lounge and the bathroom.

My fellow lodgers ranged from hard-up working men to prostitutes to those white-haired, red-eyed, gin-swilling wrecks that only ventured out at night. We were all branded as the unwanted and unloved.

I kept a small supply of food in my room in a cardboard carton. Anything left in the kitchen quickly vanished. We all tended to keep to ourselves. In the lounge you were sure to be harangued about God by one of the ravers there.

The bathroom was one place you wanted to spend the least time you could. I tended to use the toilets at work when I could and each Sunday afternoon I treated myself to a swim at the Tepid Baths. This counted as my weekly bath.

Since my banishment, Daniel's fiancée Beth and I had formed an unlikely alliance, both seeking news about Daniel and looking for some sort of spiritual solace from one other. She had no relatives in the city. Both of her parents were dead, her father killed in a Kuaotunu gold mine and her mother dying of pleurisy two years later. I had no doubt that Beth still had feelings for Daniel and hoped he would recover so they could get married. I couldn't bring myself to tell her that this was a forlorn hope because in my heart of hearts I also hoped that he would recover. There had been signs this might be happening, but then hope blinds us to the truth sometimes.

Beth was living with a couple and their one year old daughter in a cottage in Arch Hill. As it would have been inappropriate for me to meet her at the cottage we met on Sundays in Myer's Park and sat on the steps below St Kevin's Arcade. In better circumstances I would have liked to take her to lunch, but my funds barely ran to feeding myself and paying my board. Beth was also struggling to make ends meet. As part-payment for her board Beth looked after the child while both the parents went out to work.

I generally went around to Ma's on Saturday afternoons to see how Daniel was faring and could bring Beth up to date the next day. Daniel was showing signs of improvement in that he was then

215

able to speak and recognise who we were. Of course, this may just have been his recognising the people around him. We had no way of knowing if he remembered us from before the war. When I relayed the news that he was now aware of who we were, Beth came out of herself and seemed to glow. For me, regular contact with a young female also made a difference, even if it was platonic.

It was then that Beth started to visit Daniel at Ma's. She then kept me more up to date about him than I could her. She also had a woman's intuition and could relay to me how Ma was coping. To me, Ma looked just the same, but Beth could see beneath the façade she put on. It grieved me that Ma had to struggle from one hardship to the next. No doubt her faith got her through these times even if Father O'Riorden was still probably taking a proportion of her meagre earnings. After each meeting with Beth I came away feeling better in myself. I suppose it centred my life and gave me back some of my self-esteem, which had been at a low ebb for some time.

After one of our meetings, I accompanied Beth up the steps to the arcade and out onto Karangahape Road, intending to walk her part of the way home along New North Road to her lodgings. When we emerged from the arcade we ran into Emma. She was dressed in her Sunday best, as if she had just attended church. We both stared at each other for a minute. Beth saw there was history between us and bid me farewell, to continue her way home alone.

I was at a loss what to do. I wanted to accompany Beth, but she was already well along the footpath. Emma didn't look any different, still as beautiful as ever, with that slightly supercilious look she had. She looked at me in dismay before venturing a timid "George?"

"Hello Emma."

"God you look dreadful. What happened to you?"

Her words shocked me. I had washed and shaved for my meeting with Beth and was wearing my best clothes, not that they were up to much. I was well aware that both men's and women's fashions had moved on since my trial. Mine now looked old fashioned and smelled of moth balls from being stored in the wardrobe so long.

At first I resented her comment. Was she out to further humiliate me?

"Thanks Emma. You always did know how to make a man feel good," I replied.

As soon as I said it I realised what I had said and a hot flush came over me. She seemed as embarrassed at meeting me as I was in meeting her. She didn't seem to notice my gaffe, merely giving me a shy smile.

"I'm sorry," she said. "I didn't mean it to come out like that. It was the shock at seeing you after all this time. Lydia told me what happened. I'm sorry. What are you doing now?"

"I'm still out of work."

"That's awful. At least, let me buy you lunch."

I didn't want her charity, but I wasn't about to pass up a decent meal. "If you insist," I replied, feeling that her buying me lunch might make up for the humiliation she had caused me.

She took my hand in hers and dragged me back down the arcade to a restaurant. I pulled out her chair and she sat down. I sat opposite her. She looked at the menu and then handed it to me before peeling off her gloves and putting them in her handbag. I looked at the menu and decided to order the most expensive thing there. The waiter came over and we placed our orders. Emma looked slightly askance at me when I ordered the crayfish Mornay, but she said nothing. When the waiter departed we just stared at each other. I realised then that apart from her being a friend of Lydia's, I knew nothing about her.

"Have you just been to church?" I asked.

"Yes, my family are members of Pitt Street Methodist Church. It's one of my little concessions I make towards my parents. Each Sunday I attend church with them. That way I keep in touch with them without having to endure one of those long protracted interrogations by my mother about my love life."

She smiled demurely at me as she said this, challenging me to ask about her love life.

"You live apart then?"

"Lydia and I share an apartment in Symonds Street."

"How long have you been doing that?"

"A month now."

Once again she had this habit of making me feel gauche in her presence. I was saved by the waiter returning with our meals. For a while we ate in silence while I struggled to come up with something intelligent to say. As I glanced across the table, between mouthfuls, it occurred to me that her parents must be wealthy and might have some influence in this town, so I asked her what they did. She looked at me with that little smirk at the corner of her mouth, then finished her mouthful before replying.

"Dad's a ship owner. Mum makes out she's busy every day doing charity work, but I think it's really her way of salving her conscience."

"What sort of ships does your father own?"

"Oh, you know, things with masts and sails, I don't know what they're called. Does it matter?"

"It might. I need a job and I have experience on mullet boats. That could easily translate to scows or schooners."

"Would you like me to ask him next time I see him?"

"I would. I'm desperate for work and the right word in the right place always helps."

Emma and I had both finished our first course by then and the waiter swooped in to take away our plates.

"Would you like the dessert menu?" he asked, looking at me.

"Yes please," I replied, taking the menu from him and looking at it.

"What are you having?" I asked Emma.

She looked up at the waiter and ordered tea and scones while I ordered a lemon meringue pie, followed by coffee. God I hadn't had a decent cup of coffee for so long!

After we had finished, Emma asked the waiter for the bill and paid in cash. I waited while she took her gloves out of her handbag and put them on before we stood up. I then accompanied her out of the restaurant and along the arcade. When we reached the street she turned to me and held out her hand.

"It was good seeing you again, George. I'll definitely ask Dad about getting you a position."

"Thanks, it means a lot to me."

"How can I get a message to you?"

"I live in the boarding house at 136 Vincent Street."

I watched her face. Evidently she didn't know the place otherwise she might have grimaced. This gave me a sense of relief.

"I'll have a message left there if there's anything on offer," she said.

"Give my best to Lydia. I still think of her," I replied.

Emma's lips curled up at the corner at this remark and her eyes fixed on me, trying to divine if there was anything behind my remark. "She'll be surprised about me running into you," she said.

"It was a surprise for me too."

"I'm sorry for what I did to you in the theatre. I feel dreadfully ashamed of that. God knows what you think of me. It was like I had become overcome by some sort of dare."

I was taken aback that she would even mention it. I certainly hadn't been going to. When I looked at her she seemed to be genuinely embarrassed.

"Well, I won't mention it if you don't"

She smiled before stepping forward and kissing me on the cheek.

"What about Lydia?"

"What makes you think I told her?"

"I assumed that you were both in on it."

"Goodness no. I could never look her in the face again if she knew about that!"

Chapter 27

A little over a week later a telegram was delivered to the boarding house. It was from Emma saying that her father's boat, the Vindex had a position open for a deck hand. I was to report to the captain, Isaac Cobb, at the boat which was berthed at Queen's Wharf no later than Thursday, when it was due to sail. It was signed Emma Parker. Up till then I hadn't known her surname.

I wasted no time making my way down to Queen's Wharf the next Monday morning. The Vindex was a sailing scow, the type of flat-bottomed sailing vessel popular around Auckland and Northland for sailing up the many muddy estuaries and harbour inlets that abound in the area. Like many of the scows she had a clipper bow to an otherwise vertical sided hull, shaped more like a punt than anything else.

I called out to see if there was anyone aboard, but received no answer. As I waited for someone to turn up, I paced along the pier to see how long Vindex was and came to the conclusion it was about eighty feet long, almost three times the length of a mullet boat. What amazed me was the length of the centreboard. It was nigh on ten feet long. I could see it needed at least two men to raise and lower it and you could be sure that it was going to jam against the sides of the slot at times.

I sat down on a bollard and stared at the vessel. It was ketch rigged with a gaff to both masts and had three headsails. She would be a heavy old thing to sail, not like the mullet boats which took off like racing hounds in a good breeze. I could see the Vindex plugging along like an old draught horse pulling a heavy cart. The good thing was that these boats didn't have spinnakers; that I knew of, anyway.

I had been waiting about an hour before a tall man wearing sea boots, corduroy trousers and a heavy seaman's jacket came along the wharf and descended the gangplank. I remained where I was, waiting for him to reappear from below. Presently he climbed back out of a for'ard hatch and walked back towards the stern.

"Permission to come aboard," I cried.

He looked up from the locker he was peering into.

"Who are you?" he asked.

"A seaman looking for work," I replied. "I was told you had a vacancy."

"Who told you we had a vacancy?"

"Mr Parker's daughter, Emma."

"Aye, well come aboard then. Let's have a good look at you."

I clambered down the gangplank to the afterdeck and put out my hand. "The name's George Bender."

"Right, how are you. I'm Captain Cobb. Mr Parker is one of the shareholders of the vessel, so I suppose if you look all right I may as well take you on. What experiences have you in sailing vessels?"

"I've sailed on mulleties for quite a while, both fishing and harbour racing. I've never sailed on anything this big though."

"If you can handle a mullet boat in a good breeze you'll have no problem with this old girl. Scows are docile old things under sail. The main thing is that you have a strong back and are willing?"

"I've laboured a fair bit and am keen to work. I've been out of work for a while now and it isn't much fun."

"Aye, I can believe that. There's plenty round the town out of work. Can anyone give you a reference, apart from Mr Parker, that is?"

The question caught me on the hop and I hesitated answering. I saw the shadow pass over Cobb's eyes while he waited for me to answer. The job hung in the balance.

"I suppose Joe Williams might give me a good word," I said, crossing my fingers behind my back.

"Is Joe who you worked for on the mulleties?"

"Yes."

"I know Joe well. If he gives you the nod, you're on. Come back on Wednesday about ten in the morning and I'll let you know."

"Thanks, I won't let you down."

"Hah! How many times have I heard that? Away with you!"

I walked away thinking that that was that. After my last meeting with Joe I couldn't see him giving me a good referral, but you never knew for sure.

On the Wednesday I presented myself once more to Captain Cobb to be told that Joe had told him I was a good hand. I was hired on the spot and began work the next day. Never was I so glad to have a job again. It felt as though my life was back on track. With a regular wage I could face Ma as a new me, in new clothes and with money in my pocket.

The next morning we sailed out of Auckland with a westerly breeze behind us, allowing us to sail up the coast under a broad reach. The heavy canvas sails were old and stiff, having been waxed to prolong their life. The down haul lift required a man to put his back into it to make any difference, but once the sails were set you could sit back and enjoy the journey. With a full head of sail we made about five knots and the broad hull of the scow barely canted at all under the steady breeze.

Ahead of us flocks of Mother Carey's Chickens parted before us with the birds taking off in their mad little dashes across the top of the water while gannets, mollymawks and albatross glided effortlessly around us on the thermals above the waves. It had been a while since I had been out on the Milly and I now realized how much I had missed this world of sea and sky. The sea air and the salt spray spinning off the bow as it cut through the low swells invigorated me, cleansing me of the melancholy that had taken a hold of me while unemployed.

We sailed into Mahurangi Harbour late in the afternoon. There we ran up on the hard and waited for the tide to go out before loading logs off the beach. A derrick was rigged to the mast to swing the logs up onto the deck. It was all new to me and I had to see how everything was done. The petrol-driven winch was used to lift the heavy logs and manpower was used to swing the logs aboard. Once on board, they were stacked lengthwise along the deck with timber wedges driven into the sides to prevent them sliding about. We stayed there two days loading the logs. By the end of it, the logs were stacked three high on the deck with heavy chains wrapped around them. When we refloated on the high tide, the hull was much lower down in the water. To get to the masts we had to climb over the logs. It seemed to me that we were badly overloaded and that the vessel would be in trouble if we hit bad weather. However, once we were under sail again the boat settled down to a steady speed. More spray came over the side with her lower freeboard, but that didn't worry me.

In all our trips back and forth up the coast and across to Great Barrier Island and Coromandel to pick up loads of logs, firewood, shingle, sand and gravel the boat always performed well. Pushing wheelbarrows full of sand or shingle up planks onto the deck of the Vindex soon hardened up my body. I grew to respect the scows as the honest workhorses they were. The boat was now my home and I stayed at the boarding house in Vincent Street between trips, paying on a night-by-night basis. I bought new working clothes and oilskins.

It was a month later when I called in at home. It was a Sunday afternoon. Ma hadn't been expecting my visit and hadn't put Daniel out on the front porch seat as she usually did when I visited. She was loading the copper with washing when I walked in. She looked up and put her hand over her heart.

"Lawdy, you gave me a fright, where did you come from?" she asked.

"Aren't you glad to see me?"

"Of course I am. I thought you had fallen off the world. Where have you been?"

"I've been working on a scow up and down the coast."

"What, a real job?"

"Yes. I've been working for a month now. I've brought you a present."

From behind my back I brought out a brown paper covered parcel which I handed to her. She took it hesitantly, like she expected it to explode.

"It's all right. Open it!"

She untied the ribbon holding it together and carefully rolled this up before peeling back the paper to reveal the hat I had bought her. It was a felt hat with a pink ribbon wrapped around it, tied in a bow and trailing down the back. It had cost a pretty penny, but I knew how much she loved hats. It was my peace offering and I hoped she would like it. I was hoping she wouldn't criticise it as being the wrong size or colour or fashion. She put it on her head and looked at herself in the mirror.

"It's beautiful," she exclaimed. "Thank you so much."

Suddenly, a shadow passed over her face and she turned to look at me. "There's no spare room, you know."

"That's all right. You'll find some money inside the hat."

Ma took off the hat and looked under the label inside, before extracting a ten pound note. She looked at me dubiously.

"I didn't steal it. The money was honestly earned."

"Well, I won't say it's not welcome. Thank you son," she said coming forward to embrace me. I hugged her slight little body to mine; glad our disagreements were behind us.

"Where's Daniel?" I asked.

"Beth came over and took him out."

"How is he?"

"Getting better by the day. He goes for walks most days now."

"What, and manages to come home again?"

Ma gave a little titter at this. I smiled and then both of us burst out laughing. We weren't laughing about Daniel having no idea where he was when he came home from the war. Our laughter was pure relief that he was up and about. Then Ma stopped to give me one of her hard stares. "You always did have a wicked sense of humour," she said.

"What do you mean? You started it."

"Well, it felt good to laugh at something after all these months. That said, I'm still not sure if he sees Beth as his fiancée or just someone who comes around to keep him company in his illness. For all we know he might think she's some kind of nurse."

"I guess we won't know that unless he comes out and tells us. How do they get on when they're together?"

"He seems to like it when she's around. She's a possessive little thing and who can blame her. I hope she doesn't rush him. He's not ready for anything of that sort yet. Relationships are hard enough for those of us who are normal."

"You never know. It might be what he needs to snap out of it."

"I don't think so and don't you go planting any silly ideas in his head."

"Talking about relationships, what's going on between you and McFetridge?"

"There's nothing going on, and anyway even if there was, it wouldn't be any of your business."

"I was only thinking what the parish gossips would say."

Ma gave me another long penetrating glare before saying, "Do you really think that I give a hoot what they might think?"

"So there is something going on then?" I asked.

"You just mind your Ps and Qs young man. If there is something going on, as you are so keen on suggesting, then it's my business. I've given you a belt across the backside before today and I'm not afraid to do so again."

I held up my hands in token surrender, before saying, "You're right, I'm sorry."

Chapter 28

Another person I hadn't thanked was Emma. After visiting Ma I stopped in Karangahape Road to buy a bunch of flowers. I had a vague notion that different flowers meant different things and I didn't want to stuff things up by buying something that had bad connotations. In the end, I bought a bunch of red carnations. The lady in the shop told me that if I wanted to make a good impression they would be all right. They looked colourful and, as far as I knew, weren't associated with death.

It had taken me quite some time to find out exactly where Emma and Lydia lived. I had figured that a couple of single women living together would almost certainly have a telephone. Through a bit of blarney with the telephone operator I had extracted the valuable information I was after.

I walked up the western side of Symonds Street until I was opposite their apartment block. It was a four-storey building, built in brick, with a terracotta tile roof. It looked much grander than the timber dwellings that surrounded it. I crossed the road to enter the lobby where I found a stainless steel panel with the names of the occupants on. I had never seen anything like it before. I pressed the button next to the girls' names and waited. Nothing happened so I pressed it a second time. Then a metallic voice spoke out of the opening. It was so distorted I couldn't tell whether it was Lydia's or Emma's or, someone else altogether.

"Hullo. It's George Bender."

"Come on up," said the voice.

The front door opened when I gave it a push. Inside, there was a corridor leading to the ground floor apartments while a birdcage lift and stairway led to the upper floors. Not trusting the lift I climbed the stairs to the second floor. There were two apartments and I was unsure which was theirs. As I was tossing up in my mind which door to knock on, one of them opened and Lydia sallied forth, looking elegant in a long robe through which I could easily see the outline of her body. Her eyes immediately went from my face to the flowers in my hand.

"Are those for me?" she asked.

"Actually, they're for Emma to say 'thank you' for her getting me a job."

"Oh, I'll tell her," she replied.

I could tell she was a bit miffed at this. That made me realise how much stock I had put on seeing Emma. Perhaps my face showed this, as Lydia took the flowers in one hand and my hand in the other. She gave me a rueful smile before saying, "She's having lunch with her parents. Some big family event, I understand. I'm here all alone."

I was conscious of my hand in hers, the heat being transferred and the wanton look in her eyes. I knew immediately what this implied, but made no move to pull my hand away. She led me into the apartment and sat me down in a designer couch while she went to find a vase for the flowers.

While Lydia busied herself with this I looked about. Everything was very stylish in an art-nouveau kind of way. It was all plain walls, ornate trims, glass tables and black leather chairs. Everything shrieked money at me. I asked myself what I was doing there. It was then that the little imp in my head told me that it could all be mine if I played my cards right. This thought slipped into my head without any conscious thought on my part. In my old gambling days thoughts of this nature were my constant companion. I thought the little imp that had planted it there had decamped for greener pastures when I was convicted and thrown in the slammer. But no, he must have just been in hibernation.

As my eyes strayed from one statuette to a Gustave Klimt print hanging on the wall, I began to see that such a thought was not outside the bounds of possibility. My gaze then fell over Lydia's form within the diaphanous gown that hung down loosely from her shoulders. Even her clothes were art-nouveau. I had come to see Emma, but finding myself alone with Lydia to whom I had first been attracted seemed a tantalising prospect.

"There, that's done," she said, coming over to sit next to me on the sofa. I was very aware of the close proximity of her body to mine as I breathed in that particular odour that belongs to the female of the species. After spending so long in men's company, it was like a fine perfume and impossible to ignore. I wondered if she savoured my own smell or was just being polite about it. My initial urge was to slide along the sofa to put more distance between us, but I resisted the temptation, enjoying the challenge of maintaining my ground against her incursions.

"Now tell me what you have been up to since I last saw you," she asked.

"How much time have you got?" I replied, trying to sound nonchalant.

"As long as it takes," she replied, giving that side-on glance with upturned lips I had remembered.

I related how I had hit rock bottom after her father sacked me, then how I had met Emma in the street and how she had got me a job on the Vindex. I tried to hide the depths of despair I had reached. I must have succeeded in this because she suddenly blurted out, "You know that Dad has a share in the Vindex."

"Yeah, I do. Is that how Emma and you know each other in the first place, through your parents' business deals?"

"Our parents have been friends for as long as I can remember."

"Is your Dad still sore at me?"

"No, I don't think so, though damaging the boat bruised his ego more than he cares to admit. You took the brunt of his wrath at the time. I'm sure he bears you no ill-feeling."

"That's good. He's a good bloke and I was a gutted parting like that."

"Actually, Dad's not too good at the moment."

"Why, what's the matter?"

"He's just had a gallstone operation. It's knocked the stuffing out of him."

"I'm sorry to hear that. Who's looking after the business?"

"No one. The boats are all tied up."

"Can't Albie take the Milly out?"

"Didn't you hear?"

"What?"

"Albie's an invalid."

"Oh no. What happened to him?"

"He had a heart attack out on the boat. I think that shook Dad up a lot at the time. It made him feel vulnerable. It was quite amazing really. I'd always pictured Dad as indestructible, then Albie's heart attack shocked him and then he had the operation. You would barely recognise him now that he's lost so much weight."

"Please give him my regards next time you see him."

"I will and thank you. I think the thing that he misses most at the moment is some male company. Mum fusses over him, but I can see he frets to be outdoors as soon as he can, preferably out at sea."

"I can sympathise with him on that. There's nothing like it really,"

"You and he are a lot alike."

I looked sideways at Lydia in surprise. I hadn't pictured myself being like Joe until that moment.

"How do you mean?"

"Both you and Dad were brought up in the same area and you both love the sea."

"How did you know where I was brought up?"

"I made a few inquiries."

"Why?"

"Because I'm attracted to you."

She certainly wasn't backward in coming forward. Some would say she was brazen. She slipped her arm through mine and looked me in the face. There was a brief moment when I might have been reluctant to go any further, but then it passed and our lips came together.

An image of Father O'Riorden ranting on about it all being dirty unless sanctified by marriage within the church flashed before my eyes. More urgent matters then took charge. He was a fine one to talk like that when I had felt his hands on me and seen what he did to others. He had tainted every one of us one way or another. Now, for the first time since leaving prison I felt alive again. Lydia and I struggled out of our clothes and sprawled on the plush carpet. She lay back with her diaphanous gown spread out over the carpet about her, looking like a pre-Raphaelite painting as she opened her legs for me. We grappled together, thrusting and panting in an ecstasy of released emotions, lust, guilt, maybe even love, but I didn't want to push my luck in that direction.

Afterwards I lay back, looking up at the fancy plaster ceiling with tiered cornices, though not taking it in. Lydia rolled against my side and draped her arm over my chest. She let out a little sigh of contentment before saying, "That'll need a few Hail Marys next time I go to confession."

I looked sideways at her to see if she was having me on. She could have been just saying it because she now knew I was a Catholic. She grinned back at me in a naughty schoolgirl way. My heart skipped a beat.

"I didn't know you were a Catholic," I said. What had been a good romp might now turn into something altogether different if her reply was what I hoped it might be.

"I'm a convent girl through and through. We're the worst, you know?"

"So I've heard." I rolled back on top of her. "I think I could love you."

She didn't reply as we swung back into tandem. I sensed her lips set a bit tighter, but thought at the time I might be hurting her. This time we settled back to a slow rhythm, enjoying it for what it was. When it was over, Lydia got up and went to the bathroom while I lay back on the floor barely believing my good fortune. She came back out with her gown tied around her and opened the window to release the stale odour of sex that had permeated the apartment.

"You should go. Emma may be back soon."

"Right," I said, kneeling on the floor while I put on my singlet and shirt before standing and pulling on my underpants and trousers.

I tried to give her a parting kiss while she held open the door for me. At the last moment she pulled away, leaving me mystified.

"Can I see you again?"

"Next Sunday. Come earlier – around ten."

"Right, I'll be seeing you then."

I returned to the boarding house to wash and change my clothes. My fear was that the smell of sex hung over me for all to see and smell. The sense that something bad would happen as a result of what I had done came over me. I suppose it was all that stuff about it being a mortal sin coming back to haunt me. More likely, it was just that things like that did not happen to me.

All the way home, my head had been in a whirl as I tried to comprehend what had taken place. What puzzled me most was whether Lydia was again making fun of me in some way or was she genuine when she said she found me desirable. No other woman had ever said that to me before so why should I believe her? She seemed to be taken aback when I said I loved her. That had been a stupid thing to say. It was a spur of the moment thing. I think in that moment I had loved her, but now in the cold light of day I was not sure what my feelings towards her were.

After changing my clothes I went into the lounge. Some of the other boarding house residents sat about chatting or playing chess. I picked up a newspaper someone had left on the table and spent half an hour or so reading the latest news. For some reason I was holding back from visiting Ma that afternoon. Was I afraid of her reading guilt on my face? She had an uncanny ability in that respect. The mantle clock struck three o'clock and I knew I could put it off no longer. I stood up and put the paper back down on the table before heading out to the street. Would my washing and the sour fragrances of the boarding house have now masked that other residual smell? I hoped so.

Chapter 29

All my worries were baseless for when I got there Ma was pleased to see me. However, that was because Daniel had been in an agitated state since Beth returned him home and Ma needed my help in managing him. Beth had given Ma no explanation about what had happened to make him like this and had left in distress. Ma led me in to see Daniel who was lying curled up in the foetal position on his bed. I sat on the edge of his bed while Ma hovered in the doorway looking worried. When I put a hand on his shoulder he went into a shivering fit.

"Daniel, it's George. What's wrong mate?"

In response, Daniel emitted a stream of gibberish that I could not understand. He sounded like a child. When I leaned closer to hear what he was saying he sensed this and stopped his mewing to wriggle even closer to the wall. I looked up at Ma who remained tight-lipped. We weren't going to get any sense out of him so I threw a spare blanket over him and shut the door behind me.

"Perhaps he'll go to sleep. He might be more willing to tell us what's bothering him when he wakes up."

"Do you think I should get the doctor?" asked Ma.

"It's Sunday. They charge triple rates."

Ma said nothing to this. She didn't have enough money to throw it away like that, but I wasn't short of a bob or two now. "Do you want me to go and get him?"

"No, you're probably right. Let him sleep it off."

"Right, I'll put the kettle on then, shall I?"

Ma didn't answer. I wasn't aware she was sobbing at first because I had the tap running. When I turned around I saw she was holding her head face down in her hands, as though it was too heavy for her neck to support it. Now I heard the quiet sobs and saw her shoulders convulse. I had not seen her cry since I was a lad. She had been so stoical through everything that life had thrown at her, but now the sight of Daniel in the state he was in was too much for her.

McFetridge came out of his room to see what was going on. When he saw I was there he glared at me. I could see in his eyes he blamed me for causing the disturbance. I was about to tell him to take a hike when he cleared his throat and stomped out the front door. I breathed a sigh of relief. The last thing I needed right then was to have a set-to with him. By then, the kettle had boiled and I placed a cup of tea in front of Ma. She seemed to have got over her little meltdown as she looked up and gave me a crooked smile. She plucked her hankie from her sleeve and dabbed her eyes before putting it back and picking up the cup. Then she just sat there, staring into the surface of the tea, as though it was the oracle that would give her all the answers to her problems.

"It's all Beth's fault," she said suddenly.

"You can't be sure about that. You know what Daniel's like. Any little thing can set him off. It could have been a car backfiring or anything."

Ma stared at me in silence, clearly not convinced.

"He'll come out of this, you'll see," I told her.

"I suppose so. It's taking its toll though. I don't know if I can stand it much longer."

"What are you saying? Do you want to put him in Oakley, among all the loonies?"

"No, I couldn't do that."

"Well then, we'll just have to weather this little storm and hope it turns out all right."

"You're a fine one to talk. Where have you been all this time? What do you do to help?"

"Christ, you threw me out of the house, if you remember. Don't blame me if I'm not around day and night."

"Don't take Our Lord's name in vain."

"Right," I said. "I'm just trying to help. I know when I'm not wanted. I'm off. I'll be out on the Vindex most of this week. You may or may not see me next weekend."

I stood up and stomped out of the door, barely suppressing my anger. Ma always had to have someone to place the blame on. Poor Beth cared for Daniel more than either of us. My hands were clenched and I felt like I was carrying a two hundred pound weight. After a hundred yards or so up the road I relaxed enough to regret my outburst. Daniel put everyone around him under intense stress. It was no surprise that Ma and I snapped at each other. I was on the point of turning back and apologising, but then thought better of it. Ma needed to be left in peace. I would apologise the next time I saw her.

I met Lydia at her apartment the following Sunday morning. Emma had already left to attend her church with her family so there were no awkward scenes. I was pretty sure by then that Lydia would have told her we were in a relationship. We walked down to the tram stop and caught the tram to the bottom of Queen Street where we changed for one to Ponsonby. When we reached New Street, we got off and walked along to the Church of the Blessed Sacrament. It was the first time I had attended mass since my father's requiem mass. I prayed that Ma wouldn't take it into her head to come to mass here today and catch me. She usually went to the Church of the Sacred Heart in Vermont Street so there wasn't much risk of her turning up here, but you could never be sure.

The family had a pew off the side aisle so Lydia and I went in and sat down to await the arrival of her mother and sister. When they arrived, brief introductions were made with hushed voices after they sat down. The priest was someone I had not seen before. I breathed easier when he appeared, fearing that it would be my nemesis, Father O'Riorden. I wondered what the priest would think about me performing the Eucharist when I hadn't confessed for so long, but in the end, I decided 'what the hell' and went up with the rest of the congregation. I may have sinned in the view of the Church, but my relationship with Lydia felt anything, but a sin to me. I couldn't be bothered with what the Church might think. So far I hadn't been hit by lightning. I grinned to myself after the priest had been along the row and I had mumbled the phrases I had been taught as a child.

After the mass the priest shook our hands as we left the church. He eyed me like I were a visitor to the parish. I wasn't about to disillusion him on that score. I was sure that he would know all about me before an hour was up. By then, I would be gone. Lydia's sister, Priscilla, was still at secondary school, but one look at her and you could see she was Lydia's sister. She was going to be a striking woman in a few years.

Lydia's mum insisted on me calling her Mary. She was shorter than both her daughters so the girls had inherited their father's genes when it came to the physique, but had inherited their mother's dark looks, both in hair colour and in the eyes. Mary seemed a good sort and treated me kindly. I wondered if she would've treated me so cordially if she knew I was knocking off her daughter on those Sundays she didn't attend Mass. I decided it might be unwise to broach the subject.

I accompanied Lydia, her mother and Priscilla back from Church to their home in Hackett Street, above St Mary's Bay. I had dropped off gear there at night on the odd occasion, but it had been hard to make much out then. Now in broad daylight I could see their home in all its glory. It was a two-storied weatherboard house with a Marseille tile roof. Only well-off merchants could afford roofs like that so obviously Joe had done all right out of his fishing and ship owning enterprises. The house was set back off the road a couple of yards, with a small lawn between the house and the white picket fence along the road boundary. A rambling rose climbed up a trellis to one side of the entrance, spreading its scent throughout the garden.

Inside the entranceway was a hallway from which the ground floor rooms opened off. There was also a stairway leading to the upper floor.

"Why don't you go up and see Dad while I help Mum with lunch," said Lydia.

"He doesn't even know I'm here, does he?"

"Of course he does. I told him you were coming."

"All right, if you're sure he won't bite my head off."

"Go on up, he'll love to see you. You'll find him in the sun porch."

It's not often a man has to confront an old boss who fired him for incompetence. I can't say I was looking forward to it, but it was something I had to do if Lydia and I were going to have any future. My only hint that I wasn't going to get my head snapped off was Joe's support for my getting the job on the Vindex. I still couldn't believe he had done that.

As I stepped from the gloomy upper hallway into the sunroom the brilliant light pouring into the room dazzled me. Full height windows covered the length of the room, with the sunlight reflected off the sparkling waters of the harbour throwing patterns across the ceiling. The windows returned to cover both ends of the room. These were patterned in coloured glass – red, yellow and green, all made semi-opaque by a ripple pattern in the glass. The red and yellow glass formed a perimeter frame inside which a diamond of green glass sat inside white. The effect was to fill the room with a kaleidoscope of colour.

Joe was sitting in a cane chair with a blanket over his lap. Beside him was a cane table covered in glasses and bottles of all kinds. Lydia must have softened him up quite a bit before I fronted up because he looked genuinely pleased to see me when I walked in.

"Hello George, Lydia said you might be coming around. How are you?"

"I'm good. I should be asking you that question."

"Well you can see that I'm not at my best at the moment, but I'll come right. The quack says I should rest so here I am. At least I can watch what's happening on the harbour."

"It certainly is a great view," I said, taking in the fact that it was such a clear day I could see the blue outline of Little Barrier Island poking up over the horizon behind Tiri Tiri Matangi Island. "I thought that you might send me off with a flea in the ear after our last meeting."

"Yeah, well I feel pretty bad about that now. I heard that you have been through some hard times since then and I feel that is my fault. All I can say is that my pride got the better of me at the time. Pride is a bugger of a thing. It can catch you out when you least expect it. I was the champion mullet boat skipper on the harbour and had a big reputation as a fishing boat skipper as well. When we had the mishap I was afraid of how my peers would see things. I guess I couldn't stand the idea of being the butt of jokes doing the rounds. It was all pretty stupid really and I regret that I took it out on you."

"If anyone was to take the blame it was me. I admit that I reached an even lower point after that, but a man learns a lot about himself when he is down. I certainly don't hold it against you for what you did."

"That's generous of you, George. I don't know whether I'd have felt the same way if I were in your shoes. Look, I'd like to make it up to you. You've heard that Milly is tied up with nobody to run her. How about taking over as her skipper? It's going to be some time before I'm up to going to sea again."

"I'm crewing on the Vindex at the moment. I wouldn't want to let down Captain Cobb."

"I could make it worth your while. How about a share of the catch on top of a wage?"

"It's mighty tempting."

"I like your loyalty to the Vindex. That's as it should be. I respect that. I can always square it away with Isaac. He and I go back a long way. Anyway, the offer is still open. Have a think about it."

"I will, and thanks."

"So, you're seeing Lydia, are you?"

"Yeah, I went round to her place to give Emma a bunch of flowers for helping get a position on Vindex. She wasn't there at the time, but Lydia was. It just went from there."

"Well you look after her or you'll have me to answer for," said Joe. He gave me a sidelong look, but I knew he was probably relieved that someone had come along to take his wayward daughter in tow.

"You've no fears there," I answered, thinking about living the rest of my life with Lydia. The thought then struck me that she might get in the family way before she was ready. Joe and Mary would be sure to insist that I married Lydia, something which I was willing to do, but it wouldn't be the best way to start off our married life.

"Good," said Joe, giving me a grin.

I thought about Joe's offer while on the next trip on Vindex. It was a short voyage to Pahiki Island for a load of red aggregate. The whole trip only took four days. After we had brought the load of stone alongside Queen's wharf a steam shovel made short work of unloading it. We just had to hand shovel the loose material around the edges into the bucket and it was all over.

I hung back to be last in the queue as Captain Cobb paid off the crew. I took the pay packet and then asked if I could have a word in private. He looked at me askance for a second before indicating with a nod of the head in the direction of the Britomart Tavern that we should meet there. I walked off the wharf and across the road to await his arrival.

It was twenty minutes later before he entered the door to the bar. He picked me out in the crowd and headed straight for me.

"What's your pleasure?" I asked.

"Rum," he said.

"That'll be Navy Rum," I said. He nodded his ahead in agreement as I turned to fight my way through to the bar. When I got his drink I returned to find him leaning against a table. I noted he had moved my beer glass onto the table.

"Thanks for that, here's to your health," I said, raising my glass.

"What is it that you want?" he asked after raising his glass fractionally before taking a great draft of his drink.

"I understand you know Joe Williams," I said. When he gave a nod of the head again, I continued. "You'll know then that he's been crook and his fishing boats have been laid up for some weeks now."

"Aye, I had heard that."

God, he wasn't making this easy for me. "Well, I've been taking his daughter out and the other day he made a proposition to me."

"I would have thought that it should have been you doing the proposing," he said with a sly grin.

"Yeah, maybe I will soon. Anyway his proposal was that I skipper his mullet boat Milly in return for a share in the catch. I'm keen to accept this, but I need to know from you how you feel about it."

"Is this just a temporary arrangement?" asked Cobb.

"Maybe and maybe not. If Joe doesn't recover enough to go back to sea it could be permanent."

"You've got your eye on the main chance here, haven't you? If you were to marry his daughter you could end up owning all his boats," said Cobb.

His statement left me gob-smacked. I couldn't believe the nerve of the man. That wasn't why I was going out with Lydia. Even so, a little niggle at the back of my mind served to tell me that I was a hypocrite if I pretended the thought hadn't crossed my mind. "I guess you might be right, but that's up to Joe, don't you think? He may decide to sell everything up, for all I know."

"Well, if it was me, I know what I would do."

"What about someone to fill in for me on the Vindex?"

"I'm sure Joe can help me out there. You said yourself that his boats have been laid up. Some of his old crew members are sure to be looking out for work by now."

"I'm happy to stay on with you until you've got a replacement."

"We're not going out again until Friday. It's time I went to see old Joe anyway. I'm sure to find someone by Friday."

"Thanks, you don't know how happy that makes me."

"Oh, I've got a pretty shrewd idea. Good on you, son. It's time you had a bit of good luck from what I've heard."

We downed the dregs in our glasses and stood up to leave. I shook his hand, glad to have known him and wishing him well.

Chapter 30

Things were going well. I took over the skippering of Milly. This involved going out fishing three times a week and fixing nets and maintaining the vessel in between trips. I could now sleep every night on land. At first I stayed at the lodging house in Vincent Street, but then my old nemesis McFetridge got a job down country and moved out of Ma's place. She then accepted me back into the house since I could afford to pay the same board as McFetridge had paid. I wasn't to know it, but this turned out to be a double-edged sword. I now had to confront the difficulties of looking after Daniel.

Up till then my visits had been fleeting and I had not had to face how difficult he could be. He had recovered enough to be able to go out on his own, but his moods swung violently from anger to quiescence in minutes. His voice had returned, but even that was difficult. He would stutter for ages before a word got out of his mouth and then it would be in a high pitched voice embarrassing to listen to. It was always difficult to gauge how to approach him. One wrong word and he would fly off the handle. More than once Beth had gone home crying and life in the house was fraught with tension. It was only when I was out at sea or with Lydia that I felt free of this responsibility.

I would have liked to have asked Lydia to marry me, but I had nothing much to offer her and was saving every penny towards having a little nest egg. I had my eye on buying a cottage in John Street. There were several that would have been suitable. Each time one came on the market I went around to inspect it and then look at my savings, only to be disappointed once again.

Joe and I became good friends during this period. He still spent most of his time convalescing in the sun porch and watching the harbour through his spyglass. Provided someone supported him he could take walks around the garden. I was glad to assist him in this occupation, as it gave us time to talk about the boat and the crew and other matters, without the women of the family listening in or forever coming in with cups of tea and scones.

It was on one of these occasions that Joe told me it was unlikely he would ever be able to go back to sea. Obviously, he had been giving a lot of thought to his future. I guess he had had plenty of time to do so. He asked me to sit him down on a garden bench then patted the bench beside him indicating that I should sit there. That was when he said, "I want you to become a 50-50 partner in the Milly. I know you haven't a lot of money so here's the deal. I'll sign over half the ownership of Milly to you and loan you the money to buy the shareholding from me. You'll pay off the shareholding from your profits. I reckon it'll take roughly a year for you to pay me back. What do you think?"

"That's great. Thanks very much."

"You see, I've seen the way you and Lydia get on. I'd like you to be my son-in-law and to take over my holdings. I know you appreciate these

249

things and would look after them. I don't want to pressure you or anything. It's just that I know you haven't got much at the moment so I figured I should give you a helping hand. There's no reason why you can't do as well as me."

I didn't know what to say. I suppose I was a bit afraid of stuffing up a good thing by saying the wrong words. In the end I put out my hand and Joe took it in his now not so firm grip and we shook on it. Already I had it in my head to take the boat out four times a week and to cut down the time it would need to repay the loan.

"Right," said Joe. "I'll get my lawyers to draw up the agreements."

That evening I told Ma and Daniel about the offer. I wasn't sure whether Daniel understood what I was saying or whether he was just grinning for the sake of it. Ma seemed pleased for me. She gave me a hug, something that had been a rarity between us for a long time.

In the morning I was at a loss knowing what to do. I didn't want to hang around the house all day so decided to go into town in the hope of meeting some old mates. Someone needed to round up the old crew for a starter. Anyway, that seemed as good a plan as any. I could now face the future with confidence and start to put some real money together. A future with Lydia still seemed a pipe dream, but it had become a step closer with Joe's offer.

It was a clear day so I decided to walk into town. I walked up Richmond Road and turned into Lincoln Street to reach Ponsonby Road. A bicycle was leaning against the wall on the balcony of our old house. It seemed an eternity since we had lived there. I wondered who was living in it now. I stood there looking at it for a few seconds, tossing up whether to go and knock on the door, but it didn't seem right somehow.

I carried on up to Ponsonby Road and down Franklin Road. The plane trees each side of the road were now shooting up. I resisted the urge to pop into the Rob Roy Tavern and instead crossed Victoria Park to walk past Leyland-O'Connor's mill. New buildings had been erected to replace those lost or damaged in the fire. The usual line of drays and carts waited outside the gate. I felt no desire to go in and ask after anyone. That episode in my life was now shut. All the shipbuilders that used to be along Fanshawe Street had now moved on. In their place were rows of new warehouses with blank frontages broken only by sliding doors large enough for trucks.

The familiar form of Gleeson's Hotel was still there and I went in to see who might be around at that time of day. The barman gave me a nod of recognition. I ordered a seven ounce glass of lager and took a seat by the window. There was no one I recognised among the dozen or so patrons there so after finishing my glass I got up and walked out. At the bottom of Albert Street I almost ran into Mr Shaw. He saw me and hesitated in his stride, as if undecided whether to talk to me or not. I had nothing against the man, in fact I had considerable respect for him, but I didn't want open old wounds so I kept walking, just giving him the merest of nods as I passed. I suppose I was always going to gravitate to the boats. After all, that was my life now.

After watching the boats coming in and out of the ferry basin for some time I sauntered along

Quay Street to Queen's Wharf. Vindex was out, but Milly and three other mullet boats were still there. It's funny how when something is not yours you don't take much notice of the condition it is in. I found that I was now looking at Milly with a different eye. I could see the varnish on her coaming and bowsprit was peeling off, and her deck was awash with dirt and grime. In that moment I vowed to get her shipshape again. I turned to walk purposely towards the Britomart Tavern. It was by then about ten in the morning, still early for many to go to a pub, but then I knew many others who would have been down there for breakfast.

There was a new barman on duty, one that I had not seen there before. In some ways I was thankful for that. The other barman knew my history and had seen me at my lowest ebb. I ordered a handle and sat on a barstool to drink it. The rest of the bar room was reflected in the full length mirror behind the bar. I recognised some of the faces there, but was unable to put names to their faces. These were other fisherman and boatmen I had seen around the harbour and in the bars. When the barman was free I asked him if he had seen Albie Clark recently. To my surprise he said that Albie came in most days for a drink around midday. I looked at the clock at the end of the bar and saw that it was half past eleven. I sank back into dreaming about my life as the proprietor of a fleet of fishing boats with Lydia as my wife and maybe with a son. It was all possible now thanks to the generosity of Joe. I wasn't stupid enough to think that everything hinged on keeping Lydia happy. If we happened to split up then the best I could hope for was part ownership of the

Milly and even that could be jeopardised should Joe decide to call in the loan. A frown had crossed my face at this thought when a hand clasped my on the shoulder giving me a start.

"Gidday George," said a voice I immediately recognized. I turned in my seat to see Albie standing next to me beaming all over.

I stood up and pumped his hand. "I heard you were crook," I said.

"Yeah, I was. Heart attack, fair poleaxed me. I was in bed for weeks, but I'm up and about now. The quack says it's best if I get out walking everyday so here I am. The missus thinks I'm out walking anyway."

"What'll you have," I asked.

"Just a glass of draught. I have to take it easy in that department."

"Right you are then. It's good to see you."

After ordering his drink and seeing it placed in front of him by the barman I waited until he had had his first sip before asking about the others.

"I don't know whether you've heard, but Joe is making me a part-owner of Milly."

"You don't say. Well, I guess you going out with Lydia might have had something to do with that."

"That and the fact that Joe is unlikely to get back to sea for quite some time, if ever," I said.

"Congratulations then. I suppose you are wondering where the others are?"

"I'll be looking for crew. We could be going out as early as the end of the week."

"I still see Mattie and Bill regularly. Do you want me to tell them?"

"If you would. I guess I'll need someone to take your place as well."

"My nephew's looking for work. He's a likely lad."

"Has he been out before?"

"He's a keen yachtie. He sails a 16-footer."

"All right, I'll give him a go."

"When will you know when you are going out again?" asked Albie.

"I should know by Wednesday. We could meet here at noon on Wednesday and I can then tell you whether it's a goer or not."

"Fair enough. I best be getting back on my round. The missus will be expecting me home for lunch."

After shaking hands I watched Albie shuffle back out onto the street, then finished my glass and stood up about to leave. I wanted to visit Joe, but it might seem that I was being a bit pushy.

On Wednesday morning I received a telegram from Joe's lawyer asking me to go their offices and sign the documents that afternoon. I put on my best clothes and rushed out of the house. I needed to get to Albie at midday and then to the lawyer's after that. By then, I was running late so caught a tram in Richmond Road and paid the thruppence fare. It dropped me off at the bottom of Queen Street and I was able to walk along Quay Street to the pub with time to spare. They were all there when I arrived. I got plenty of gentle ribbing about being all dressed up until I explained why. Mattie and Bill shook my hand and then I bought them each a round.

"I'm hoping to take over Milly by Friday," I said. "It all depends on how long it takes Joe to sign the documents and get them back to the lawyer. You can guarantee that they will need to be lodged with the court or something so I can't say how long that will take. Either way, I want you all on standby to go out on Sunday night."

Mattie and Bill exchanged glances and grinned. I guess they were relieved to be back at work. I knew all about being unemployed.

"What about your nephew?" I asked Albie.

"I'll see he's there," said Albie.

"Righto then, I'd best be off and sign the deal."

Chapter 31

The offices of Joe's solicitors were in a four-storey building in Kitchener Street. I entered the tiled foyer of the building and looked at the directory board. The firm was on the top floor so I climbed into the birdcage lift and closed the concertina doors behind me. On pressing the button, the lift gave a lurch and then settled into a smooth, but slow, motion. The various floors passed by, as did the stair which coiled around the lift shaft like a serpent. It came to a halt six inches below the floor level. I opened the door and climbed over the step. Four doors faced me, two of which were the men's and women's toilets. The other two had the name of the firm written in gold letters on them.

I opened the door to Cox, Garlick and Rennie and entered. As soon as I said who I was, the receptionist got up and ushered me into a small meeting room. After a five minute wait, a man in a three piece suit came in and introduced himself as David Rennie. He then spread a sheaf of documents across the table and pointed to where I should sign. Joe had already signed the documents, so it was all over in minutes. I shook hands with Rennie and left the building. I suppose I was in a state of disbelief. Certainly I had never been happier. I wanted to share this happiness and the obvious person to do that with was Lydia, but she was at work. Instead I walked down to the bottom of town and around Freeman's Bay to Hackett Street.

Mary Williams gave me a big hug and kiss on the cheek before ushering me inside the house and sitting me down at the kitchen table. She called out to Joe that I was there and he came in from the hallway. I told him the deed was done and thanked him, perhaps a little too effusively, but I was so grateful to both of them. Mary made tea and brought out sponge cake.

"What's your next move then?" asked Joe.

"I've got a crew all teed up to go out on Sunday night. Mattie and Bill have agreed to come back on board and Albie has a nephew keen to join."

"Yeah, I know. Albie told me. What I mean is, right now."

I was a bit nonplussed that Albie had stolen my thunder. It seemed as though Joe still had his fingers on the pulse even though he was housebound. I stared at Joe wondering how I was going to fill in the rest of the day. Staying there to wait for Lydia to come home had been at the back of my mind, but Joe evidently thought I should be doing something else.

"I hadn't given it too much thought," I said. "I suppose I should go down to the boat and take possession, so to speak. The deck certainly needs a good wash for starters."

"Good on you," said Joe. That was it then. I had planned to tidy up Milly though somehow the order seemed to come from Joe. As I got up Joe also stood and walked across to the sideboard where he opened a drawer and pulled out something. He turned and said, "Here's the key to the padlock. You'll need it."

I took the key in my hand and knew that this was a symbolic handing over the boat to me. I looked him in the eye as I once more thanked him.

"Go and make us some money," he said.

The tide was well out by the time I reached Queen's Wharf. Milly was a good eight feet below the level of the wharf. I climbed down a steel ladder fixed to the side of the wharf and dropped the last couple of feet onto Milly's deck. The boat rocked gently as I landed on her deck. The familiar sensation caused me to smile. I unlocked the padlock and slid back the top to open the doors. A waft of stale air smelling of diesel and old fish assailed me as I climbed down into the low cabin. The light inside was dim, but I knew my way around the cabin like the back of my hand.

I made my way forward to the anchor locker and took out some over-trousers. After putting these on I climbed back out to the cockpit. There I retrieved a bucket from one of the side lockers and dipped it in the sea to swab down the deck. When I had finished I put the bucket back in its locker and spent the next half an hour tying up the down hauls at the base of the mast before locking up again. I took one more proprietary look over the vessel before climbing back onto the wharf. Joe was right. I had needed to do that. She was mine now. I had taken possession.

The Ferry Building clock struck five o'clock as I walked along Quay Street. It had been a long day and I was feeling weary but happy. I paused at the foot of Queen Street undecided as to whether I should catch a tramcar home. In the end my frugal upbringing got the better of me and I set out on foot.

I had no sooner stepped through the door when Ma came rushing out and demanded to know where I had been all day. I was about to reply that I had been to Joe's lawyers to sign the ownership papers for Milly when I saw the look on her face. Instead I asked her, "What's the matter?"

"Daniel has been gone all day."

"He'll be back" I said.

"I've got a bad feeling. I'm afraid he's gone and done something," she said.

"What makes you think that?"

"I don't know; it's a feeling I have."

I had learnt over the years not to take Ma's intuitions lightly. She had an uncanny ability to divine what other people were going to do before they knew themselves.

"Did he say where he was going?"

"No, that's the trouble. I don't know where to start looking."

"All right, I'll go and look for him. I'll start at Beth's. You stay here in case he comes home."

My feeling of weary jubilation was now shattered. Ma had managed to make me feel guilty for not being home to watch over Daniel. That familiar curtain of despondency I had endured threatened to overwhelm me once again, but I was determined not to let it. I trudged my way up Richmond Road and along Scanlan Street to Arch Hill.

Beth had just arrived home from work when I got to her place. She was about to put the key into the lock when she saw me coming.

"Hello George," she said.

I could see the question written all over her face asking what I was doing there, so I said, "You haven't seen Daniel today have you? He hasn't come home yet and Ma's worried."

"Sorry, I've been at work all day."

"It's probably nothing," I said.

"Do you want me to look for him?"

"No, I'm sure he'll turn up in due course." As I said this I knew in my heart that he wouldn't. Perhaps some of Ma's psychic powers resided in me after all. I wished Beth a good night and then decided to check Karangahape Road and Ponsonby Road all the way to Three Lamps before heading home.

By then I was really tired. The emotional highs and lows of the day were taking their toll. Ma made me cheese on toast and a hot cocoa before inveigling me to make another tour of the town. By now she was beside herself with worry and it transmitted to me. I did a round of St Mary's Bay along to Point Erin, then the Herne Bay beaches before cutting around Cox's Creek past Cashmore's Timber Yard and then zigzagged my way home through back streets. It was after midnight by then and both Ma and I decided to call it a night in the hope that he was with one of the homeless that he hung about with. I had a fitful night and woke early in the morning to darkness all around. I'd dreamt that Daniel and I were kids and playing in in a field of long grass. I could see a row of large trees. I think it was this image that jolted me awake.

I got up and looked in Daniel's room. There was no sign of him and his bed hadn't been slept in. When I peered at the mantle clock in the parlour I saw it was a quarter to five. I then did my morning ablutions before grabbing some bread and butter for breakfast and poking my head through Ma's bedroom doorway. She was asleep so I left a note on the kitchen table saying I was out looking for Daniel. Now I was really worried. He hadn't stayed out all night since returning from the war. I took a jacket and scarf off the peg by the back door and put on my boots before setting out.

The sun was just breaking over the horizon, turning the eastern sky the colour of butternut. High overhead it was still blue, but graduated through new blue to yellow to butternut the closer to the horizon one looked. The air was still as I buttoned up the front of my jacket. It was going to be a fine day, but cold.

Daniel seemed to have reached a point in his life where he had made a decision, a resolve of some sort. This had not been communicated to me in words, more in the look of his eyes and a stillness that descended over him each time I spoke to him. He always headed up the road towards Ponsonby Road where there were lights and people to keep him entertained or, more likely, for him to keep entertained as they made fun of him. I'd seen those trees in my dream and I felt they were further down Cox's Creek towards the harbour.

The fetid waters of Cox's Creek lay sluggish as I crossed the causeway. The muddy banks lay gleaming in the morning light. A red stain marked the inter-tidal zone on both banks where the brick dust coating the surface of the water had spread down the banks with the receding tide. Upstream the brick stack from the factory belched black smoke into the clear morning air. There were no footprints in the mud, not that I expected to see any. Bracken and blackberry grew thick along the sides of the creek. An occasional lichen-covered fence post poked out from the scrub, usually at some drunken angle. I couldn't imagine Daniel forcing his way through all that. I walked further up the hill past the causeway. Farmland opened out on both sides of the road. Cattle grazed amongst clumps of gorse and bracken. On my right there stood a stand of Monterey Cyprus bent before the westerly wind. A splash of white caught my attention.

I stood still, but couldn't see it anymore. I began to think it was my imagination when I glimpsed it again — just a shimmer of white high up in the branches. My heart caught in my throat. I climbed over a seven-wire fence and began running, tripping constantly in the clumped grass.

There was a shape high up in the branches. I raced ever faster, mindless of the cow pats and obstacles in my way. With a heaving chest I came to a standstill beside one of the massive trunks. It took a conscious effort to look into the branches above.

A pair of bare feet gently rotated high up above me. They looked so white against the browns and greens. I recognised Daniel's trousers above them. Above that, all I could see were his limp arms hanging by his side. It amazed me that he'd managed climb so high up. I knew then that Daniel had taken the only course left to him and how little time I'd given him. When he'd needed me I hadn't been there. Being thrown out of our home seemed a poor excuse for not providing the comfort he needed from me.

I slumped to the ground and cried. Images flashed before me of Daniel on his grocer's bike when he was trying to put some money together after Da died; the wicker basket and the tiny front wheel on the bike and him barely able to reach the ground with his feet. How was Ma going to come to terms with him taking his own life? Had she an inkling that he was going to do this? I wasn't sure. I looked around the field. We were all alone. The least I could do for him was to cut him down and carry him home.

It was only as I pulled myself out along the branch that I realised that he had hung himself using his own bed sheets. Surely Ma had noticed they were gone. When I was directly over him I tried to pull at the knot he had tied in the sheet, but came away with broken nails. His weight had pulled it too tight to untie. He must have sat on top of the branch tying the end of the sheet to the bough before tying the other end to his neck and then sliding off the branch into oblivion. His neck would have broken immediately. I took grim comfort in this.

A small gust of wind ruffled through the tree making the branch move. Daniel swung in a slow pendulum action for several seconds before slowly spinning around. His tongue protruded from his mouth and his eyes looked unusually large. I thought I was going to be sick for a second then he spun around once again, his face now away from me. My only thought was to get him down. The knot looked daunting. He certainly wasn't taking any chances with it slipping undone. I attacked it with both hands while clamping my knees each side of the branch.

Bit by bit I worked the end free until I was down to a single knot. The sheet was taut and I was hesitant to untie this since he would fall some twenty feet to the ground. There was no way of lowering him gently. He had to be dead yet I couldn't bring myself to just let him drop twenty feet. There was that faint chance he might still be alive. A fall from that height would certainly kill him. The knot began to slide undone in front of my eyes. It began slowly then picked up speed. I made one last grab at it, but had to let it go as it began to pull me over the side of the branch.

A soft crump erupted below as Daniel hit the ground. He lay on his side with the sheet heaped over him. I began edging my way back down the branch towards the trunk. My focus was getting myself down. I had become aware of how high up I was. I froze, unable to move. It was only when a pair of pigeons alighted on the branch above me and began walking up and down the branch cooing at each other that I came out of my daze and concentrated on getting down.

Once I reached the ground I walked across to the crumpled form and checked my brother for vital signs. When none were forthcoming I wrapped him up in the sheet and lifted him on to my back in a fireman's grip. Rigor mortis had set in making it nigh on impossible to move arms and legs. However, the fall must have broken his right arm so I was able to grip this.

Tears streamed down my face. I heaved myself up and staggered through the long grass. At each fence I rolled him over to land in a heap on the ground before climbing over myself, then heaved him back up over my shoulders and started all over again. I thanked God there were no houses down there, and for the early hour. I didn't pass a soul on the road during our journey back up the road to the house.

Chapter 32

Ma was waiting at the front gate. She told me afterwards that she had had a premonition that he had taken his life and was half expecting me to come home with him. She held the gate open to let me pass through then ran around me to get the front door open. We lay Daniel down on his bed and Ma bent over him to kiss his forehead before throwing a sheet over him.

"Where did you find him?"

"In the wind break on Fearnley's farm over the creek."

She nodded, as if already knowing this. I wanted to put my arms around her and comfort her, but something held me back. I suppose it was partly resentment at my having been thrown out of the house, and partly the look of disappointment I always saw in her eyes.

"What do we do now?"

"Go and get Father O'Riorden. It may be too late, but I want the Last Rites read to him anyway."

"Right you are, Ma."

As I was walking out the door she called, "You'll find him in Vermont Street. He's now at the Church of the Sacred Heart."

I already knew that and was taken aback that she might think I didn't know.

I found Father O'Riorden getting dressed. When I was ushered into his presence he turned his great head with its protruding ears towards me. He looked much the same, just older. His bulbous nose was redder and more heavily veined than the last time I had seen him.

"Well," he said in his usual sarcastic tone, "if it isn't the biggest failure of me life. So 'tis."

I ignored his comment. "We need you at home, Father. Daniel is dead."

"What? That is truly terrible. How did it happen?"

"He couldn't stand it any longer."

"You mean he took his own life?"

"Yes, Father. He suffered greatly."

"'Tis a mortal sin that, no matter what the circumstances."

"Ma wants you to give him his Last Rites."

"Does she indeed? Well, Oi may not be able to do that in the circumstances. Anyway, she'll have to wait until Oi've had my breakfast. I doubt whether young Daniel will mind too much."

There was little doubt that the priest was going to be as difficult as always so I sat down on a chair while he ate his breakfast. Little was said while he spooned his porridge and then ate his toast and eggs. It was not lost on me how well he ate compared to our family. As soon as he had finished his cup of tea he took off the napkin he had hung from his collar and placed it on the table before getting up.

"Oi'll be out for a while, Mrs Black," he called out to his housekeeper before taking down his hat and coat from the hall stand. Without a word of acknowledgment to me he set off at a fast clip down the road with me rushing to catch up. In the end I didn't bother, not wishing to talk with the bellicose priest any more than I had to. I let him walk ahead of me. At the end of the road we turned into John Street for the fifty yards or so needed to take us to Richmond Road. There we turned downhill heading for our house.

Ma was waiting on the veranda when the priest opened our gate. He was mumbling words into her ear as I reached them. Ma's face looked stricken at his words. I was sure that he was filling her full of trepidation about Daniel's soul and I hated him for it, but Ma was a true believer so there was nothing I could say. He then walked through the front door to see to Daniel while Ma and I waited on the veranda. She was visibly shaking and I took her in my arms to comfort her. No matter what had taken place between us, I couldn't leave her in that state.

The door crashed open and Father O'Riorden came back out, his face not quite as ruddy as it had been when he went in.

"'Tis a terrible shame, that it is," he said, while leaning his back against the weatherboards. "Oi've read him the Last Rites, but I fear for his poor soul. The best we can do is all pray for him now."

A visible tremor passed through Ma while the priest said this. I could see that she feared he wouldn't be able to sit with Jesus and the angels, but might be destined for warmer climes. She believed in such things. I wasn't quite so sure myself, but wanted the best for Daniel too.

"We'll have to advise the police," said O'Riorden.

"Can't we just get a doctor to certify the time of death?" asked Ma.

"For a man of his age they'll want to do a post-mortem. There can be little doubt that he took his own life with those burns on his throat, but the police will need to be convinced of that."

"There must be another way?" said Ma.

"I don't see any, Mrs Bender."

"He was a good boy. You know that yourself. You can't let him go to his Maker in this state," she said.

"Have you a telephone, Mrs Bender?"

"Goodness no! I can barely make ends meet as it is. What would I be doing with a telephone?"

"Right! I'll call the ambulance and the police when I get back to the rectory. Oi'll leave you both to pray for poor Daniel's soul. Good day to you both."

Father O'Riorden put on his hat again and opened the front gate. I put my arms around Ma once more.

The ambulance arrived first. This acted as a magnet for a crowd to form on the street outside out house. The police arrived soon after. To my dismay one of the policemen was my old nemesis, Detective Inspector O'Donnell. Both Ma and I gave statements about the circumstances of Daniel's death before he let the ambulance take Daniel away. I was grateful that he showed us sympathy and didn't look at all threatening towards me.

Ma then got up and went around the house to draw the curtains. Out of respect, the crowd dispersed, no doubt to fuel rumours about what had happened. I made Ma a cup of tea which she stared at but didn't drink. It was as if she had fallen into a trance. She didn't speak a word all day after that and I couldn't get her to eat or drink. When night came it was all I could do to lift her out of her chair and carry her to her bed where I laid her down and covered her with a blanket. I don't think she was even aware of any of that.

The following day she lay in bed with her eyes open, but unseeing. In the end I went next door and asked Mrs Flynn to watch over her while I went to fetch Father O'Riorden again. Mrs Flynn was very sympathetic when I told her what had happened. You could be sure that she would later broadcast a true account of what had happened to the neighbourhood. I left her sitting in a chair watching over Ma's inert form on her bed and set off for the rectory.

I found Father O'Riorden supervising the ladies putting flowers in the church. I'm sure the ladies could have managed perfectly well by themselves, but I suppose it gave the old priest a sense of his self-importance. I still couldn't bring myself to like him even though Ma was in need of him. He had treated me like shit over the years and a person doesn't forget that sort of thing. They all stopped what they were doing as I entered the church and walked up to the priest. I could tell that he was waiting for me to go through the rituals of entering the church, but I wasn't going to give him the satisfaction of seeing me paying obeisance to it or, more specifically, to the likes of him.

"What brings you back so soon?" he asked.

"Ma has withdrawn from the world. I can't get through to her. I think she needs some spiritual guidance."

"Coming from you, that's a bit rich."

"Will you come, or not?" I asked.

"I'm sure these ladies won't mind if I speak my mind. You come into this church like it was the local hotel and ask for my help. You, who I have

269

not seen at church since your pappy's funeral. I take it you've not been to confession in all that time. In all that time your mother has been in dire straits financially, had to sell her house and rent. Meanwhile what have you done? Oi'll tell you what. You've been a torment to her, 'tis what you've been. Always drunk and carrying on, gambling so I hear and going on to prison. Your father was a fine upstanding man. To be sure, he'd be turning in his grave right now. Here you are now asking me to help your poor Ma. Well, let me tell you that any help I give her 'tis for her and not for you. She's a God-fearing woman who has worked hard all her life. The reason she is in this state is because she wants her only other son, the decent one who went to church and fought for his country, to be buried in consecrated ground in the churchyard. 'Tis not much for her to ask, is it? I'll let you dwell on that while I go and get my hat and coat. You wait here and we'll walk back together. I have a little proposal for you."

As soon as he stopped his tirade the women busied themselves with their flowers, pretending that they had not heard his little sermon. For me, it was all water off a duck's back. I knew I had been a disappointment for her, but I had sorted my life out and now I was all she had left. What really surprised me was that Ma was only renting the house in Richmond Road. She had led me to believe that she had bought it with the money left over from the Lincoln Street house. I had no idea she had been living on the capital. Anyway, she needed me now more than ever and I wasn't going to let her down again. Whatever he had in mind wasn't going to change my mind. I left the women to it and walked out of the door to stand outside in the yard where I rolled a fag and lit it. Father O'Riorden took a long time to come back from the rectory and I was beginning to think that he was deliberately standing me up when he came out the door.

"Sorry for that. I had a parishioner on the line," he said, falling into step beside me. "Shall we go then?"

"Right," I replied, taking a drag on my cigarette and then holding it in my hand as I strode out to keep up with him.

We walked in silence until we reached the corner into Richmond Road where he stopped and turned to me.

"You may be wondering what my proposal is?"

"Not especially," I said.

"Well, be that as it may. Oi'll tell you anyway. 'Tis almost guaranteed that based on the evidence the coroner will announce that Daniel died by his own hands. That being the case I'll be forced to deny his burial in consecrated ground. However, if you were to go to the police and say that you killed your brother after he had pleaded with you to do so, I'm sure the court would be lenient on you. Let's say you are sentenced to four years for manslaughter, there's a good chance you might only serve two years. In the meantime, I will be able to bury him in the churchyard and your mother will achieve some peace of mind. What do you think?"

"Not only are you a cold-hearted bastard, you're mad! It's bloody obvious you don't know what it's like in prison. If you want to talk about souls, I'll tell what prison does to a man's soul. It rots it until nothing's left. A man comes out of prison as a hollow shell. You now have the gall to ask me to go back there just so that you can bury my brother in consecrated ground?"

"That's about it."

"The cops'll never believe it anyway. What's the point? And anyway, who will look after Ma if I'm inside."

"The parish will sort that out."

"Oh great, like they've done for the last six years."

"Yes," he replied, and he set off down the road. I stared at his back, shocked, as it had not occurred to me that the parish had been supporting Ma.

Chapter 33

The central police station hadn't changed since my last visit. The sergeant at the reception desk looked up as I entered.

"I'm here to see Detective Inspector O'Donnell," I said.

"Have you an appointment?" he asked.

"No."

"Wait over there and I'll find out if he's in," said the sergeant, pointing to the hard benches by the opposite wall.

By the time I had taken a seat the sergeant had vanished out the back and a constable taken his place at the desk. We stared at each other for a few seconds before he found something to read on the desk.

After ten minutes had passed I went outside to light a ciggie. The sunlight filtering through the plane trees was creating a dappled pattern across the ground. I stared down at these patterns trying to make out shapes, like you do with clouds sometimes. I walked back and forth in front of the entrance, stepping only on the patches of sunlight. All the time, I puffed away like an old steam train. I don't suppose I looked up once the whole time. Then I heard the sergeant calling out to me. I ground out the remains of my ciggie with the sole of my shoe before re-entering the building.

"The Inspector will see you now," he said, lifting up the top of the reception counter to let me pass through.

I followed his bulky frame through a maze of corridors to emerge into a yard littered with dry leaves. We crossed this to enter another building. O'Donnell was waiting inside. The room was dingy with everything painted beige. It had no windows and was illuminated by a single light bulb suspended from the ceiling. O'Donnell pointed to a table barely big enough to place a tray on.

"Take a seat," he said.

By now my initial resolve was beginning to fade.

"I'm sorry about your brother, George. I presume that's why you're here?"

"Yeah, it's about his death."

I was glad he had opened the conversation. I had been wondering how best to broach the subject.

"Go on," he said, fixing me with an unequivocal stare, like a bird of prey.

I knew he wasn't going to make it easy for me; he never had in the past. But somewhere inside this gruff Ulsterman there had to be some compassion.

"I was wondering if you've had the results of the post-mortem yet," I asked.

"Maybe I have and maybe I haven't. That's official business. Why are you interested?"

I leaned forward to rest my hands on the little table between us. I didn't want him to see this as provocative. I just wanted to get nearer so that I could speak quietly.

"My Ma wants him buried in consecrated ground. That won't be possible if it's decided he took his own life."

"How does that concern me?"

O'Donnell must have sensed my nerve faltering. He held my gaze while waiting for my reply. I couldn't back down now. It was in for a penny, in for a pound, as Da would have said.

"I was wondering whether there was any way that the result could be worded so as to ease Ma's mind on this matter."

My words hung in the silence between us. O'Donnell's gaze shifted to some far off point in his imagination. A full minute must have passed before he replied.

"I hope you're not asking me to pervert the course of justice. There are penalties for that."

"Yeah, I know."

I knew I was stepping on glass. I had to be careful how I chose my words. That was when I leaned forward once more to ask, "What say he asked to be killed?"

"Did he?" he snapped, the words sounded like a gun going off in the little room.

"No, just supposing like."

"Go on…"

"Well, supposing it was a mercy killing. How would the court view that?"

"They would treat it as murder. The person who killed him would have had to have gone about it in a premeditated manner. In that case it would be a hanging offence."

"What about the mercy aspect. Surely the court would look at any extenuating circumstances?"

"I've never known the court to have any compassion when it comes to murder."

"Thanks," I said.

"Is that all then? You're not going to make it easy and confess, are you?"

"Not today, no. I was trying to find a way to make it easier for Ma."

"What you've said today is between you and me. If I'd had a mind I would have had a constable in here taking down everything we said."

"I appreciate it."

"Well then, on your bike then and don't do anything stupid."

My head was in a total muddle after our meeting so I went into a pub for a drink and to mull things over. It didn't seem fair for anyone to want me to give up my chance of happiness and a secure future, yet there were those out there asking me to do just that. After an hour or more of beating my brain to bits on all the different possibilities I got up and headed home, determined to have it out with Father O'Riorden. When I got to the corner of Victoria and Chapel Streets, I paused and looked down Chapel Street towards St Patrick's Cathedral. Without any bidding from me my feet turned down the street and carried me there.

As I passed through its portal the familiar hum of the city died away to be replaced with a low hush. I lit a candle for Daniel and walked down the aisle towards the confessional boxes. All were closed so I sat in a pew waiting my turn. Presently, a door opened. It was my turn.

It had been a long time. I sat down and muttered the usual "Bless me Father, for I have sinned."

When a voice responded, I poured out everything that had happened in my life and my relationships with women and anything else that came to mind. I guess I laid it on a bit thick, making out that I was a victim of circumstance with myself barely able to direct my own life. At the end of my diatribe I stopped to a heavy silence. For a minute I wondered if the priest was even there. Wouldn't that have been typical! I was about to say "Is anyone there?" when I heard the slight movement of the priest shifting his position in his chair. Then he spoke. He sounded young. That gave me hope that I would be heard and that he might absolve me of my worst sins and give me freedom for the future.

"For your many sins I want you to say ten Our Fathers and ten Hail Marys each day for the next month and to attend church every week."

"Yes Father."

"Apart from that it appears that you are asking me to resolve a question in your life."

"Yes Father. Should I give up my future happiness with the woman I love?"

"It seems to me that the Lord has placed both Joe and Lydia in your path as a means to redeem you. In that case it would be a sin not to accept what is being offered. On the other hand, we have the question of your brother Daniel. For him to take his own life is a grievous sin in the eyes of the Church. However, from what you say, he was badly affected by the war and not of sound mind. If that is the case it could be argued he had the mind of a child. Our Lord Jesus said: 'Suffer little children, and forbid them not, to come unto me: for such is the Kingdom of Heaven.' If Our Lord has given us such implicit instructions in this matter then who are we to contradict Him? I take it that Daniel was a good Christian prior to his mind being afflicted in this way?"

"Yes, Father. He attended Mass every Sunday with Ma."

"Very well, I shall speak to the bishop on this matter. What was your brother's full name?"

"Daniel Cyril Bender."

"Remember your penance and the next time your mother goes to Mass I expect you to be with her."

"Thank you Father. You have eased my mind."

I left St Patrick's walking on air. I felt that way all the way back to Ponsonby and down Richmond Road. This mood evaporated as soon as I turned the last bend in the road and saw an ambulance outside our house with a crowd of people clustered around it. I broke into a run. The driver had closed the rear door and was walking around to open the driver's door when I slammed into the side of the vehicle. All heads turned to me as I rebounded off it to come to a stop.

"What's happened," I gasped.

"A woman's taken a turn. We're taking her to hospital," said the driver. "Who are you?"

"George Bender. Is that my Ma in there?"

"You had better hop in."

The driver turned around to open the back door for me and I climbed in. Ma was lying on a gurney looking pale. Her feisty spirit always made her appear bigger than she was. Now she looked small and pale. I wanted to tell her everything that had happened that day, but she was out to it, just like you are now, Steven. I sat on the gurney opposite her and the ambulance began its journey. I gripped the edge of the gurney as we lurched forward over the kerb.

Ma was kept in hospital overnight for observation. She hadn't had a heart attack, which was what Mrs Flynn told the ambulance driver she thought had happened, but was suffering from heart palpitations brought on by worry, or so a doctor told me. I brought her home the next day and she sat on the front balcony enjoying a certain amount of attention from the neighbours. The fact that I had told her the bishop was looking into the matter of Daniel's funeral put her mind at ease. When I also told her part of the deal was that I'd take her to church each Sunday she almost fell off her chair. I did put my own condition on that though. I insisted we took the tram into the city and that we went to St Patrick's. I wasn't about to subject myself to the acerbic attention of Father O' Riorden.

Several days later, the funeral director came around to say that the coroner had released Daniel's body and that he had arranged his funeral for the coming Saturday. We agreed to that and travelled out to Waikumete by train, like we had for Da's funeral. One of the priests we had got to know from the cathedral officiated.

The Williams family arrived in Joe's truck and I was able to introduce them to Ma. When she met Lydia, Ma was all over her. After raising two sons, the idea of having a daughter-in-law gave her something to look forward to after so much

279

tragedy. I lost no time in asking Lydia to marry me after that. To have seen a married life with Lydia appear like a dream and then to almost lose it again made me anxious it didn't slip away.

We married in St Patrick's and went on the weekly steamer to Hot Springs for our honeymoon. We walked on the beach, sat in the hot pools and made love. I have never been happier. We returned to Auckland and moved into a cottage in Blake Street. My earnings were enough to allow us to rent this. It was midway between Ma's place and Lydia's parents and was within walking distance to the Church of the Blessed Sacrament down College Hill.

As a married man I kept up my attendance at church. I discovered there were other priests able to restore my faith not only in the church, but in humanity. Father O'Riorden had all but destroyed that in my youth, but I could now put all that behind me. The last I heard about him was that he had been retired and sent off somewhere where old priests are put out to pasture.

Chapter 34

My throat is hoarse and my mouth is dry. I'm stiff from sitting in one position for so long. Steven hasn't moved a muscle the whole time I've been talking to him. I would have liked to have had some sort of response from him. It seems strange talking to somebody who is so unresponsive yet I don't know whether I could have recounted this much of my life if he was there to interrupt me with questions all the time, as he is prone to do. As time has gone on, I've begun to sense that maybe he is listening to me. I hope he is, because I don't want to have to repeat all this when he wakes up. Not with him looking me in the face anyway.

As I lever myself out of my chair my chest cramps. I pause a second before it goes away. It's a bastard growing old.

I pull back the curtain surrounding the bed. The lights in the ward are muted. It's dark outside and the lights in the container terminal throw a soft light onto the ceiling. A siren wails in the distance. As I walk up the ward towards the doors leading to the nurses' station I'm conscious of the dark stain on my shirt and my trousers. If I was younger I might have felt embarrassed by this. Half eaten meals sit on trays on the beds as I pass by. Once again I've missed having a meal, not that I have any appetite anyway. I have got past any desire to eat now.

At the nurses' station I help myself to a paper cup and fill it at the water cooler. The nurse on duty glances up and seeing it's me, she goes back to filling in forms. That's all people seem to do these days, fill in forms. The water tastes good as I slake my thirst. I go in search of a toilet. After a day with no food or drink it amazes me there is still something to come out. At the washbasin I splash water over my face. The face of a stranger stares back at me in the mirror. It is thin and haggard, strands of grey hair stick out from my head making me look like a lunatic. There are black rings under my eyes. I poke out my tongue at the image only to see it coated white. What happened to the boy, the not-so-young father? The trials of everyday life are etched into my face. The image depresses me.

I make my way back down the corridor to the ward. The lights in the ward are still dim. I am thankful for this. It seems appropriate nearing the end of my story. As I settle back into my chair I look at the monitors and listen to Steven's shallow breathing. What caused him to cut his wrists is anyone's guess; heartbreak over being jilted by a girlfriend perhaps or angst over an exam. It doesn't really matter. That he was driven to attempt suicide seems incredible. With Daniel I could understand it. He was faulty goods and he knew it, but Steven is fit and healthy. My assumption that he had been of sound mind has now been shaken. If something was troubling him, why did he keep it to himself?

There is a little tic in Steven's breathing and I leap out of my chair. A wave of dizziness overwhelms me and I put out my arms to steady myself, but cannot stop falling onto the bed beside him. I feel the wetness of his breath on my cheek. Our breaths mingle. The feeling of dizziness passes and I climb off the bed and slump back into my chair to resume my story.

"Your mother came along soon after we moved into John Street. She looked just like Lydia, something I was grateful for. I wouldn't have wanted a daughter looking like me. That would've been a millstone for any girl." A small hiccup of a laugh erupts from my throat.

"Old Joe died when your mother must have been about ten. Mary, his wife, followed soon after in one of those situations when a partner loses their will to carry on without the other. We were left their house in Hackett Street and moved in there. Things went well for us then. Your mother attended St Mary's School not far from us. The fishing fleet had grown. I rarely went out on the boats much by then. Your grandmother and I looked after the company accounts and bought and sold boats as required."

I look back at when everything was so good in my life. At the time it seemed compensation for all the hardship I had endured. I wonder now whether it was a reality or whether I dreamed this episode in my life. I look at the still form in the bed before me. My reality now is to save him from himself.

"One day your grandmother went to the doctor complaining of a sore stomach. At the time we didn't think it was serious, but before we knew what was happening she was here in the hospital having tests. That's when they told us she had cancer. It was all through her. She was dead in three months. I brought your mother up by myself after that. She was what kept me going. When she brought your father home to meet me I knew immediately they were made for each other. I guess you know the rest of the story. When you wake you can fill me in on the rest of yours. I'm feeling a little tired right now. I'm going to rest for a bit."

I can't say I'm feeling that great. Bile is burning my throat and my right arm is all a-tingle. It isn't the first time I've felt like this. If I shut my eyes and take deep breaths it usually goes away.

I don't know how long I was out for. Perhaps I blacked out or maybe sleep finally caught up with me. When I open my eyes I see a doctor and the Ward Sister fussing over Steven. His eyes are open. Whether he is aware of what is going on or not I can't say. Nevertheless I say, "Gidday, young fella. Welcome back to the world."

The Sister turns her head. "We could say the same for you," she says.

"Why, was I out for long?"

"The night nurse found you slumped in your chair. We were about to put you into a bed when your grandson woke up."

"Is he conscious?"

"Yes, but it may take him some time to orientate himself."

The doctor shines a torch into Steven's eyes and writes something on a chart.

The Sister fluffs his pillow and props up his head before turning to say. "I'll leave you to talk for now." As an afterthought she whispers in my ear, "The police will want to talk to him sometime."

"Thanks," I say.

Steven and I are alone. His eyes focus on me. "What's happening?" he asks.

"You're in hospital," I say.

He looks at me with a quizzical look on his face.

"It's okay. I've been here the whole time. You did something to yourself and I don't know why. It doesn't really matter for now. The main thing is that you're okay. We can go through why you did it later. I'm sure you had your reasons. I'm not here to judge. I only want you safe."

This seems to relax him, and he lies back on his pillow. It's then that he lifts up his arms to peer at the bandages swathing both wrists. I wonder what it is going through his mind.

"My younger brother Daniel tried to do what you tried to do, only he was successful. I couldn't allow you to do the same thing. I've never told you about Daniel before, so when you're up to it, I'll tell you about him."

"I'd like that," he says.

I take hold of his hand and feel the life force pulsing in it. I wonder if he senses the same in me or whether he can detect my life force ever so slowly fading away. We stay like that until he dozes off again. I take away my hand, feeling as though I've been drained of all my energy.

Suddenly there's a vice-like clamp across my chest. I'm helpless in its grip. In my mind's eye I have a vision of a mullet boat canting over in a squall. It has passed that point of no return and is about to capsize. I know that boat is me.

Everything is bright. White light shines all around me. My vision is fuzzy. I hear noises. People are speaking. The bright light moves away and I can see a ceiling above me. A head moves across my vision. It is the Sister with the white veil framing her face.

"You gave us all a scare there, Mr Bender. You've had a heart attack. You were very lucky you had it here."

Her voice resonates back and forth. It has a lovely cadence, almost musical in quality. I suppose I've been given drugs of some kind. That's why her voice sounds strange and why I feel no pain. Through the oxygen mask fixed over my face I ask, "Steven, is he all right?"

"He's in the next bed. He's very concerned about you."

I shut my eyes, grateful that there is still time.

About the Author

Miles Hughes lives in Auckland, New Zealand. After graduating from the University of Auckland in 1970 with a BE (Civil), and in 1972 with a post-graduate Diploma in Public Health Engineering, he worked as a professional engineer from 1970 to 2007 in New Zealand, Australia, Malaysia, Singapore and the United Kingdom. Between 1998 and 2007 he wrote novels in his spare time and retired from engineering in 2007 to take up writing full time. In 2009 he graduated with a Master in Creative Writing from Auckland University of Technology.

Seven of his books, all published during 2012 and 2013, are currently available as e-books on Kindle. These include, the novels; *The Coconut War, Birthright-Mātāmuatanga, Catalan, Servant of the King - Part 1 of the Templar Trilogy, Knight of the Temple - Part 2 of the Templar Trilogy, Defender of the Realm - Part 3 of the Templar Trilogy,* and the travel narrative *Egyptian Escapade.* His non-fiction work *150 Years of New Zealand Shipyards 1795-1945*, also published in 2012, is currently available in pdf format on CD-ROM. He has extensively revised this text and is soon to publish a second edition of this work in soft cover. *Richmond Road*; is his latest work to be published. This will soon be followed by his YA *novel Enki's Ark* in which he introduces a new teenage hero, Toby Briggs.

Miles Hughes was short-listed in the 2011 Graeme Lay Short Story competition with his story *Farewell;* was co-producer of the award winning spoken-word event 'Spit.it.Out' at the 2013 Auckland Fringe Festival; and was also short listed in the 2013 National Flash Fiction Competition with his story *Buried at Sea.*

By the same author

Egyptian Escapade
Birthright-Matamuatanga
The Coconut War
Catalan
Servant of the King: Part 1 of the Templar Trilogy
Knight of the Temple: Part 2 of the Templar Trilogy
Defender of the Realm: Part 3 of the Templar Trilogy
150 Years of New Zealand Shipbuilding 1795-1945

Coming soon: *Enki's Ark*

To be notified when I am about to publish a new book, please join my mailing list by sending me a note at writermiles@gmail.com.

You can also keep up to date on what I am working on through my blog at http://www.mileshughes.co.nz/.

Thank you once again.